"Kate? What are you doing here?"

Keeping one eye on the road, Tony watched in the rearview mirror as Kate climbed over the back seat of his SUV. Somehow her dress ended up over her head, exposing her legs...her *great* legs.

He couldn't drive while being distracted like this!

After pulling the car onto the shoulder of the highway, he twisted around and fixed her with what he thought was a stern glare. He couldn't be sure, because he kept thinking about her legs.

"Do you know what you've done?" he demanded.

Kate sighed. "Sorry, I didn't mean to startle you. Look, I'll just climb up there and we can chat about this."

"Chat?" He couldn't have her in the front seat with those legs so close to him! He'd lose it. "You want to have a chat? You ditch your wedding. Then pop up out of nowhere in my car. And you want to chat?" He noticed his voice getting higher with each sentence, but he was too upset to prevent it.

He was such a goner. He had the hots for the runaway bride.

For more, turn to page 9

"Adapt?" Desi asked, not sure she liked the sound of that.

"Yeah. And I think I've got it." Seth studied her, a crooked grin on his face. He tossed her bodily over his shoulder in a fireman's hold.

"Seth, I don't think this is what the romance novels mean when they say, 'He carried her into his bedroom.'"

"Ah, but as a scientist I've learned there are often a multitude of solutions to any one problem."

Desi was laughing, and she noticed he was, as well. "Put me down!"

"Not yet. I'm carrying you to my bedroom, and then...what's the proper romantic word?"

Make love. That's the phrase she wanted to blurt out. Instead she kept her tone light. "Ravish. You're going to ravish me."

"Oooh, that sounds good. Seth Rutherford— gentleman, academic, ravisher of one beautiful, smart, sexy woman, herewith now in my bedchamber."

Desi could not stop giggling; that is, until Seth placed his eager mouth over hers.

For more, turn to page 197

HARLEQUIN DUETS

ISBN 0-373-44150-9

Copyright in the collection:
Copyright © 2002 by Harlequin Books S.A.

The publisher acknowledges the copyright holders
of the individual works as follows:

THE GREAT BRIDAL ESCAPE
Copyright © 2002 by Bonnie Tucker

HOW TO CATCH A GROOM
Copyright © 2002 by Holly Fuhrmann

The Great Bridal Escape

Bonnie Tucker

HARLEQUIN®

TORONTO • NEW YORK • LONDON
AMSTERDAM • PARIS • SYDNEY • HAMBURG
STOCKHOLM • ATHENS • TOKYO • MILAN • MADRID
PRAGUE • WARSAW • BUDAPEST • AUCKLAND

Dear Reader,

Several years ago I gave a workshop at a writer's conference in Houston. After the workshop several people said I had to meet a woman named Holly Jacobs. During the luncheon that day more people told me I had to meet Holly Jacobs. It went on like that all day until finally, at the book signing, I had the opportunity to meet the one and only Holly Jacobs!

The bond of friendship was sealed immediately. We are kindred spirits. We both love storytelling and writing. One day Holly called to tell me she had an idea for two books—one about a runaway bride and the other about the groom left at the altar. She asked if I'd like to write one of the books, and of course I said, "Yes." That's how *The Great Bridal Escape* and *How To Catch a Groom* were born. Working with Holly has been wonderful. She's funny, imaginative, and her creativity is extraordinary. Of course, I know she feels the exact same way about me!

So, in the spirit of love, marriage and happily ever after, keep your eyes open as we spin more stories about the Romano and O'Malley families to tickle your funny bone and bring laughter into your life.

Happy reading!

Bonnie Tucker

Books by Bonnie Tucker

HARLEQUIN DUETS
2—I GOT YOU, BABE
50—GOING IN STYLE
64—A ROSEY LITTLE CHRISTMAS

HARLEQUIN LOVE & LAUGHTER
18—HANNAH'S HUNKS
52—STAY TUNED: WEDDING AT 11:00

To Barbara Daly
With heartfelt thanks
for your advice, encouragement and support

1

_____

A FANTASY IS A TERRIBLE thing to waste...

...and the fantasy Mary Kathryn O'Malley had
the night before her wedding rehearsal dinner was
definitely too good to waste.

She'd gotten to bed at exactly 10:00 p.m., just as
she always did. A totally normal activity. Only between the moments of lethargic drowsiness and actual sleep, the fantasy began. While having a fantasy may have been normal for other women, it was
anything but normal for Mary Kathryn—boring,
play-by-the-rules Mary Kathryn. And lately, this
particular one had been recurring with startling fre-
quency. Not even when she was awake did she
think about the things that were filling this fantasy.

It always started out in the same.

She and Seth were on their honeymoon. Floating
on Presque Isle Bay in his boat, *The Guppy,* they'd
spend the daylight hours taking water samples for
their research at Gannon University.

But at night, when the sun went down and the
moon rose in the sky, ooh, that's when the magic
would take place as the gentle waves rocked Seth
and her into uncontrolled passion.

She was naked, lying on the deck, gazing at his body. His silhouette outlined by the backdrop of stars and the full moon. He was fully aroused. Primed and ready. Her own body heated and moistened in anticipation of what was sure to come. He stretched his arms up and out, and arched his back so that he looked longer and thicker and bigger than even she thought possible, before he stood straight once again, turning to face her, so hard, so ready.

Her hands twitched in anticipation. She so longed to touch him, to have him come to her. Her pelvis gyrated naturally, beginning the rhythmic dance of what they would finally do when they came together as one. Her breasts became heavy, her nipples taut and painful, needing to be touched, fondled, played with. The apex between her legs already moist and ready for her man to fill her.

His body, clearly defined, taunted her, teased her. She wanted to see his face. Needed to see his face. The face of the man she would marry. The man she would love and whose children she would bear.

If only she could see his face, to make sure it was Seth. But of course it was Seth. Who else could it be? She didn't know anyone else. So it had to be Seth. It just had to be.

He moved closer to her then and she reached out, wanting to touch him, wanting him to come to her. To lie next to her. To cover her with his body. To enter her slowly, erotically. To make her one with him. She stretched out her arms in invitation, and he approached her.

His face. Always in shadow, only this time, this time, she could almost see his features. The outline of a strong nose, a chiseled chin, broad forehead. Almost, but not quite.

No sooner did she think she could touch him with her fingertips than he vanished, the dream broken, leaving her wide awake, throbbing, unfulfilled. And downright testy.

Testy was not what she needed to be on the afternoon of her wedding rehearsal. At this very moment she shouldn't be thinking about a face that she could almost see in her fantasies, and wondering who it belonged to. She shouldn't be having longings about kisses and touches that led to lovemaking so thunderous that she wouldn't be able to breathe for the excitement. Or of what would come afterward as they lay in bed together, legs and arms wrapped around each other in peaceful slumber.

What she should be thinking about was the here and now. The fact that she would be married tomorrow. That at this moment, Seth—a man she cared about deeply—waited for her at the altar. He did look a bit impatient, which could mean either he was hungry and wanted to get to the rehearsal dinner, or that he was in a hurry to give her the practice you-may-kiss-the-bride kiss.

Given that neither of them had eaten much today she knew it was more likely that Seth was hungry and wanted dinner. Once again, much to her dismay, hunger, not passion, ruled their relationship.

Her father's arm, linked through hers, had tightened, as if he could sense her turmoil. "Nervous, Mary Kathryn?"

"A little," she said, counting her blessings that her father couldn't possibly read her mind. She would never intentionally do anything to hurt him or her mother. She knew if she voiced her doubts about Seth or getting married, it would tear her parents apart. They were so looking forward to this union. "I'll be glad when it's all over." That much she could say and it was the truth.

He squeezed her arm reassuringly. "You were never a person who liked a big to-do."

"That's true," she said and smiled at him. Mary Kathryn never liked to be the center of attention. She was happy in her anonymity. She could admit to herself that every once in a while she wished she could take center stage, but that only lasted for a second and then her normal, practical self prevailed over any momentary sexually frustrated insanity.

She didn't think too much about the noise when she heard the heavy sanctuary door opening and slamming against the wall out in the church's corridor. Nor did she pay attention to the hot jolt to her system when a deep voice boomed from behind her, "I'm here."

She did twist around to see who had come in, but the man ran, like a tornado at ninety miles an hour, right past her, almost knocking her into her father.

All she could take in as he sprinted down the aisle was male, tall, muscular and fit. He had mumbled, "Sorry," as he sped past, his voice deep and sexy. He jumped onto the altar and was immediately surrounded by the men, but not to the extent that she couldn't get her fill of him from where she stood.

"Who's that?" her father asked.

"I'm not sure," she said slowly. She couldn't stop looking at him, and the longer she looked, the faster her heart beat. Her fast beating heart was doing something to her insides because a knot had formed in her throat. She tried to swallow. It was hard, but finally she did, and the knot moved from her throat, and landed in her belly, which made her knees weak and her head swim. This was not normal.

The organist who had started to play the opening music stopped abruptly.

Mary Kathryn had a few moments to get her mind back to its normal practical self and analyze him. It should be easy since analyzing is what she did best.

It wasn't as if he was great-looking, unless a woman was attracted to a man taller than her Seth. A man whose ruddy skin made Seth's pale, sunscreen-protected complexion look almost sickly in comparison.

And who needed dark hair, thick and wavy, the color of unsweetened chocolate, when Seth's blond hair was so much more appealing?

Definitely *not* her.

So now that Mary Kathryn knew that the reason her body temperature rose about fifty degrees, her mouth went dry and her super scientific brain had turned to bacterial mush was a purely sexual reaction to a man she wasn't attracted to in the least, she could get on with the rehearsal.

She let out a deep breath. Her father patted her arm in a sympathetic way that she didn't deserve. All she knew was that despite the need to drool, she would do what it took to talk herself out of feeling that the man who had just stormed the church was droolingly gorgeous. She immediately got to work on suppressing the unfamiliar weak-in-the-knees feeling racing through her body.

Now Seth and his groomsmen, including the just arrived Mr. Drool-babe—if a woman happened to like that type, which she was working very hard at not liking—were slapping each other on the back, landing blows on biceps and shooting pretend sucker punches in abdomens.

If she hadn't known who Mr. Drool-babe was before, as soon as the men began to chant, ''Tony, Tony, Tony'' she knew exactly who he was. The best man, Tony Donetti. Seth's best friend.

TONY DIDN'T WANT TO BE here. No, that wasn't right. He *did* want to be at Seth's wedding rehearsal and the dinner that would follow immediately afterward. In fact, he even wanted to be at the wedding and was honored, but not surprised, that Seth had asked him to be best man.

It was Erie where he didn't want to be. If Seth had to do something totally noble and Seth-like, as in getting married, Tony wished he'd done it in Pittsburgh, or Miami, or anywhere else. But not Erie.

It never failed that whenever Tony came home to Erie, something bizarre and completely unexpected seemed to happen to him. Like thirty minutes ago when he had gotten himself engaged to his friend Cara Romano.

His mother had invited both Cara and her mother, Cecilia, to lunch. They were all in the kitchen doing lunchtime preparation things. His mother stirred the spaghetti sauce—a sauce he wouldn't be eating since he was allergic to tomatoes. Cecilia rolled out the pasta dough. Cara grated the parmesan. He leaned against the counter and watched her. They talked about the kinds of things friends talk about when they haven't seen each other in a while. Catching up kinds of things. He told her some funny stories about his sushi chef, Hataki, and she told him about the kids in her kindergarten class.

Suddenly the quiet lunchtime preparations became loud. There was a flurry of conversations going on at once, half in Italian, half in English. Ques-

tions being shot to both him and Cara, more rapid
and complex than any person who didn't speak flu-
ent Italian—and especially being a male person as
he was and not quite able to follow the conversation—had a right to be subjected to.

The gist of it being something about the mothers
not getting any younger, and that they had already
waited too long to have grandchildren and if they
had to wait any longer, they'd be dead when they
finally got some.

"What kind of son or daughter wouldn't have
children and give his own mother grandbabies that
she would be alive to enjoy?" his mother, Teresa,
demanded to know.

"Haven't you two been thinking about it?" Cecilia asked.

"I know you have," his mother answered for
him. "You want to give me grandchildren, and
what better person to do that than our own little
Carabella." Teresa reached over and pinched
Cara's cheek, rolling her tongue over the *bella*.

"Momma," he said. "Cara and I are friends. We
love each other like friends. We're not getting married. At least not to each other."

He looked at Cara, smiling at her, waiting for her
to back him up. Instead she looked back at him, her
lips moved, but no words came out. He couldn't
tell if she was trying to agree, or disagree. Or if
she, too, felt so overwhelmed that no words were
possible.

"If I had to wait until you two fell in love," Teresa yelled, hitting him on the head with a wooden spoon, "I'd be ten years in my grave."

Finally Cara spoke. "Mom. Teresa. I love Tony, but I'm not in love with him. There's a big difference."

"I didn't love your father when I married him," Cecilia said. "But we were good friends and after a while the love came."

"Maybe I want something more." Cara tried again.

"You're almost thirty," Cecilia accused.

"I just turned twenty-nine."

"Your eggs are spoiling." She poked Cara in the stomach with the rolling pin.

"Momma, please," Cara moaned, her face turning red.

Finally Tony got the two mothers to calm down enough, and stay silent just long enough to convince them that Cara and he would take their suggestion under advisement. They would go outside and talk about it.

They left as quickly as they could from The House of Motherly Pressure, and walked side by side to the park a few blocks away. It was a nice day for the beginning of June. Not too hot, not too cold. She sat on one of the old swings and he stood off to the side of her, looking at the kids playing, the mothers chatting on benches while gently moving strollers with sleeping babies in them back and forth in a kind of hypnotic rhythm.

He hadn't thought too much about marriage. But occasionally the thought of settling down went through him. Usually when he felt lonely. Or horny. Or both. "Are you dating anyone?" he finally asked Cara.

"No."

"Has there been anyone serious for you?"

"There have been a few possible prospects, but no one who lit my fire. I guess I've been too picky. Or that's what my mother tells me. I've been waiting for the man whose kisses make my insides clench. So far no clenching," she told him. "What about you?"

"I've gone out," he said and quickly added, "I haven't been a monk." He needed to get that straight right away. "But there hasn't been anyone who set my burner on fire either."

"Why do you think that is?" she asked.

"Maybe because I haven't given anyone a chance. Maybe because the idea of falling in love and having some kind of out-of-body experience is all in books and movies, but not real life. I don't know."

"I don't know either." She used her foot to push the swing.

"I will say this though, for me to search for someone who can set me on fire would be pretty hard right now. The restaurant business is an unforgiving taskmaster.'' Donetti's Irish Pub and Sushi Bar was a twenty-five hours a day, eight days a week job. Since a day only had twenty-four hours, and a week only seven days, there was no time for any social life. The joke on him was that despite being named one of Houston's most eligible bachelors, he never had time to go out on a date.

''Same with me. I teach during the school hours, then do all the administrative paperwork they demand we do after school is over. Six hours of classroom and six hours of paperwork, classroom preparation. Meet men? I have to laugh at that one. If my mother wasn't pushing blind dates on me whenever she can find someone, I'd never go out.''

He took a real good look at Cara, trying to see her as if he had never seen her before. She was a beautiful woman, long dark hair, creamy skin, a perfectly fine-looking face, great figure. But as far as lighting his fire, she didn't do it. Then again, he apparently didn't light hers either, so maybe they were perfect for each other.

''You're pretty, Cara. I would think you'd get lots of dates. Men would be banging at your door.''

She shook her head, a sad smile across her lips. ''Tony, all the good men are either married, engaged or gay. There's no one out there.''

''So what do you think?'' he asked. ''We should get married by process of elimination?''

''Maybe,'' she said. Then with a little more energy she asked, ''Why not? You and I know each other really well. We're friends. That's a good start.''

He was lonely. He wanted companionship. Cara was a great girl. She was a good choice. He'd known her since the day they were born in adjoining delivery rooms at St. Mary's Hospital.

"I want to have lots of babies..." she tilted her head towards the mothers on the benches. "Do you?"

"Babies are okay. My mom wants to be a grandmother."

She nodded. "Tell me about it. So does mine. But I want them for me, not her."

He didn't have the heart to tell her he didn't want a family right away. Women didn't take that well. He should know, he'd been telling his mother the same thing for the past few years and she never stopped nagging him to find someone to deliver the goods. That being a child.

Maybe now it was time. He'd hit the big three-oh in less than a year. He knew Cara better than any other woman. They had shared a baby buggy as infants, a bathtub as toddlers, the same bike as little kids. They even shared answers on tests, and had only been caught a few times.

Tony's thoughts were whirling, but they all ended on the same note. "There have been thousands of marriages that have been successful based on a lot less of a start than we have."

''We're friends. We do love each other. What better way for a marriage to begin?''

He pulled her off the swing and took her in his arms, kissing her lips, sealing the bargain. So the kiss didn't give him an erection or make his blood boil. Maybe in time all that would happen. He took Cara's hand and together they walked back to his mother's house to tell the soon-to-be in-laws the news.

The idea of being married to a good friend, for convenience sake, to ward off loneliness, wasn't such a bad idea. He just wished they were both a little more enthusiastic about the whole thing.

Oh, hell, it didn't matter. For whatever lack of enthusiasm the bride and groom may have had, their mothers were thrilled. As soon as he and Cara announced their intentions, Teresa and Cecilia started speaking in rapid Italian, making their plans. He and Cara might as well have been living on another planet for the amount of attention their mothers paid them.

Tony glanced at his watch and almost swore. He stood up, walked around the table and kissed Cara on the cheek, a very fiancé kind of thing to do, even if he didn't feel any kind of spark when his lips touched her skin.

''I'm late,'' he told her. ''I'll call you when I get back to Houston.'' He was leaving right after the wedding tomorrow and heading back home. He had to get back to his restaurant. There wouldn't be time for any more socializing.

He drove his Suburban to the Gannon University chapel where he was sure Seth's wedding rehearsal had already started. The idea that his own wedding would be right around the corner didn't scare him. He accepted the fact that it was time to settle down. So far, being engaged wasn't too bad. Maybe being married wouldn't be so bad either. All in all, Cara was a good friend, and she would make him a good wife. He would do whatever it took to make her a good husband.

He parked the car, and ran to the church, hating to be late. He vaulted up the church steps and mumbled an apology to the inanimate door when it slammed against the wall. He mumbled another, "Sorry," to the woman and man standing at the entry.

He had gotten a brief look at her as he brushed passed her on his toward Seth and the altar. He ignored the heat in his side where he had touched her, and didn't pay attention to the way her perfume sucked him in. If she was the bride-to-be, she was a stunner. If he hadn't looked away when he had, he probably would have ended up doing something stupid, like falling over his own feet. Seth was one lucky sonofabitch.

When Tony leapt on to the altar, bypassing the steps, he immediately told Seth about his new status as an engaged man, which lead to chanting and back slapping. He took it all in like how he thought a newly engaged man should take it. Not very well. Especially when Seth asked, "Where's Cara?"

"Who?"

"Your fiancée?"

He must have given Seth a blank look, because he asked, "The girl you're going to marry? Why didn't you bring her?"

Tony shrugged. "I didn't think about it." And that was the crux of the matter. He didn't think of her in that way. Then he remembered his mother and Cara's mother, and decided if he, a good Italian boy, could run a very successful Irish pub and sushi bar, then he sure as hell could learn to remember to include Cara in his social life.

That thought was put into his memory and once there, he promptly forgot about it. Not because he wanted to forget about her, but because all the while Seth and his buddies were congratulating him on his future marriage, he couldn't stop gazing at the bride-to-be. That Mary Kathryn woman, standing all the way at the head of the aisle, a good fifty yards away, holding on to the arm of her father, looking all sweet and innocent and vulnerable. His side still felt hot where he had brushed past her.

She—Mary Kathryn—had done something to Tony that he had just told Cara would never happen. Just one casual brushing had rammed a fistful of desire and lust for his best friend's bride-to-be right into his gut. His Italian jewels had stirred, his hands and feet went numb.

He was pond scum. That was Seth's woman and Tony knew he was a sinner and was going to hell. How could he feel desire for Seth's woman? Seth, his very best friend. His high school mentor.

Tony accepted the fact that he had now become the lowest form of mold spores existing on earth. No, he was even lower that that, if that were possible.

But even knowing how low he was didn't stop the case of full-blown lust he found himself inflicted with for the woman coming down the aisle.

2

"MARY KATHRYN, COME DOWN here," Seth yelled out in a very uncharacteristic Seth manner. "I want you to meet Tony."

She started to shake her head no. How could she even think about meeting, talking to, having a conversation with a man who looked like Tony looked? Who reeked of male sexuality. Without knowing him, she knew he was more than she could handle. She would never be able to carry on a normal conversation with someone who looked like him. No way. No matter that she was an extremely intelligent woman, that her IQ bordered on genius, she was not equipped to handle that man.

"Come on Mary Kathryn," Seth said. "Hurry up. Tony wants to meet the woman of my dreams." They elbowed each other like little kids.

She dropped her hand from her father's arm and walked towards the men, with what she hoped was a neutral, nonsexual smile plastered on her face. She wanted to meet him. Only she didn't want to. There was too much attraction, at least on her part. How could she possibly control her drool?

But control she would because she was a woman

with the ability to use certain female rational thought processes to stave off runaway hormones. Tony was only a man. A friend of Seth's. He may be gorgeous, he may reek of male sexuality, but still he was of the male species and her reaction was nothing more than that of two amoebae seeking to reproduce. Her biological clock ticked away, and she actually heard it ticking.

When she reached the altar, and put one foot on the bottom step, Tony hurried toward her, hand held out, an open invitation to place her hand in his and grasp. How could she do that? How could she touch him and not melt?

Seth should stop this. Couldn't he see what was happening inside her heart? Apparently not. He stayed back, grinning, approving. If only he knew. She felt as if she were cheating, and she wasn't. Nothing had happened. Nothing. It was all in her head and no where else.

So Mary Kathryn placed her small hand in Tony's large one. A big mistake. Heat. That's what happened when they touched. Hot. Electrifying. She glanced at him. Did he feel it, too? Apparently not, since he returned her smile in a friendly way, but there wasn't anything in his eyes to indicate he felt the same charge. In other words, where she expected smoke to be pouring from his eyes there was nothing.

She tried to pull her hand away, only couldn't. He held on fast. She glanced at him and saw the smile and then knew, just knew he must have felt something. A little something, but something nonetheless. "How're you doing?" he asked.

"Fine." Her voice was a hoarse whisper.

Then he released her, leaving her hand a tingling mess. She stretched her fingers out, trying to get the blood flowing again, to send the tingles away. She knew at that moment that she would have to stay away from Tony. She couldn't be alone with him, not even alone with him in a large crowd. Not if he felt one iota for her what she felt for him. Did he feel it, or was it all in her head, her runaway fantasies?

Desi Smith, her wedding coordinator, came running down the aisle. "Let's get this show on the road everyone." Desi held out her hand to Tony and he took it. After a very quick shake, she added, "Glad you could finally make it." The condemnation was lost by the smile of her voice.

Father Murphy stood on the altar, waving his hand, his bible held to his chest, a slightly harried look on his face. "Thank you so much, Ms. Smith. I was getting ready to say the same thing. Come on children. We must get moving here."

"You're welcome, Father." Desi then began doing what she did so well. Ordering with extreme organization. "Mary Kathryn, you need to get back down there where your father is. Mrs. Elgin, are you ready to fire up that organ?" With her hands on her hips she turned to the men at the altar. "Fun is over boys. Now it's time to get to work.'' She clapped her hands. ''Chop-chop.''

Finally, Mary Kathryn sighed in relief. She had been handed an opportunity to get away from Tony and the mixed up feelings she had inside her. She hurried up the aisle and once again took her place next to her father. The organist played only three notes before Desi stopped her. ''One moment. Boys,'' she said to Seth and the groomsmen, ''I want you to move over here.'' She pointed to a spot on the altar. Then, as if not quite satisfied, she re-directed the men to move there, to stand closer to the front or farther away.

Mary Kathryn stared at the stained glass windows while waiting for the rehearsal to resume. She loved the beautiful old buildings at Gannon and if she had to get married, then this chapel was where she wanted the ceremony to take place.

Listen to her. *Had to get married.* She didn't *have* to get married. She *wanted* to get married. Really. She wanted to get married.

She sighed, still not knowing why they had to have this big wedding. She was a scientist, not a froufrou kind of woman. She would have been happy going to the judge, saying the vows, and then it would be over.

There she went again, wishing it were over. Truth was, she wasn't even sure she was wishing it would start.

Must be some kind of bridal cold feet. That had

to be a common ailment among brides to be. Her parents had introduced her to Seth. They had hinted that the marriage would be a good thing and had pushed both her and Seth toward the institution.

She had to stop thinking along those lines, as if marriage were a jail, instead of a wonderful institution. Jail, institution, what's the difference?

The music started again. Desi ran up the aisle and directed first the flower girl, then her two bridesmaids and finally her maid of honor—her sister, Shannon—down the aisle to the beat of some song that Mary Kathryn had no idea what it was, but Desi and Shannon picked out and it seemed pretty.

Finally the "Wedding March" started with its big, flamboyant beginning.

Holding on to her father's arm, they marched slowly down the aisle. It was only practice. She could do it, one foot in front of the other. The bridesmaids were standing to the side. Shannon, looking way too happy, stood on the altar with a big, encouraging grin slapped across her face. Seth looked like Seth, cool, confident and distracted. He must be thinking of his microbes. She could understand that. Anything would be better than this painfully slow rehearsal.

Then there was Tony. He looked too good.

She should amend that actually, now that she'd had all this time to observe him as she slowly made her way down the aisle. He wasn't really *that* cute.

Totally different from the handsome, debonair man who was a night and a morning away from being her husband.

She wasn't even attracted to Tony's kind of devil-may-care looks. Oh, no. She liked the steady, deliberate manner of Seth. She simply adored his scientific mind and his predictable ways. She always knew how he felt, what he was going to do. Those were qualities that she admired in a person. In a man. In Seth.

Still… There was something kind of wild and carefree about his friend. Or so it seemed.

"All right, Seth, Mary Kathryn. From this point forward, I'll take over from Ms. Smith." Father Murphy smiled at Desi, and she nodded in agreement, as if handing them over to the Father was putting them in expert hands. "You'll repeat after me, say your 'I do's', kiss the bride, and that will be it. Now I'll see all of you back here tomorrow."

"Father," Mary Kathryn asked, "is that it? Is that all the practice we're going to do?"

"There's nothing left, my dear," he said, his voice kind and gentle. "You've seen the movies. You know the drill."

"But, Father," Mary Kathryn said. "Don't you think we should practice the kissing part?" She looked at her groom-to-be and smiled shyly. His face had turned a light shade of red.

"Mary Kathryn," Father Murphy softly admonished, "I doubt you'll be needing any practice before the wedding."

Seth looked relieved. Not a very good sign. She wondered if he'd kiss her tomorrow, or if a public display of affection would turn him away from her. Again.

A glance at Tony, and his sexy, knowing expression embarrassed her. It was as if he knew that there was no passion between Seth and her.

When Mary Kathryn thought about it, she didn't even know why all this passion and romance stuff had come up now, of all times. In all the years she and Seth had known each other, passion had never been an issue. Maybe because there hadn't been any.

They had so many other things working in their favor. It was only because of those stupid nighttime fantasies she'd been having that she now couldn't quite remember what all those things in their favor were. But they'd come back to her.

The wedding party began to break up, and everyone left the church for the rehearsal dinner at The Bayside Inn.

A pianist played soft, romantic music as people milled around before the dinner started. Everything seemed to be going along fine. Her parents and sister, and Seth's parents were all laughing, which was pretty much a phenomenon. She couldn't remember her mother, of all people, laughing.

Her mother was also partaking in a little wine,

something else she normally never did, and she was obviously feeling no pain. Of course, the final bill for the wedding weekend hadn't arrived yet either. Then she'd really need a bottle or two of wine.

Mary Kathryn saw Seth across the room talking to Tony and Desi. She should have gone over there. After all, he was the groom and she was the bride, and they should be inseparable. But she didn't make a move to enter the throng of people, just stood in the entryway and waited. Waiting for what she didn't quite know.

Then Seth turned in her direction and noticed her. He waved, signaling her to join them. She smiled at him, a smile that felt almost bittersweet to her, and waved back. He looked happy. Or maybe content would be a better word. As if he hadn't a care or thought in the world. As if the wedding was only another day to get through before he could be back on his *Guppy,* studying his sea creatures. Not that she minded that. Not at all. It was just that a honeymoon on the boat, gathering seawater and looking for bacteria wasn't very romantic.

But she had agreed to it, because at the time she hadn't been having fantasies and because nothing about her and Seth seemed romantic, which was probably why she had been having those fantasies to start with.

In every book she'd read on the subject, a fantasy was a good thing. It was healthy, something normal men and women did. But to her, having a fantasy about a man making love to her—a man she assumed was Seth, because after all, they were getting married, but since his face never came up in the dream she couldn't be sure—seemed, well, not normal.

She made her way to Seth. She linked her arm through his and was grateful he didn't move away from her as he had so many times in the past.

Tony said, "I feel as if I know you already. Seth's told me a lot about you."

"He has?" she said, grateful she didn't stutter over her own two words. The man simply made her normally staid thoughts turn positively wicked. "Tell me three things he said."

Tony stared into her face, gave her a smile that melted her knees, and said, "Kate, I can't possibly repeat all the things he's said."

Which meant Seth hadn't talked much about her at all. She understood.

Seth said, "Hey, Tony, her name's Mary Kathryn, not Kate. You knew that."

Tony took a sip of wine, and in his deep, sexy voice said, "My mistake." She knew he didn't think it was a mistake at all. Even while answering Seth, he didn't take his sexy, pure male gaze off her face when he added, "She looks like a Kate to me." Then he winked at her.

All it took was the wink for her to lose her romantically lusting heart to him. She had been Mary Kathryn all her life. Never a Mary. Never a Kathryn. And certainly never a Kate. No nicknames allowed in her life.

Suddenly nothing seemed the same. One wink, one name, one fantasy man and her life took new direction. Grandma O'Malley—Mary Kathryn crossed herself and looked up—would have said it was a sign and she better heed it, because if she were too stupid to heed the signs when they were hitting her over the head, then she deserved to get what she got and there would be no more signs.

But, Mary Kathryn, being a scientist, knew she'd have to think about it, analyze the whole thing, figure out if there were more than one sign, and decide what to do. One thing she did know was more than anything in the whole world, Mary Kathryn didn't want to be a Mary Kathryn. She wanted to be a Kate.

3

THE SUN WAS SHINING brightly on her wedding day. Maybe too brightly. Mary Kathryn stared at herself in the mirror, but it seemed the longer she looked, the less she looked like herself. Maybe it was the sun hitting the mirror that blurred her vision and distorted her image.

Or maybe it was she, herself that was causing it to happen. Because as she looked at the image in the mirror, her mind once again filled, not with the wedding that would soon take place, but with the dream that had awakened her this morning.

So vivid, so powerful. So intense, so real.

That dream. That fantasy. Stupid. That's what it was. That's what she was. Scientists didn't have fantasies. Their whole existences were based on reality.

It was easy to explain, really. She and Seth hadn't made love—not once—and they were getting married. If they had made love first she wouldn't have had the fantasy or any of the doubts she had been having about this marriage.

But, through no fault of her own—she'd certainly tried to entice Seth—they hadn't made love. Instead, it was up to her own imagination to figure out what it would be like. And clearly her imagination—not often used because she was such a logical, rational person—had gone wild. They were the fanciful yearnings of a woman who wanted some loving, was not getting any and was getting pretty damn frustrated by the whole thing. There was no other reason for what was happening.

Mary Kathryn had changed from straitlaced professor, working her way toward tenure into the woman in the mirror who looked like a real, life-size bridal Barbie doll. If only she could get her old self back, the doubts would be gone, too. But it was hard to become the old Mary Kathryn when these past few weeks had been filled with silk and lace and everything feminine and womanly. Everything, that is, except her sex life.

So now she was wearing this floor-length gown made of bone-white satin with the tiny seed pearls hand-sewn to the bodice. That had been Desi's idea, but then her wedding planner's job was to make a bride look like a bride, and she had earned her fee. Especially because Mary Kathryn had not been a willing participant.

If it hadn't been for Desi—with a lot of push from Shannon—Mary Kathryn's blond hair would have been in a ponytail. Instead, an antique lace veil had been attached to hair that had been curled and teased and pinned until the now highlighted straight blond hair was piled at least ten feet above her head. Or so it seemed.

Everything she wore under the gown was Shannon's doing. All that Victoria's Secret underwear. Wait. Not *underwear*. Shannon would kill her if she heard her refer to the three layers of expensive white silk and lace see-through, made-to-seduce-a-man-and-have-sex-for-life underwear she wore right now as underwear.

Lingerie. That was it was called. A French word that meant *underwear.*

If not for Shannon and Desi dragging her from store to store, insisting she act like a bride and not a dud, Mary Kathryn would, at this very moment, be wearing the practical beige silk suit she had wanted to wear as a wedding outfit but had been talked out of buying. Not talked out of exactly, more like worn down until she'd given in and said a weary "yes" to the traditional white dress.

It seemed to her as if she went along with everyone, like a puppet on a string, even when she knew in her heart it wasn't in her own best interests. She could have reused the beige suit next month when she was tentatively scheduled to lecture to women environmentalists at the Smithsonian. She doubted she could wear the wedding gown to her lecture. She knew that much at least. The gown was a total waste. And the fact that she thought her wedding gown was a waste was only another indication something was drastically wrong.

Mary Kathryn's eyes closed on the bridal image in the mirror. That might have been a mistake because last night's fantasy did an instant playback across her mind.

Last night. Mary Kathryn's fingers clenched, her body tensed.

As she lay on The Guppy's deck, her arms stretched out from her sides, she ran her toes up the cords of her fantasy man's calf. She was as fully exposed to him as he was to her. He knelt between her legs and began the slow, scorching process of kissing her. Starting at her knee, his lips and tongue nibbled her, moving up the inside of her thigh, higher and higher, until he kissed her where she wanted him most.

She reached out and touched his face, lightly caressing his cheeks with the tips of her fingers. He looked at her with love and lust, and she saw his face. For the first time she saw the man who was about to make love to her. Tony Donetti, Seth's best man. Seth's best friend. He stood before her splendidly naked, hugely erect and proud.

That's when she'd shot up in bed, her body covered in a cold sweat, her female parts, still able to feel where his mouth had been, throbbed in unfulfilled frustration, her arms and breasts twitched from tension. Her blood burned inside her. *It's not real,* she'd tried to reason with herself.

That didn't matter. Tony. Oh, God. Tony. How could she fantasize about Tony Donetti when it was

Seth she was marrying? She practically wept at
what she'd been dreaming. What in the world had
happened to her?

"Mary Kathryn, what's wrong?" Shannon was
standing next to her, shaking her arm. "Are you
okay? You look funny."

She just bet she did. "I'm fine."

"Nerves." Shannon smiled, only the smile didn't
quite reach her eyes. "It's normal."

"Maybe it is." But it wasn't normal to have
dreams about the best man. Not the erotic kind she
had anyway. "I'll be okay."

"Do you need some aspirin? Or seltzer? Is your
stomach bothering you?"

"No." It wasn't her stomach, it was lower. And
there wasn't a magic pill or drink that could fix it.
She wanted her wedding night, and she wanted it
now. Only she didn't want it with the groom.
"Shannon." Mary Kathryn grabbed on to her sister's arm as if she were a lifeline, which at this
moment she was. "I'm a terrible person," she
whispered urgently. "A terrible, *terrible* person."

"No, you're not," Shannon said teasingly.
"You're the good one. Remember? Everyone says
so."

"They're wrong. I'm not. I'm bad, really bad.
You just don't know." Her lips and mouth were
dry and she needed water. She looked around the
room, desperate, only there wasn't anything to
quench her thirst. So now she could be frustrated

in two different places in the same body at the same time.

"Let's talk about this," Shannon said soothingly. "You look beautiful."

"If I do it's because you and Desi took me by the hand and took care of me."

"Hey," Shannon said with a big smile. "We had to have the material to work with, right?"

Mary Kathryn smiled back. She couldn't help it. Shannon's happy outlook on life was simply contagious. "I wish I could be more like you." Free.

Shannon gave her the are-you-crazy? look. Then she laughed. Only the laugh wasn't a happy one. "Me? You're the lucky one. You're getting married. I'll be an old maid forever at the rate I'm going."

"Yes," she said. "Very lucky." If your goal in life was to marry a man who was more like a brother than a lover. A man who, until last night she'd thought about in terms of a comfortable, but not passionate life together. A life doing research, getting grants for the university. A life publishing papers and seeking tenure.

"Did you notice the best man?" Shannon teased. "Now that's one good-looking hunk-o-man. Do you think he's available?"

"Didn't notice him. Not at all." Mary Kathryn tried to sound disinterested, terrified that her face would reveal where her thoughts had been.

"You're such a liar," Shannon teased. "You'd

have to be dead not to notice him, and even then I'm sure you still would.''

''Are you interested?'' Mary Kathryn tried to sound as if she didn't care, when she did care. A lot.

''No, Tony's not my type. He's so male, it's overpowering.''

That was the truth, Mary Kathryn thought. It was the way he stood in the room. Or commanded a room. It was the way the muscles in his arms and shoulders flexed under his shirt, even just from lifting a glass of wine. He radiated male sexuality to her. He stood well over six feet, making her, at five-seven, feel diminutive. No one had made her feel so utterly feminine before. Not ever.

Last night, at the rehearsal dinner, she had kept her distance from Tony, because she knew that was proper. When the dinner broke up, and it was time to go home, she did. Alone. Like always. She had tried one last time to take Seth home with her, and all she got from him was a kiss on the cheek and a, ''Darling, not before the wedding. We'll save it.''

Who could have blamed her for being frustrated and disillusioned? Who would blame her for having that fantasy? What in the world was she going to do?

Tony Donetti.

Well, nothing. Mary Kathryn was just as practical as Seth. The whole fantasy thing was silly. It really was. It wasn't like she had real feelings for

Tony. Seth had talked about Tony often and she felt as if she knew him even before they'd met. That familiarity and her frustrations combined to torment her with those wicked fantasies. That was all.

But she knew that on their honeymoon, Seth would never make love to her on *The Guppy*. He wouldn't be spontaneous. He wouldn't do luscious and exciting things to her. He would never allow her to do those things to him. She had nothing to look forward to but a long life of affectionate companionship, boredom and bacteria.

"DO YOU, MARY KATHRYN O'Malley, take this man to be your lawfully wedded husband, in sickness and in health, until death do you part?"

"I..." Mary Kathryn started, then stopped. It wasn't just that Seth didn't make her toes wiggle, or her heart jitter, or her stomach flutter, or any of those other double-consonant adjectives that would describe the bloom of love. It was that while she loved him like a friend, she didn't love him like a lover. She didn't dream about him. "I..."

"Do," Seth whispered. "You have to say *do*."

"But," she whispered, her eyes opened wide, "I don't." She covered her mouth with her hand, not quite believing what she'd just said. Out loud yet. Her gaze darted first to the people sitting in the chapel, to her mother and father, and then back to Seth. She didn't know where she'd found the courage, but as soon as the words escaped from her mouth she realized it was true.

"You don't what?" Seth asked.

She didn't want to marry Seth. The marriage had been her parents' wish. She and Seth had fallen into their plans because it seemed so easy, and logical, and the right thing to do.

Above all else, Mary Kathryn had agreed to marry Seth because she would never intentionally disappoint her parents. She had never, ever gone against her parents' wishes. She had never defied anyone. But marrying Seth was definitely not the right thing to do.

Mary Kathryn took Seth's hands in hers. He was shaking, or maybe it was she that shook. Her heart was beating so fast, her breath was coming in short gasps. She couldn't believe she was about to do what she was going to do. She tried ignoring the questioning looks from the priest and the quiet whispering amongst their guests.

She leaned closer to him and said softly in his ear so he alone would hear, "Seth, I love working with you, and I love you like the wonderful friend you are, but I'm not in love with you. It wouldn't be right. It wouldn't be fair, not to you, not to me."

He gave her hand an encouraging squeeze. "Honey, it's just cold feet."

"No, it's more than that. You need someone who can give you more than I can."

"Mary Kathryn, what are you saying?"

"I can't marry you." She dropped his hands, turned to the guests, held out her arms and said, "I'm so sorry."

She ran down the aisle, out the double doors and down the steps of the church. She ran right past the white limo that wouldn't be taking her and Seth on the honeymoon ride out to the bay where *The Guppy* would be waiting. She didn't slow down until she reached the parking lot over a block away. She gasped for breath, leaning over, hugging her waist to relieve the painful stitch in her side. It was then that she realized the enormity of what she'd done. The finality of it, the courage to defy, to be her own woman, was overpowering and hit her with such force she started to tremble.

Mary Kathryn looked around at all the cars. Hers was parked at her parents' home. What in the world had she been thinking? She had no place to go. She had nowhere to run. Even if she had somewhere to run, she had no way to get there. She wasn't even carrying a wallet or her driver's license.

She looked behind her. She could see the church's steeple. For a moment she wondered if it would be wise to go back and get her identification. Then she spotted the navy Suburban with the Texas license plates. She didn't want Mary Kathryn O'Malley's identification. Not yet. Right now she wanted to be Kate. She knew what she had to do. There was no choice. Not any longer.

Because…

…*a fantasy is a terrible thing to waste.*

4

TONY DONETTI WATCHED with a combination of horror and admiration as the bride ran away. Her footsteps fell silent on the red runner that stretched down the aisle of the chapel, the only sound, the swish of her dress as satin crashed against satin.

The door slammed behind her. It took a moment for the echoes reverberating throughout the chapel to fade. Finally, the drama just witnessed registered with the guests, and the realization she wasn't coming back seemed to take hold.

A quiet hum started up as all the guests, family and wedding party spoke at once. Tony faced Seth, keeping a hand on his shoulder, watching, feeling momentarily helpless as his friend's normally confident face turned from shocked white to embarrassed red and finally an ashen gray.

"I can't believe she did that," Seth murmured more to himself than to Tony or anyone else. He began repeating the words, shaking his head as if in denial.

"It's better to find out now than later," Tony stated.

"She loves me, I know she does."

"Women. They're fickle." A statement of fact meant to be sympathetic.

"Not Mary Kathryn. She'll change her mind," Seth said with confidence, while at the same time looking as if he were going into shock.

"Sure she will," Tony agreed, but he doubted it. From the moment he had first seen her, standing in the aisle at the wedding rehearsal he'd had a sneaking suspicion that she was one unhappy lady. Then last night at the dinner, when he'd called her Kate, he'd seen her eyes light up, and the shadows reappear when Seth corrected him. Small things, insignificant by themselves, but put them together, and they could very well spell trouble.

"Just now, I told her it was cold feet. She should've believed me."

Tony could only nod. There wasn't anything to say. Seth was a good friend and a great guy, and Kate—he couldn't bring himself to call her Mary Kathryn since that name was synonymous with his ninth-grade algebra teacher, Sister Mary Kathryn— might look a little prudish, but she was definitely no nun. "You're right. She'll realize her mistake and come running back."

"Probably in a few minutes," Seth said sounding confident. "After all, she's dependable. And smart."

Tony nodded, only he could pretty much bet his restaurant that she wouldn't be coming back. A future husband thinking of the woman he was going to marry in terms of dependable and smart wasn't the same as *I love her, can't live without her, I'd take a bullet for her.* He could tell, even if Seth couldn't, that the passion wasn't there. Maybe underneath Kate's cool exterior simmered one hot tomato and maybe that tomato needed to be peeled and brought to a boil. But hell, who was he to say? He was allergic to tomatoes. If he hadn't been, he'd be the owner of an Italian restaurant instead of an Irish bistro.

Desi had gone over to Seth's left side and was whispering to him. Tony took the wedding ring that wasn't going to be used this afternoon from his pocket and handed it to his friend. Seth glanced at the simple gold band, then back at Tony. Finally, he shoved the empty reminder in his pocket.

Tony stepped off the raised platform where the canopy of flowers that the ex-bride and ex-groom had stood under for a few moments now seemed to droop, their scent turning sickly sweet. He moved among the guests, answering questions about what had just happened with ''I don't know,'' or ''It's a mystery to me.''

He didn't have the answers any more than anyone else did. Except for the runaway bride, that is. She had all the answers and she took them with her.

Tony was standing in the middle of the church surrounded by guests when he heard the announcement that the reception would take place anyway.

He approved of that move. Maybe Seth could work out his hurt, turn that hurt into anger. Anger helped heal the wounds of a broken heart. Tony knew that for a fact.

The wedding planner who hadn't planned for this to happen shuffled the guests toward the reception hall. Seth stood at the head of the buffet table, Kate's sister, Shannon, looking a trifle bewildered, stood on one side of him, Tony on the other.

A beer kept Seth's left hand, the one bare of a wedding band, occupied. As the guests made their way down the buffet line, anyone who made even the smallest token of sympathy received Seth's assurances that everything would work out fine. With every gulp of beer, things with Seth seemed to become even finer.

Finally, there was a lull in the line and Tony pulled Seth away. His now slightly wobbly friend gave Tony a buddy punch in the shoulder that more missed than reached its mark, and with a slightly slurred voice said, "You're a good friend."

"I know. Had enough to drink yet?"

"I'm still standing, right?" He swayed to the left.

Tony nodded.

"Then I haven't had enough." Seth belched. Only being Seth, even the belch was dignified.

"Life sucks, huh?"

"You know it." Seth took another long swallow. "She was a fine woman. Real smart."

"Yeah, that's nice. But was she a good kisser?"

"Kisser?" Seth gave him a blank look. "All right, I suppose."

"Don't you know for sure?" There was a main ingredient missing from this corned beef and cabbage recipe.

"Sure I know." This time he swayed to the right and Tony propped him back on the vertical. "She was a great kisser." He got a woebegone look on his face. "We didn't kiss much. Saving it."

"For what?" Just like Tony had figured. No passion between those two. As far as he could tell from an outsider-looking-in-through-the-window vantage point, Kate needed passion. He'd felt heat from her body when he brushed into her yesterday, and when he shook her hand. She was hot.

But, when it came to passion, he knew he wasn't one to cast stones. There wasn't any passion between him and Cara either, but at least they had a history. And they were good for each other. Passion would come.

Seth started to mumble again, almost incoherently, between gulps of beer, "Too busy for those kinds of things, you know. Things to do. Research. No time."

Tony could only think that if Kate had been his girlfriend, he would not have been able to keep his hands and mouth and every other part of his body off of her. Maybe Seth was now drinking enough beer to float his own boat because in retrospect he regretted not making the time for loving when it came to his former fiancée. Tony would never know for sure, because that was something guys didn't talk about. But the one thing Tony did understand was a man's need to drown his sorrows. There had been a time or two when he himself had had the need to binge, although getting left at the altar hadn't been one of them.

He stayed at the reception until he was sure Seth would be okay. Not that he had any doubt, but still, he had to be sure Seth would be okay before he'd leave.

"Hey, buddy, I'm heading back to Houston."

"Why?"

"The restaurant calls."

"You got people there," Seth hiccupped. "Let 'em take care of it. You and me, we need to go celebrate."

"We'll celebrate another time." He held his palm against Seth's shoulder, making sure he stood and didn't fall over.

He wished he didn't have to go, but he did. Donetti's had three full-time chefs, and one, Letty, was about to have a baby. She'd flat out told him that she could only keep the baby inside of her for so long, because once it wanted to make its appearance, nothing would stop it from coming out.

Tony had called the restaurant before he had left for the wedding. Him calling wasn't unusual, he called at least five, maybe ten times a day. Letty took the call which surprised him since she was supposed to be in the kitchen, and not near a phone. "Where are you?" he asked.

"In your office," Letty said, her breathing heavy.

"Whose minding your stove?"

"No one. Your temporary chef didn't show up."

"Get back there then."

"I'm calling the doctor, Tony, and I'm hanging up on you."

"You can't do that," he yelled into the mouthpiece in case the receiver was halfway between her ear and the cradle and she could still hear him.

"I can and I will. I'm having a baby. Now."

Then the phone went dead.

Tony had to get back. Now.

Donetti's Irish Pub and Sushi Bar didn't shut down because Tony traveled to Erie and Letty decided that today was the day her baby was going to pop out.

Tony left the building, letting the same door the bride had escaped through slam shut behind him, too. Once on the front steps he rotated his shoulders, getting the kinks out, trying to ease the stress. Then he stretched his neck and loosened the knot in his tie.

By the time he reached the Suburban, climbed inside and started the engine, the weight and responsibility of what had just happened started to dissipate. He knew why he felt responsible even though he had no reason to feel that way. Even though he had the feeling last night that Kate seemed so unhappy.

He should have warned Seth. But about what? A feeling. "Hey buddy, take care of that girl. I have a *feeling* she's gonna bolt if you don't do something." Yeah, right. Seth would really heed that kind of warning. Not likely. He hadn't seen anything out of the ordinary in the first place. Tony wouldn't have either, if he hadn't seen the way she looked when he called her Kate and Seth had corrected him.

Tony pointed the Suburban south on 71 and figured in about twenty-two hours he'd be pulling into his driveway back home. Now that was a novelty, him thinking of Texas as home. When over the last few years had that happened?

He scanned through the stations on the radio until he found one that played the country music he had grown to like since he'd moved to Texas. He could belt out a mean bass to George Strait's tenor and did just that. He let loose and started harmonizing. He thought he sounded pretty damn good, too.

He had been driving for about two hours when a soft feminine voice coming from the rear of the Suburban said, "I have to use the bathroom. Please."

The Suburban swerved to the right, running on to the shoulder. He drove over rubber, soda cans and who knew what else. He had no idea he hadn't been alone. The person behind him could have a gun, a knife. Could be a deranged killer, a psycho in his midst.

He jerked his head around. "Kate?" Then turned back on the road as the Suburban shot back on the interstate, almost taking out a Mustang and Blazer at the same time. He didn't honk at those drivers when they made obscene hand gestures to him. He deserved it.

"What the hell are you doing here?" How could this be happening to him?

He had the runaway bride. With a sinking feeling, he watched through the rearview mirror as she uncrunched herself from between the very last seat in the truck and the back hatch. She spoke again, "Please Tony, it's an emergency."

"My crashing into some car would have been a real emergency."

"Why would you have done that?"

"You scared the hell out of me, that's why." His voice boomed. Didn't she understand?

"I'm sorry. I didn't mean to startle you. I don't want to distract you anymore. Let me just climb over these seats and we'll chat."

"Chat?" he growled. "You want to have a chat? I almost got us killed because you pop up out of nowhere and you want chatting?"

"Now, Tony. I said I was sorry." Her voice was muffled as her wedding dress somehow landed over her head as she climbed over seats.

He was having a lot more trouble watching the

road since the scene unfolding in the rearview mirror was so much more entertaining. Finally, for both their safety sakes, not wanting to rear-end an eighteen-wheeler, he drove the car off the highway and onto the shoulder—on purpose this time—slammed down hard on the brakes and brought the Suburban to a screeching halt.

Twisting around, watching her every move, he asked, "Do you know what you've done?" A white dress, petticoats, legs, feet and lots of blond hair rolled over the back and into the rear seat. Pretty hair. Nice legs.

"Oh, yes. I've been waiting forever to do it. Maybe longer. But I fell asleep, I think." She sat up, holding the top of her dress tight against her chest. Then she let it go, placed both hands on the next back seat and slung one leg over the back. "What took you so long to leave?"

"That's it? That's all you have to say?" He wasn't going to look at her climbing over the seats. But he did look. Long and hard. "Everyone's crazed with worry about you. You had a wedding to be in." She didn't have just nice legs. Hell, no. She had great legs. Long, femininely defined and shapely. Legs she'd kept hidden under the long skirt she'd worn when he first met her. And she was panting in these short little breaths that were damned erotic.

"I doubt that." She sucked in some air before the rest of her crawled over the back of the seat to join her leg, any sounds she may have made momentarily muffled under more wedding dress and petticoats. She landed in the middle seat, looked at him and gave him a big smile. "Crazed, that is. But I'm going to be crazed if you don't get me to a rest room. Immediately."

"How bad?"

"Bad."

He reached across the back seat, stretched his arm towards the door, accidentally grazing across her breasts as he grabbed hold of the handle, unlatched the door and pushed it open. "It's all yours." He waved toward the pasture.

She looked outside. "There?"

"The cows do it."

"Are you calling me a cow?"

"I would never call you a cow."

She scrunched up her forehead, as if trying to figure out if he were telling the truth or not.

"Sweetheart, if you really have to go, a little thing like a big pasture isn't going to stop you." Kate, with her dress all spread out like it was, with her pretty face and slender body sticking up in the middle of the dress, looked like the doll on top of the wedding cake. "Have at it," he said. "I'll wait for you."

"Why are you being so mean?"

"Mean?" Didn't she know the position she had put him in? What was he supposed to tell Seth? "You're the bride..."

"Ex."

"You're the *ex*-bride," he ground out, "of my best friend. What do you think he's going to do when he finds out you ran away with me? Do you think we'll still be friends."

"He'll understand."

"He's not going to understand." She may be one hot-looking number, but her thinking Seth would understand made him want to throttle her. Why couldn't she have picked someone else's car to hide in? Why him? Seth would kill him. "Not only won't Seth understand, I doubt Cara will either."

"Cara?"

"My fiancée."

"You're getting married?" Her eyes widened, her already pale skin seemed to get even more so, if that were possible.

"That's the plan."

She seemed to think a long moment about what he had said, and he didn't think what he said required any thought at all. "Well, how 'bout it." He gestured to the field. "Gotta go?"

"I can't go out there." Her voice took on a desperate edge. Her face twisted in a pained kind of look, her eyes seemed glazed.

But this was the woman who didn't have to be stuck in the middle of a cow field on a lonely stretch of freeway if it hadn't been her own choice. She could have been tucked in her marriage bed with Seth. All it took was one flashing memory of the expression on Seth's face when the bride bolted, and he didn't feel that compelled to give in to her female pleas for nature's release. There was no reason to make it easy on her since she hadn't made it easy on everyone left behind at the church. So he asked a simple question. "Why?"

"Because there's no toilet paper. There's no sink. I need a sink. You know, to wash my hands." A reddish flush appeared over the plump parts of her breasts revealed by the low-cut neckline of the dress.

"That's the answer to one why. Not the why I was asking about."

"Oh." She covered the tops of her breasts with her hand. A small hand that didn't cover much.

"The other why." He wasn't even sure he cared right now. Not that there was a lot of breast showing, or that he was looking or anything like that. Or noticing on purpose, but he was, after all, a breast man. And Kate's were just there.

He was sure she hadn't that much breast material when he'd first seen her because he would've noticed. He was only newly engaged when he'd first seen her. So at that time, yesterday, he could have legitimately noticed because as a newly engaged man, versus an old engaged man, he was still more single than attached.

Cara had big breasts, too. Wait. He thought a second. Maybe they were medium sized. Hard to say, really. He had never noticed that about Cara.

He made himself a mental note to notice Cara's breasts the next time they were together. Not her breasts together, Cara and him together. There. That was better, he thought.

Kate's blush made its way up her neck. She had a long, slender neck. He could see her tendons, and her pulse beating. There was something about a woman's neck. No doubt about it. He was a neck man, too. Cara had a neck, of that he was sure. He must have seen it hundreds of times. Thousands even. Her neck was…was…well, it held up her head.

Finally the blush crept up to Kate's face. She had the face of an angel. Her hair had come loose from its pins and strands of it were covering her cheeks and neck. The veil was still attached to several pieces of hair and hung on in desperation with wire pins. She had nice golden hair. The kind the sun would kiss—if suns really kissed hair. The kind that would be soft if it hadn't been so stiff with the gunk women used to keep it in place. He was a dig-his-fingers-in-a-woman's-hair kind of guy. He liked to feel its soft, silky texture, smell its fragrance, sleep with his face buried in the curve of a woman's neck, feel the tickle on his cheek. Yep, no doubt about it, he was a hair-without-the-gunk kind of guy.

Now Cara, that woman had hair. Thick, dark brown hair. He thought it might be straight. No, now that he thought about it, her hair was curly.

Wait a second. He tried to remember when they were kids what it had looked like then, but he didn't remember ever seeing her wear it down. It was always in a ponytail, and then, as they got older, a bun. He was sure though, on their wedding night, she would wear it down. Maybe. He wondered about his wedding night. He looked at Kate and knew her wedding night wouldn't take place. "Why did you ran away?"

"I'll try to explain. But not right now, okay? Now I have to go. Can we stop at a gas station?"

"What's to stop me from turning around at the next crossover and taking you right back to your grieving groom?"

She turned from her blushing bride blush to a very nonbride color of pastry dough white. "You wouldn't, would you?"

"Give me one good reason why I shouldn't?" He didn't have time to drive her back, but he could put her on a bus. Didn't he owe it to Seth to send the bride back home? Morally it was the right thing to do. But looking at her beautiful face with the unhappy, dejected and woeful expression he had to reconsider the wanting to send her back.

Kate lowered her gaze then looked straight back at him with eyes as sharp as glass shards. Her nose was small and straight, her nostrils slightly flaring. Her mouth, pink and full, was set in a pink full line. He knew she thought she looked serious, thought she looked stern and formidable. Only her lips were too kissable for that to happen. It took every muscle he had and a lot of willpower to stop himself from leaning over the back of the seat that separated them and planting one right on her. He wanted to do that badly. So badly he hurt.

Only he'd be a real schmuck to lust after the ex-bride of his best friend. Especially since, as of twenty-four hours ago, he wasn't available. Old habits were hard to break, and the idea he was suddenly attached hadn't really had a chance to sink in. He was working on it though. He had a duty to Seth. And to Cara. Lusting after the escaped bride was not part of his plan.

Mary Kathryn—no, wait, she was Kate now—gazed into Tony's eyes, and the heat she felt going through her blood made her arms and legs weak, made her mind totally vacant of everything except the need to kiss him and not stop. But he was engaged, and that put a crimp in her intentions. She would never go after an attached man.

Then again, she had never really gone after any man, and her inexperience showed, she was sure.

So she might have analyzed the whys and why nots of actually carrying through the kissing fantasy if she hadn't the need to take care of urgent business. "Please, Tony. Don't make me beg." At least not beg for something like going to the bathroom, she thought.

He gazed back at her with incredible dark brown eyes that, at least to her, seemed both compassion-

ate and suspicious at the same time. She admired
him for his suspicion. She probably would have felt
the same way had she been him.

"Beg not to go back, or the bathroom?"

"Both."

"You sure you don't want to go over there?" He
pointed to the field, the cows, the very few trees.
"This is your last chance."

"No. I couldn't." She breathed a half breath of
almost relief. She felt him giving in and when he
sighed, a deep exasperated sigh, as if he knew he'd
have to, but didn't want to, but would anyway, she
finally took a deep steadying breath.

He faced the front, giving her the back of his
head to look at. He had nice, thick hair. Dark, wavy,
just over the collar. The kind of hair she'd like to
run her fingers through while she brought his head
down to hers for a deep, wet kiss. A kiss that she
could dream about, only knew it would never happen. Because Kate may be a lot of things—things
that caused her to leave her wedding, for instance—
but she was noble, upstanding, righteous and moral.
And being moral meant she would never kiss another woman's fiancé. Although thinking about it,
dreaming about it, was a whole other matter.

Tony turned the signal on and merged back into
the interstate. She looked down at her painted pink
fingernails. They looked nice. She'd never thought
about how nice hands could look before. She'd also
never thought she'd have a fantasy about the man

who was in the driver's seat. She didn't have a lot of experience when it came to men and none at all when it came to seduction, but she had a feeling nice fingernails helped. Kind of went with soft, warm hands rubbing backs and chests and things like that. God, she was such a loser when it came to all this.

She stared out the window as fields of green and cows of black whizzed by.

"You should have seen Seth after you left," Tony said, almost casually, breaking the silence.

"How long have you been engaged?" she asked.

"He was crushed. He was crying. He was threatening to commit suicide."

Mary Kathryn's eyes widened, then she squinted at him. "You liar. You're not engaged. Seth would have told me."

"Don't you care about how Seth felt?" he demanded to know.

"Seth's not the type to do any of that."

"You got me."

"See, I told you you weren't engaged."

"Oh, I'm engaged all right. It's Seth. He wasn't crying. He didn't threaten to kill himself, only you couldn't have known that when you took off, could you?"

Tony being engaged was depressing. She wished she wasn't so moral. "I knew Seth would be better off without me."

"He wasn't. Do you know what he did?"

"I have no idea." He could have done anything as long as it was dignified and planned out. He wouldn't have had much time to plan, but Seth could plan quickly.

"He got drunk, that's what he did."

"He'll be okay," she said softly. "He's a smart man. He'll soon realize what happened was for the best."

Tony snorted.

"He will," Kate insisted. "He'll thank me one day."

"I don't know about that. What if he stays drunk forever? What if you ruined his life? What if he never trusts a woman again? What if—"

"What if you stop imagining all these things that aren't going to happen. Seth is sensible. He'll be fine. I know it." She had to believe that. "So how long have you been engaged?"

Tony pulled the car into the parking lot of a bed and breakfast chain that had cropped up over the countryside. He parked near the front door, turned off the engine, then faced her again. "Two days."

"Oh." The reality of his situation was a crushing blow to her.

"When did you decide not to get married?" He sounded more curious than condemning.

She didn't think it would be a good idea to tell him the idea had come in a dreamlike fantasy and he had been the main attraction. Especially since he wasn't available to act out even a portion of her fantasy. Instead she looked out the window and asked, "Why are we here?"

"So you can use the bathroom."

"A gas station would have been fine."

"This is closer." He got out of the car, came around to the passenger side and opened the door for her, extending his hand, offering, without words, to help down.

She gladly took hold of his hand. Strong, rough, big. Big hands, big feet, big— Nah, she had to stop thinking that way. It made her heart race and moisture pool in her woman's very center. Not a good thing to be happening at this moment. Shannon had insisted she buy the crotchless panties.

They walked side by side, without touching, into the lobby. The woman behind the counter clasped her hands together. "Oh, a bride. How delightful," she twittered.

"It's not like that," Kate started to say, but got jabbed in the ribs for her effort. She jabbed him right back. "May I use your rest room?"

"Of course, dear. It's down the hallway, to your left. We have many weddings here and the bathroom is built for a dress like yours. Enjoy it." She pointed. "Do you have reservations for our bridal suite?"

"No." Kate started down the hallway when it dawned on her that leaving Tony might not be a good idea since he might take off without her.

"Come with me," she ordered, grabbing his hand and pulling.

"It's available," the lady called out as they hurried down the hallway. "The Bridal Suite. Ah, true love," she sighed.

Tony got this wicked grin on his lips when the reached the door marked Ladies. "Did you need help?"

"Of course not," she retorted, going inside, closing the door in his face. She quickly opened it again, held out her hand and said, "Give me your wallet. Please."

His sexy grin stayed in place as he handed it over to her. She tried to ignore the tingles jumping all over her arms when she heard him laughing after she closed the door.

The lady at the front desk was right. This room was more like a private dressing area than a public facility. Mary Kathryn could hardly take it all in. She'd never seen anything like it before. The commode was hidden away in a room by itself. The sink was in another room. It was on a pedestal. Next to the sink was a table full of lotions, hair spray, mouthwash, disposal toothbrushes, hair pins and all kinds of other feminine things that a woman might need. She went back into what seemed like a dressing area. Candles in silver and crystal holders, and spicy potpourri in china bowls were placed on every available surface. A chaise lounge in burgundy velvet leaned against one wall, an antique

makeup table with a lighted mirror was against another. The carpet, an old-fashioned burgundy, rose
and green floral design, matched the wallpaper.

She went back to the door and listened for
Tony's breathing, only didn't hear anything. She
cracked it open, and without looking out in the hallway, called out, "Tony, are you still there?"

"Right here," he called from the other side.
"You've got my wallet, remember?"

"Good." She shut the door and locked it.

The dress took up a good part of the room. Oh,
what she'd give for that beige suit right now. There
was more satin and crinoline and layers of slips and
petticoats sewn into the waistband than she knew
what to do with. Not to mention the garter belt, the
G-string underwear that had no bottom, the silk
stockings, and the bustier—which was just another
word for rib crushing lung compressor. How she
ever let Shannon talk her into all this she would
never know. It would never happen again.

She gathered satin skirt and crunchy petticoats
and lifted them up. The material slipped out the
back of her arms since her arms simply weren't big
or wide enough to hold it all up, nor were they long
enough to reach over, above, across, around or below all the material and be able to grab hold and
disconnect the hooks and eyes that held her underwear together. Now that she got a good look in the
mirror at what she was wearing under the dress, she

wasn't even sure she had put it on in the right order to begin with.

All she knew was that unless someone undid the bustier she wasn't going to be able to get any of what was underneath off her body.

There was only one person who could help. She went back to the door and cracked it open again. "Tony?" She peeked her head out.

He was slouching against the wall opposite the door. He didn't even stand straight when she called his name. "Can you ask that lady at the front desk to come here and help me?"

"With what?" he asked.

"It's personal." She hissed back.

"What'll you give me if I do?"

"Your wallet?"

"Not good enough."

"I'll start flushing money and driver's license…"

"Damn, women blackmailers—" He took off muttering about her gender adding a seemingly sermon about PMS. When he knocked on the door a few minutes later and gave her the news, she was distraught. "There's a note on the registration desk that says she'll be back in an hour." He shrugged and headed back to his wall.

She must have looked upset, because he stopped for a moment and looked back at her, then asked, "Is something wrong? Can I do something?"

She had no choice really. Her fantasy could turn

into reality by simply letting circumstances happen as they will. She looked up at him and licked her suddenly dry lips. Fantasies of Tony naked, primed and ready, slammed into her full force. She asked him, almost shaking at the thought, ''If it won't be too much of a bother, can you undress me?''

5

HIS MOTHER HAD NEVER TOLD HIM there'd be moments like this. Pop hadn't either. Or had anyone else for that matter.

He tried to keep his excitement at bay. After all, it wouldn't be any good to let Kate know it was times like this little boys wonder about, teenager boys hope for, and grown men dream will happen, but never think really will. Not without flowers, candy, dinner, dancing, a minimum of three dates and promises of undying love and devotion.

Tony gulped. There she stood, a beautiful, desirable, albeit skittish woman in need to take care of life's most basic urge—besides sex that is—and she needed him to get out of her underwear. All thoughts of Cara ran out of his head. He was a jerk. He was a philanderer. Then again, he hadn't done anything wrong. He was only thinking about the possibilities, and thinking wasn't doing.

Besides, Kate needed him. Him. He had the power and her blue eyes had the desperate look of a cornered cat. Her full lips were set in a grim line which worried him. A lot. Because what he wanted were for those lips to pucker up. For him. The overwhelming desire to feel her lips on his skin broadsided him with such an intensity that if he hadn't been a person used to controlling his emotions, he would have lost control right then and there.

He could act cool. Detached. And all the while his hot Italian blood burned a fire inside him. She would never know.

When he reined in his libidinous thoughts he realized her expression had that certain pleading look only women can muster up. He had to ask the obvious. "Why don't you pull them down?"

"Don't you think I would if I could, you idiot." Her words slid through clenched teeth.

"Idiot?" Strong arms complete with those muscular biceps he was pretty proud of, if he said so himself, crossed over abdominal muscles years of lifting boxes of fruits, meats and vegetables from crate to workbench had made washer-board tight. He flashed her his Tony the Tiger grin. "You're calling me an idiot? You're the one who can't get out of her own underwear."

"O-o-o-h. That has nothing to do with it. I didn't want to be in this underwear in the first place."

"This keeps getting better and better," he murmured, sweeping her from lopsided veil down to the tips of white shoes with an appreciative gaze. He closed the dressing room door behind him. And locked it. "A bride with no panties on. The fantasy of every male."

"*Any* woman with no underwear is a man's fantasy," she stated.

"You bet your life it is."

"Well, this is not your fantasy." She was turning red and sputtering. "This is my nightmare."

He only smiled as he watched her stomp her pretty little white shoes. "Temper, temper."

"I'm not having a tantrum. I'm having an emergency." Her look implored him. "Please. Please help."

He made what he hoped sounded like a sympathetic sigh, when truly he couldn't wait to get his hands underneath that skirt. By invitation yet. Cara would understand, since he was only helping out. It would be a totally detached moment for him. He wouldn't even think about it. Not at all. "What do you want me to do?" He hoped his tongue wasn't hanging out and the panting was under control.

He got down on his knees in front of her legs. Not seeing her legs under the dress was even better than seeing her legs. He put his hand around her ankle. Slim. "This is good." His fingers could almost wrap around it.

"Not there. Higher," she said.

"Oh, yeah, mama. This gets better and better."

She whacked him on the head. "You're engaged."

"I know, I know. I'm only giving you a hard time." And himself one, too.

Tony might have been in a rush to get back to

Houston, but for some reason, at this moment, he felt like taking his sweet time taking care of the task at hand. He let his fingers wander slowly up her leg. It was covered in silk, all soft and smooth. Her calf had muscled definition. When he reached the back of her knees, he massaged them in slow circles with his thumb. She quivered slightly under his touch. Now he was convinced. He was a blind man with a leg fixation and he'd just died and gone to leg heaven.

"Hurry," she urged.

"This isn't something you rush," he told her, gliding his fingers up her middle thigh. And women claimed they wanted foreplay. Hah! *Hurry, she had said.* Liars, all of them.

He reached the part of the garter belt part that clasped the top of her stocking, and touched the silky smooth skin right above. She gasped when his fingertips made contact with her soft inner thigh. He had to close his eyes for a moment, stop and find control. Her scent, sweet and musky, emanated through the layers of her skirt. He wanted to bury his face inside the warmth between her legs so much, the wanting almost choked him. *Pond scum.* That's what he was.

His hand felt a warmth as he moved closer to the apex between her legs. Her woman's center. He felt the bottom of lace touching the top of his hand and something more. Soft curls, warm, damp skin. His hand hesitated, she moaned. He was now rock hard, throbbing and urgent. This situation was not good. Not good at all.

Finally, when he could talk, he had to ask, "What exactly am I looking for?" He knew what he found. As much as he wanted to touch her more, to cup her with his hand, fill her with his fingers and let her ride, bringing her to a whimpering climax, he couldn't. He wouldn't.

He glanced at her face, her lips were slightly parted, her eyelids half closed, and her breathing coming in rapid bursts.

He moved his fingers a fraction down her leg, away from temptation, across her hips, heading toward the small of her back.

"I don't know what you're looking for. I think that my bustier has to be undone so I can get my panties off." Her voice strangled around the words.

"You're wearing panties?"

"Those lacy G-string kind. There's no bottom," she whispered almost shyly. "So be careful."

He didn't move. He couldn't. The image of what he had touched but didn't see, what he could only imagine was under the dress, was almost more than a red-blooded male should have to bear without any hope of fulfillment. "We're doing this backward. You should take the dress off first, and then I'll unhook you."

"No. Just undo the bustier."

He tried to reason with her. Not for any selfish reasons of course. "Kate, you're not making sense.

I'll be happy to help you out of the dress. Only if you want me to, of course,'' he tossed out for good measure. He didn't want to beg. It took a lot of effort to sound nonchalant, because in a moment his boner was going to make him keel over.

"No." She was adamant. "You can't see me in this thing. It's like being naked."

"What do you think I'm doing now?"

"You're only touching. Feeling. It's not the same."

"Oh, come on, Kate. I'm a guy. Seeing you in that lacy thing isn't going to do a thing for me. It's not going to give me ideas. It will be like seeing my brother in his underwear."

"Really?"

"No, not really." This woman had a lot to learn about men. But who was he to give her lessons? No one. Just a poor slob with a hard-on and no hope for relief at the present time.

She let out a soft groan. He put both his hands under her skirt this time, took her by the hips and turned her so her backside faced him. The material of her wedding dress now covered his shoulders, her legs almost straddled both sides of him. He reached around her until he felt the hooks and eyes of the contraption she had on, and he started to separate both of them. Without much luck.

"I'm afraid I'm going to tear it," he told her as he pulled and heard a ripping noise.

"I don't care. Rip it." She sounded sleepily sexy as all get-out.

"What are you going to wear if I do that?"

That perked her up for a minute. She glanced down at him over her shoulder. Then she gave him a heart-stopping smile and he could tell she was ready to say, "I'll wear nothing." Then she'd ask him for a quickie, just to dull the reality of not having a wedding night, and because his incredible fingers felt so good on her quivering skin. It was so obvious what she wanted.

Only for some strange reason she asked, "Can I borrow something of yours?"

"What?" Hell, he had no plans on giving in to her lust for a quickie anyway. Even if she had asked.

He had to gather his thoughts, which were spread out on a floor somewhere in images of the two of them rolling around together. She apparently took his silence as a no, because she asked hesitantly, "A T-shirt maybe?"

"I guess I can help you out there. I'll go to the car and get the clothes."

"Thank you so much, Tony. Really, I appreciate all your help and understanding."

"I don't mind helping. I need to change out of this tux anyway."

She shot him a relieved smile and turned away. His gaze followed the long line of buttons that needed to be undone. The dress was almost as low cut in the back as it was in the front. Her shoulder blades were erotic and he had to stop himself from rubbing them, massaging them, and then continuing down her spine. He reached for the top pearl button.

"Just rip the buttons." She was trembling, standing first on one high heeled foot then the other and back again.

"I can't do that." He'd never ripped a dress off a woman. He went to work on the tiny pearls as best he could and tried to control the fire that ran through him when his fingers touched her skin. She bounced from one foot to the other, her breathing just short gasps. He knew she was feeling what he was feeling, only she wasn't as experienced at controlling it as he was.

"Hurry, please. I've got to go."

"I'm hurrying as fast as I can." The buttons are the size of pinheads. His frustration at the situation grew. Why did he have these feelings for Kate and not Cara? He didn't realize he had pinched her until she said "ouch."

"Hold still," he mumbled and went back to his torturous work. Each button revealed more skin that was more satiny than the material of her dress.

"I can't help it," she whispered. "Hurry."

He finally, almost regretting that he reached that point, got the last button undone. She let the dress slip off her body. It billowed on the carpet in a pool of white. She stepped over the dress, arms crossed, holding the corset to her breasts. She never turned around. He saw all of her back, the firm, rounded cheeks of her bottom that weren't covered by that sexy lace harness she wore, and those incredible long legs that were still wrapped in silk and garters and high heels. Legs that could pass for a Las Vegas showgirl's.

Then she bolted and a lot of male fantasy ran with her into the adjoining room. Just before she disappeared for good, she turned and faced him.

He couldn't help staring. The woman was built. Tiny waist, breasts pushed up and almost overflowing out of that thing she wore. Breasts that looked like they were longing, no hungering, for his touch.

"Tony," she said softly. "When you go out to the car, you're not going to drive off and leave me are you?"

"No," he denied. "You haven't given me back my wallet."

She smiled and nodded. "Still, thank you for helping me." Then she disappeared.

Tony let himself out of the dressing room and shut the door behind him. The lady in the front check-in area still wasn't back from her break when he passed her desk. He went outside and took a deep breath, trying to cool down. He didn't know what to do. Call Seth, not call Seth. Take her back to Erie, not take her back. This came at the worst possible time for him. There wasn't time to go back to Erie. He had to get home.

Until Kate popped up in his back seat, he'd

planned on driving straight through to Texas, making the minimum stops, until he got there. Now he'd have company and he was going to make sure she understood that under no circumstances was she to slow him down. He'd buy her a one-way ticket back to Erie when they got to Houston.

He took his sports bag out of the Suburban and rummaged through, finding his favorite old Astros T-shirt and an extra pair of jeans for her and another pair and a T-shirt for him. The clothes would be too big on her, but they were better than nothing.

Well, on second thought, he smiled to himself, her wearing nothing but that corset thing was pretty dammed nice. Almost as nice as her wearing nothing at all. Well, a guy could imagine couldn't he? Being engaged didn't mean being dead.

He changed quickly in the men's room, and when he was finished, he knocked on her dressing room door. She opened the door a crack and peeked through. When she saw it was him she opened it wider, and gave him a big smile. "You came back."

"Big surprise."

"Well, I did have that insurance," she said sheepishly.

"Sure did. Wallet, money, credit cards. That's enough to keep any guy on a short rope."

"Good." She grinned at him. "That's just the way I like it. I'll be right out."

After she closed the door in his face for the second time, he went back to leaning against the same wall as before. This time though, he rubbed his chin and his eyes in frustration. How the hell was he going to keep his hands to himself when he wanted them all over her? Had she been dropped in his lap to test his resolve? If she had, the test wouldn't be easy, but he had yet to flunk any test.

Kate pulled the T-shirt over her head, covering up the sexy underwear. It smelled like Tony.

Tony. He had skimmed his fingers up her leg and she about died. No one had ever taken the time to do that before. Then he touched her. In that place. That secret place that Seth had never even shown an interest in. Yet Tony had gone right up her leg, and he reached her in the place that had been yearning for his touch, and he knew, he must have known. He had brushed against her, and felt her, and she had almost collapsed right there and then.

She knew he had been affected, too. She could tell. His breathing had come faster and he had lost that cockiness that seemed so much a part of him. He had swallowed, and she could see his Adam's apple go up and down. He wanted her, she knew that. But he wouldn't do anything about it. She didn't know how she knew, but she just did. And she was glad he had the morals and strength to be true to his fiancée. Somehow, it made him more appealing.

She tied his T-shirt in a knot at her waist relishing the feel of soft cotton against her skin, knowing he had worn the same shirt. She rolled up the cuffs of the jeans, running her hand down the zipper, imagining Tony in the jeans, Tony behind the zipper. Finally she slipped her wedding shoes back on. The waist was too big, but maybe she could find some safety pins to tighten it up, or a piece of rope to hold it up. Maybe he'd lend her some money so she could buy something that would fit. But not yet. She didn't want to give him back his clothes, not for a little while.

She gathered the wedding dress under her arm, and bunched the waistband with her free hand, then called Tony's name through the door.

He opened it for her and she walked out. "Need any help?" he asked.

She handed him the dress. "Don't make such a face. It's only a wedding dress."

"Real men don't hold wedding dresses."

"Would you rather hold my pants up?"

"Yep." He handed her back the dress, and took the back of the jeans and pulled her back into him.

Her rear end came in contact with one rock-hard Tony. When he said, "Just walk like you normally do. I'll be right behind you," she hoped walking normally would be an option, and that her knees wouldn't buckle out from under her.

When they got to the car, he took the dress from her and she grabbed the waistband. He threw the wedding dress in the back, the same place where she had been hiding. They walked to the passenger door together, he opened it and helped her into the seat.

He didn't start the car. Instead he sat for a moment, hands on the steering wheel, gathering his thoughts. Finally he looked at her. "I have to know. Didn't you love Seth?"

She knew it was going to come up again, in one form or another. But the, "Didn't you love Seth?" question was a lot easier to answer than the, "Why did you run away?" question.

"I did love him. But I wasn't in love with him. Do you know what I mean?"

He was looking at her, a funny kind of expression on his face. "Maybe," he said. "Some inkling. Although small."

"I wasn't in love with him in the marriage forever after kind of way."

"When did this revelation hit you?"

She chewed on her lip. "It's been building a long time." That much was true. Although she didn't think telling him that the catalyst was a fantasy in which he was a star would be politically correct. "Then last night, or maybe it was this morning, I knew I couldn't go through with it."

"You should have thought of it before. A lot of people came a long way to be at the wedding. I flew down."

"I thought you drove."

"I'm taking the car back. My sister, Angie, had

flown down to Houston to visit and help me out in the restaurant. She drove it back to Erie so she could take a few things back for my mom. I had known I was going to the wedding and so there wasn't a problem getting it back to Houston.''

''Then this was a good thing. That you came back home.''

''No. I've problems at work and I need to be there. If you had called it off when you first doubted you'd marry him, it would have been a lot better for me.''

All she could say was, ''I wasn't sure until I stood there that I would not go through with it.''

''I wish you had known sooner. Seth is my best friend and being left at the altar is embarrassing and humiliating.''

''I know I'm not perfect,'' she said. ''But I certainly saved Seth a lot of future unhappiness.''

He gave her a sidelong glance and a sardonic grin. ''No. You're not. Then you chose my car. By doing that, you also gave me with the honor of telling Seth that the bride ran off with the best man.''

''He'll understand that you didn't sweep me off my feet.''

''I hope so.''

''I like the idea of going to Texas.'' She settled herself in the leather. ''Starting a new life. With a new name, too.'' She looked at him and with a big smile, she said, ''Tony, from now on, I'm going to be Kate.''

6

No SOONER HAD HE STARTED the Suburban and backed out of the parking space than the enormity of what had happened today hit him. He was in the car with Kate. Would Seth understand? Or would he accuse him of stealing his girl? Which he wasn't doing. Had no intention of doing. Not ever.

"You're not thinking about taking me back, are you?"

"It would be the right thing to do."

"It's the most wrong thing to do."

"Stop worrying. I can't take you back. I have to get to Houston as quickly as possible. But I have a problem." He had a lot of problems with the situation, but he'd only share one or two with her. He certainly wasn't going to tell her she turned him on, and that he had very single male thoughts about what he wanted to do with her, which contradicted with his very engaged status. "You're a woman."

She grinned. "I know that."

"And as a woman you do things that are a little, how can I say this without sounding chauvinistic?"

He glanced at her for a second, her forehead was furrowed. He'd have to tread lightly. "You know, kind of irrational. You change your mind about things.''

"Change our minds?'' One curved eyebrow shot up.

"It's a woman thing.'' He shrugged. She should know that. She was one of them. "How do I know I won't hit the Texas–Louisiana border and suddenly you'll start boo-hooing and want to go back to the man you love?''

She started giggling. He didn't think what he had said was funny and he told her so.

"But it is. Because you're being a real jerk,'' she paused before adding, "in a nice sort of way, of course.''

"Of course,'' he mumbled. Jerk he was not. How dare she? "I thought I was being extremely clear-sighted, coming up with all the possible scenarios of what might happen as we travel down the road.''

"It's not going to happen.''

"You don't think that after you've been away for a day or two, you'll realize your mistake, and want to go back. That once you see him again, you'll fall into his arms, and declare your love and beg for his forgiveness.''

Now she was really laughing, from deep within her gut, and it was making him a little angry. How could she be so insensitive, when he was being such a sensitive kind of guy? He didn't get it.

When she finally got her laughter under control,

she told him, "Our love was of a purely friendly nature. Not at all romantic."

"Okay, if that's the case, tell me the reasons why you were getting married."

It took a few minutes for her to answer. "Our marriage would have been a wonderful partnership based on the tenure track and biological microbes grants. Not on passion. Which is why I'm not getting married. I need passion."

"It was going to be a marriage of convenience?"

"Something like that. My parents made it seem as if this was the marriage of the century. They both wanted it so badly for us, and Seth and I got sucked in."

He couldn't really say anything like she should want to marry for love and not research grants. He certainly couldn't comment on parental pressure when it came to the marriage vows. That's why he was engaged to Cara right now. Because of biological clocks, family pressure and loneliness. Passion or no passion.

She grabbed his bicep and dug her nails through the cloth. "I hope you can understand. I need to have the sparks. The chemistry. The zing."

Her eyes were big and blue and beautiful. He wished she wouldn't look at him the way she was, because he didn't care about her eyes. Or anyone else's for that matter. Eyes weren't anything but a window into confusion.

He placed his hand over hers and loosened her

grip. She relaxed her hold, and very slowly slipped her hand from his arm, letting it fall back in her lap. He wished she'd put it back where it had been, almost grabbed it back, but common sense prevailed.

Common sense though didn't quell the urge to lean over the seat and kiss each eyelid shut and then watch them slowly open so he could look at her look at him. He was lying to himself. Her eyes were special.

He shut his own for only a brief second, then focused on the road ahead. He couldn't look at her face. At her eyes. He had no business of thinking about kissing her lids.

''I couldn't convince Seth that the marriage was a bad idea. I had tried, I really had. I would beg him to kiss me. To sleep with me. He refused.''

''Maybe he was waiting for the right moment.''

''There were plenty of right moments.'' She puckered out her lower lip and looked down at her swirling thumbs.

''The wedding night? Is that what he was waiting for?''

''I suppose. But I doubt it would have been any different then.'' Her voice had become quiet and sad. She twisted in her seat, looking out the side window as the strip centers, and green fields flew by. ''I don't think Seth and I were meant to be.''

''There's another problem with all this, Kate.

Now we're going to have to deal with Seth's ego. Ego is a terrible thing to crush.''

"It's better to crush an ego now, than to go through a marriage lacking in love, and to live a lie. He would have hated me after a while.'' She came right back at him.

"I doubt he would have hated you.'' His tone softened. How could any man hate perfection? At least in body.

Tony had to clamp down on the sudden—or maybe not so sudden—image he had of the two of them locked in a passionate kiss. A kiss that started slow, and deepened. A wet kiss. A kiss where one tongue would slide over the other, raising blood pressures, raising other parts along with it.

Forget it. He wasn't allowed to have those kinds of thoughts about her, not now. Not ever. Those kinds of thoughts were past thoughts, from a previous life, a life of a single guy. They didn't belong in the life of a soon-to-be-married guy, whenever that marriage was supposed to take place. He guessed he should call Cara sometime and find out.

Then he decided to cut himself some slack, and give himself a strong talking to. After all he had control. When he thought about it rationally, he reasoned that since he was a newly engaged man, he could be forgiven for thinking of Kate that way. True, being engaged he had no business thinking the thoughts he had been thinking. Old habits had to be given up, but sometimes that took a little time.

He did what he could to help himself get on with his new status of an engaged man. He immediately ordered his brain to substitute Cara whenever he had any thought about Kate that was lustful instead of sisterly or friendly.

His brain, being highly intelligent, did just what he'd ordered it to do.

Sort of. For a guy who'd known his own fiancée for all his life, he had a pretty difficult time remembering exactly what she looked like.

That would soon be rectified. Cara would come to Houston. They would get married. She'd set up house. She'd learn to love the rice fields and humidity, the tall buildings and petrochemical refinery purified air, and she'd make it her home.

He had to move the conversation to some neutral, not personal kind of ground. He didn't want to think about his marriage. "Do you have any pets?" he asked. Safe.

"No."

"Oh." That conversation didn't take long. "How about hobbies?" She probably quilted, or cross-stitched. Women did things like that. He played football.

"No."

Cross that conversation off the list. "What do you do?"

"I work."

"Okay." He wasn't going to delve into the work habits of science researchers. No matter what she would tell him in that department, he doubted he'd understand what she was talking about. She did the same kind of work Seth did, and Tony didn't have any idea what Seth did, no matter how many times his friend had tried to explain about bacteria and microbes and all that stuff Tony didn't want to know anything about.

Maybe if he brought the conversation back to the present, as in today, she would talk. "What were you thinking when you climbed in the back of my car?

"Huh?"

"Versus anyone else's car that you could have picked." He expanded.

"Technically, you know, this isn't a car."

"Excuse me?"

"I'm not sure it's an SUV either." She seemed to be wandering off in whatever world that brain of hers was taking her. "Not that it couldn't be a sports utility vehicle, but a Suburban is more the size of a pickup truck with very elegant rear seats— I like your leather—and a lot cargo room. That's why I was so comfortable. Why I fell asleep. So I'm not sure I'd call it a car."

She was distracting him from the issue at hand. "What does any of that have to do with you picking my car?"

"Your almost-but-not-quite car, you mean."

"What difference does it make? Just answer the question. In as few words as possible. Think of this as an exercise in getting your thoughts into some kind of concise order.''

''Are you insulting me?''

''Not at all. The less words you use, the more conversations on a variety of other topics we can have.'' Or maybe she would take another nap so she wouldn't distract him with her honey voice, and her pretty hands that became animated when she talked, her blond hair that swayed, and her breasts, ah…her breasts. Not that he was looking. Because he wasn't, really.

Although she was looking at him in a funny kind of way, as if she didn't believe him. She was certainly a suspicious woman. She told him, ''I can't be concise. Not in conversations. It has to do with writing grant papers. The more words used, the more money gained. Why say with one word what you can say with two. Or five. Or ten. Words have great meaning. I never speak without having something extremely important to say in a lot of words. By now, you should know that.''

He wasn't going to give up. ''Okay, in as many words as possible, tell me what you were planning when you climbed into my car.''

''You mean semi-SUV.''

''Kate…'' his tone was a clear warning.

''I just explained…''

''You weren't planning anything when you got in my car, were you? This is a woman thing. A spur of the moment, not thought out, not planned, woman thing.''

"Oh, no." She got all haughty. "There you go again, getting that male attitude. Really, Tony, I had higher expectations of you."

"I'm the least chauvinistic man you'll ever meet."

"Sure, I believe you." She rolled her eyes. "Anyway, I don't talk about my plans."

"In other words, you did just what I said—a spur of the moment—"

"No, I can't tell you." She had crossed her arms over her chest and looked at him in defiance.

He didn't even blink. "Don't you think, since I'm your chauffeur, that you should let me in on your secret?"

"I would, only I'm afraid you'd disagree. And then if you disagree, what would I do then?"

"You won't know unless you tell me."

"Oh…I'd know."

"Trust me."

"Anyone that says 'trust me' can't be trusted."

That was true, although pride made him get all huffy and say, "That's not true."

"Oh, really?" That arched eyebrow called him a liar.

"You put me in a very bad position. I'm trying to help. To make it easier on both you and me."

"How did I do that? Put you in a bad position?"

"Kate, concentrate here. Seth is, or maybe by

this time I maybe I should say he *was* my best friend. His girl is in my car—'' And before she could go on another automobile correcting binge, he added ''—or whatever you want to call it, and I'm not sure he'll understand.''

''How did you meet him?'' she asked. ''You two seem so different.''

''High school.'' Tony and Seth went back a long way. They had a long history together.

He looked over at the woman sitting in the passenger seat. She was beautiful and Seth had to be devastated. Right at this very moment he must be drowning his sorrow in beer. Or more probable passed out on the floor, since he never could hold his liquor.

Seth was a guy who had never failed at anything, and losing a bride had to be the biggest failure a man could face.

Things naturally came easy for his friend, and Tony knew he deserved all his good fortune, because he was, above all else, a great guy. He was smart and the word failure had never been in his vocabulary. He told Kate, ''Seth and I both went to St. Agnes. I got a scholarship. They said it was because of academics, but the truth was, they wanted my throwing arm.''

''Throwing arm?'' She looked confused. ''You threw your arm? Where?''

''No, it's a football term. I played football. There was some kind of rivalry between Father Flanagan and Father Lindsey of St. Pious. It went back forty years of St. Agnes defeats. Until me, that is.'' He couldn't help being proud.

From the time he'd entered St. Agnes as a freshman, there had never been any misunderstanding on either Father Flanagan's part, the board of trustees' part or Tony's on what his role was supposed to be. St. Agnes needed a quarterback that could throw down the field, and actually connect with a teammate, not someone on the other team.

There was never any misunderstanding either that if Tony failed in school, throwing arm or not, he'd be out the door. Father Flanagan did what he could to make sure Tony succeeded on all fronts, and the key to that success had been Seth.

Seth had become Tony's mentor. The brain and the jock. The brain tutored the jock until science, history, math and any other subject had been drilled into him so deep there was no way it would escape.

Tony was not going to fail out of St. Agnes. There had been too much at stake. Father Flanagan's pride and life savings. One hundred thirty-two dollars and seventy-four cents. And Tony's ego. He would prove to all of them that he wasn't just an arm. He could succeed on all levels, even if he died trying. He'd do it for the school. He'd do it for Father Flanagan. He'd do it for himself. And most of all, he'd do it for Seth, because Seth had worked so damn hard to make sure Tony would pass everything.

"You and Seth were a pretty great pair. That's nice."

"I would do anything for him. Even take care of you, keep you safe."

"I'm a big girl."

"I know. So tell me, if you weren't here with me, where would you be?"

She didn't even have to think. Her words were laced with passion. "I would go anywhere, as long as it was far away from Erie. I want to start over, I want to be a new person. Not a scientist worried about tenure. Not a Mary Kathryn anymore. I am Kate. I am free. I am unencumbered."

"Interesting." This was not good. It meant that if he took her to the Houston bus station, and bought her a ticket back to Erie, she'd trade it in for a ticket to anywhere.

This was payback time to Seth. He had Seth's bride, and as much as he thought she was one hot number and as much as he knew he should get rid of her if only because of Cara, he felt obligated to make sure nothing happened to her. He owed it to Seth. He'd consider this his duty as a best friend, to give something back for all those hours Seth pounded trigonometry into his brain.

He'd keep Kate safe until both Seth and she figured out what they wanted to do.

They were about five hours out of Erie when Tony pulled into a truck stop. "We still have about an eighteen-hour drive left. Why don't you go inside and get some food,'' he said, taking out his wallet, handing her a credit card.

Kate shoved it in her pocket then held out her hand again.

''What?'' he asked.

''I need the keys.''

''I'm driving.''

''I know. But I want to make sure that I'll be in the car with you when you start to head south again.''

''I wouldn't take off, Kate. I said I would take you, and I will.''

''Look at it from my point of view.'' She smiled sweetly at him, and began to talk to him as if she were talking to a child. ''You didn't expect me to be with you. You are used to traveling alone. It takes longer for a woman to use the rest room than it does for a man.''

''That doesn't mean I'll leave you.''

''Picture this situation. You fill up this almost-SUV, but not quite SUV, with gasoline. I bet it takes about eighty gallons, right?''

He shook his head. ''Not eighty.''

''I'll be inside,'' she pointed to the truck stop, ''getting our rations, doing my womanly thing, and when I come out, arms full of groceries, you'll be long gone.''

''That's ridiculous.''

''I don't mean you'll leave me here on purpose. Oh, no, not at all. It's because you will have forgotten all about me. You will probably be halfway through Kansas—''

''We don't go through Kansas.''

Her hands went to her hips. Beautiful, soft hands. Slender hips. Hips made for a man to ride. *Scum.* That's what he was.

''It doesn't matter where we go, Tony. Don't you understand, you're not used to having me with you. You'll forget.'' She gave him another sweet smile. ''Because you're a man and men forget important things, like birthdays and anniversaries, and me in the truck stop.''

He was shaking his head. His brain on overload.

''And wherever you are, by the time you remember me, you'll be close enough to Texas that you won't turn back. I'll be stranded.''

Did she say what he thought she said? ''I'll be straddled.'' No. She had said stranded. He had to stop thinking this way, about how much he wanted to pull her hips close to his, to feel her rub against him. Straddle her. *Worm.*

He looked up at the bird sitting on top of the truck stop's sign advertising the gasoline prices, and not directly at her when he answered. That way his thoughts would be pure. ''I wouldn't forget you.''

She punched him lightly in the arm. ''You can't even look at me and say that.'' She plucked the keys right out of his hand before he had a chance to realize what she had done, and headed toward the truck stop.

As soon as Tony saw her walk through the door, he took out his cell phone and dialed Seth's number. Finally, after six rings the voice mail picked up. Tony whispered, although why he felt the need to do that, he didn't know, since he was alone. "Seth, I've got Kate. She climbed in the back of the Suburban, and I didn't know until I had already driven into Ohio. I'm taking her with me to Texas. That way I can keep an eye out for her. Protect her for you, buddy, so she doesn't pull anymore stupid things. Call me at the restaurant and we'll talk. She's okay. Just a little confused. Hope you're holding up, good buddy."

After he filled the Suburban's tank, he followed Kate inside the truck stop. The clerk added the gas to the bill. They came back out carrying six plastic bags of groceries and over one hundred dollars on his card.

Once they were settled and back on the road, Kate asked, "Can I use your cell phone?"

He handed it to her. "Are you going to call Seth?"

"Oh, no. I can't do that now."

"Good, because I tried, and he's not there."

"You tried?" She didn't look happy. "You didn't have to do that. I was going to, but I was waiting until he cools down."

She punched in the numbers and then said, "Hi, Shannon," in a cheery, happy tone.

He did his best not to pay attention to her conversation, only it was hard not to because she was sitting right next to him. He heard her ask, "How's Seth?" and then her response, "Oh."

Then she asked, "Are Mom and Dad okay?" There was a long silence, and when he glanced at her, he knew her mom and dad were not okay.

"Will you mail my wallet?" she asked next, her voice softer, sounding more unsure. Not like the bold Kate he had come to know in such a short span of time. "I can give you an address." She looked a question mark at him, so he nodded.

Soon very un-Kate like words were pouring from her lips. Words like, "Uh-huh, oh-no, really, oh-my and geez." Now Tony knew for sure there was something terribly wrong with Kate. When she handed back the phone and didn't say anything, he became concerned. A not-talking Kate was worse than a nonstop talking Kate.

She leaned back in the seat and closed her eyes.

"Was that your sister? I met her at the wedding that wasn't."

"She's a nice girl." Her voice drifted off.

"Kate? Are you okay?"

"Not really."

"Do you want to talk about it?"

"No. I don't want to burden you."

"Okay." He would respect her privacy and silence.

"But, I'll tell you something, I love my mom

and dad. I think they're wonderful people, even if they are a bit shortsighted.

"I'm sorry I put them through so much heartache today. But I don't think they have the right to hold my personal belongings as hostage. I just don't."

She crossed her arms over her chest, and Tony couldn't help that his gaze may have slipped for a brief moment to what most men refer to as the women's breast area. After all, she was wearing his T-shirt. He had every right to see how it looked on her. Even if he hadn't, he'd have been blind not to notice it didn't look the same on her as it did when he wore it. He also observed, however briefly, that the soft cotton fabric outlined her breasts, made them look voluptuous, rounded and soft. Sort of made his hands itch to touch. He'd have to be a eunuch not to see how the logo for the Houston Astros splashed across the erect peaks.

Damn, that T-shirt was lucky.

Of course, since he was a rational kind of guy and he'd already had this discussion with himself, he could ignore the way she looked in his T-shirt. However the way his Italian jewels hugged his jeans beneath the zipper was a whole other situation. He shifted uncomfortably in the driver's seat, and counted raw ravioli, without tomato sauce, in his head.

Kate shifted, too, moving her body a little to the left so she faced him. She waved her hand as she talked, as if the hand would punctuate her sentences. "I'm a very qualified person in a lot of different areas," she said. "I don't need my parents. I don't need anything. I can get a job, I can start a life, a new life with a new name, and go from there." She sounded so positive. So cheerful.

"That's good," he said. "What are you planning on doing?"

"First, when I get to Houston, I'll get the want ads and I'll see what kinds of jobs are available."

"You don't have a car." He pointed out.

"I'll get one."

"How do you plan to do that? You don't have any money."

"That could be a problem." She looked ahead now, biting her lip, sounding a little less optimistic.

He liked the way her teeth gnawed. He wasn't going to even go to the place where his thoughts were trying to stray. "It could be," he agreed. "There's also a problem with lack of identification."

Now she glared at him. "You sure know how to spoil a party."

"I'm only stating the obvious."

"I know there are places that sell fake IDs." She started to sound excited again. "There must be a lot of them in Houston. I could buy a fake ID, and then get a job. No one will know the difference."

"How do you intend to pay for it?"

"Would you lend the money to me?"

"No."

"Why not? I'd pay you back as soon as I get the job, which I should be able to find in no time at all."

"I won't lend you the money because that would be the same as me giving you permission to do something illegal." Tony had to keep her safe. He had to watch her until he talked to Seth live and not via voice mail. "Once you think the whole thing through, I'm sure you'll see I'm right." She was giving him the evil eye again. "Why are you looking like that?"

"I didn't know I was looking any particular way, but, if I was, and I'm not saying I was, it could be because you're being so jerky."

He shrugged. "I'll tell you what I'll do to help. You can work in my restaurant until you figure out what it is you want to do."

"You'd let me do that?" Her perfect cupid's bow mouth opened. Her eyes widened. Her breath came in short quick intakes of air.

"Can you wash dishes?"

"I suppose so," she sounded a little less enthusiastic.

"I know it's not a job for a multi-degreed scientist like you, but it's a job, and I won't require an ID."

"I don't mind washing dishes, as long as you have rubber gloves." She held out her hands and showed them to him. "I just had a sixty dollar manicure and would like it to last a day or two."

"Nice," he murmured, then got his thoughts back on track, where they should be, which was protecting her, not ogling her hands. "You can stay at my house."

"Really!"

"For a short while." He would have to leave another message for Seth. "Until you figure out where you're going and what you're doing." It would be dangerous on his libido, and he hoped Cara would understand. Shoot, he hoped his body would calm down. But he had to offer, because there was no other way he'd be able to keep a watchful eye on her until she came to her senses. He hoped she did soon, because he could tell that it wouldn't take much to lose his grip on being a righteous man.

"Oh, Tony. I don't know how to thank you." She clasped her hands together. "This is all so wonderful. I'll do something nice for you, too, as soon as we stop again, which I know won't be for a long time, and that's okay, I can hold it, I promise I can. Even though I have to go just a tiny little bit, I can still hold it."

"Great, you hold it."

"And I would hold it, too, Tony, but you know bladder infections are not good things. We should stop. It won't take a second."

"Kate, we left the truck stop not thirty minutes ago. Can't you wait at least another hour?"

She was pulling on his shirt. "Maybe when I said

I had to go 'a little bit' I was exaggerating in the wrong direction. I have to go badly, Tony, really badly."

"You just went at the gas station," he said.

"I went shopping at the gas station. I forgot to go to the bathroom."

He was slowly realizing that sexy, luscious Kate could also be a total pain. He pulled off at the next exit and handed over the keys at the gas station. He had to give it to her, she didn't take long at all, and when she got back into the car, she closed her eyes and didn't say a word.

Soon her breathing grew regular, and he was glad for the quiet he'd have while she napped. He needed to get all his thoughts together, to figure out how he would fight the attraction and stay true to what his future would be.

It should have been an easy task to accomplish. Except that Kate, in her sleep, began to stretch out her arms and make her body go all pliable and soft looking. Then she began to moan. A moan the likes of which he hadn't heard since the last time he had taken a woman to bed.

7

THE SMOOTH ROAD, the hum of the engine, the steady thump-thump as the tires rotated over asphalt added to the stress of a wedding that didn't take place and made for an exhausted Kate. Try as hard as she could to stay awake, it was a losing battle, and so, wrapped in the comfort of leather seats, the soft country music Tony had going on his CD, and the steady sound of the wind as it passed over the vehicle, she dozed, and the dreams appeared.

She was being held hostage. Oh, my, to be held hostage by Tony. She would do so willingly. She would never want to be rescued, she thought with a longing sigh.

He striped her naked and tied her to the bed. "It's not fair," she told him, tossing from side to side, her hair caught under her neck and shoulders. "You're dressed. You can't be dressed." He didn't say a word. Not one little word. He didn't undress either. Not seeing him naked was as torturous her lying there fully exposed to his gaze and not being able to do anything about it.

He didn't touch her, not with his hands, not with his mouth, not with his tongue or any other part of his body. Instead he gazed intently at her. He began at the top of her head, and the intensity of his gaze made her moan. Bit by bit he lowered his gaze, paying special attention to her breasts. Full, needy, hurting, nipples peaked and taut, wanting his touch and not receiving it. Him not touching her was torture, pure torture and she moaned again in frustration and desire.

"Hey," Tony was calling her, shaking her arm. "Kate, wake up."

She moaned again, mumbling, "Leave me alone."

"Wake up. You were having a nightmare."

She shook her head, only he wouldn't be able to see her in the dark. "No, I wasn't."

"You were moaning and groaning very loudly. You were practically crying. What were you thinking?"

She didn't answer.

"You're sorry you left your wedding. Is that it? Is that what this is all about? Do you want to go back? Try and make it up to Seth? See if he'll take you back? I'll be happy to find the closest airport and drop you off."

He was so far off track, and she certainly wasn't going to help him get on. "You know, I've been thinking," she said.

"'Bout what?" Tony asked cautiously.

She had been such a bad person today. The whole month even, with all her fantasies. That was the cause of what happened today. She was very wicked. Maybe evil even. "I need to go to confession."

"Confession?" He smiled slow and easy. "Are you crazy?"

That took her aback. "I'm sure I don't know what you mean." It hurt, that accusation.

"What can you possibly have to confess?"

He wasn't taking her seriously. "I've sinned," Kate stated with force. She wrung her hands together as if they were sponges and she had to make sure every drop of liquid had been expelled.

"Is this about ditching your wedding?"

"No, Tony. It's never been a sin *not* to marry a man you don't love. By the same token, it's not a sin to marry a man you don't love either."

"Then what did you do?"

Oh, sure, she could see telling him all about the starring role he had in all her fantasies. Those fantasies had to be a sin.

"Did you break one of the ten commandments?" he asked.

"No." Thinking about the best man and what he would do to her was all in her head. She hadn't acted on any of it. That couldn't possible be a sin. "At least I don't think so."

"Then don't worry about it."

"But what if I did? What if I have sinned?" She had to convince him. She needed to get to a church.

Now. "Now that I think about it, it's very possible."

"We all do things that may not be perfect," Tony said. "Even me, as hard as that is to believe."

"You've got to be kidding."

"I'm learning a lot about myself. Unfortunately, some of what I'm learning I'm not very happy with."

"Then you'll find me a church."

He smiled at her. "Sure, I will."

Relief and gratitude shot through her. "Thank you so much," she whispered.

"No big deal." He patted her knee.

The feel of his hand on her knee left her legs weak. She let out the breath which she had to hold while he touched her, so that she could soak up all the feelings his touch did to her.

They continued down the interstate, going at least eighty miles an hour. Not that she was counting, but, since he had said he would take her to church, thirty minutes had passed, and so did three small towns. Then forty-five minutes, and still he didn't seem to be inclined to slow down and exit the interstate.

Finally she had to ask. "How soon will we be there?"

"Where?"

"At church."

"You mean you want to go now?"

"Of course I do. What did you think I meant?"

"That when we got to Houston you would go to confession. I didn't know you meant now. There's no time now."

"But, Tony," she leaned over as close as she could within the confines of her seatbelt. Then she touched his arm. Her fingers went warm and tingly from the touch of his skin. "I've got to go now. So I can confess and ask to be forgiven."

"Kate, I don't know where there's a church. We're in the middle of nowhere."

"We're in Tennessee. That's not nowhere." She tried to read his expression, but it was difficult. She didn't know him well enough to know what he was thinking.

She only knew that when she looked at his face, even in shadow as it was now, she wanted to touch him, to feel the stubble on his cheeks and chin, to run her fingers down his neck and knead his shoulder. That's what she saw. That was it. "I need to go to confession."

"I need to get to Houston."

"This is important."

"So's my business."

"So's my soul."

"I won't have to worry about your soul if I can't get back home and take care of my restaurant."

"I'm going to help you, remember?"

"By washing dishes?" His laugh was shallow. "I can always find a dishwasher."

"I don't have to wash dishes, Tony. Although

that's an honorable job. I'm very resourceful.'' She gave him a sidelong glance. He didn't know her, but still, how dare he question her ability to do something as mundane as working in a restaurant. She was a scientist.

"Listen to me, Kate. I'm doing you a favor by hiring you. So tell me, what do you think you can do? Have you ever worked in a restaurant before? Maybe in college?''

"I'll write out my résumé,'' she said. "You'll be impressed. Maybe I didn't work in a restaurant, but I did work with all things that are served in restaurants. Like food.''

"You do that. Give me your résumé. And I'll put it in my circular file.''

"Ouch! You would trash my résumé. That bites.'' She paused, and then said quietly, "All I wanted to do was go to confession.''

Tony took the next exit. "I'm not a wimp,'' he told her in no uncertain terms. "Just because you said you need to go to confession, doesn't mean I'm running to take you to a church because you're insisting on it.''

"I understand,'' she said.

"I don't do things just because some woman tells me to.''

"I know, Tony.''

"I'm my own man. *I'm* not a wuss.''

"I never thought you were.''

"I'm doing this for Seth, not for you.''

"Really?" That she didn't understand.

"He would do it, so I'm doing it."

"Of course he would." She agreed with him only because he was doing her a favor, and she didn't want to argue, or point out how wrong he was. Not to the man who had the mode of transportation.

"You bet he would. Seth's the kind of guy that if you said jump, he'd ask how high."

Kate wasn't sure about that either. Seth was pretty much his own man, except when it came to agreeing to a marriage of convenience set up by her parents. In that instance he had gone along just as fast as she had.

"Seth would take you to confession and do it with a smile. That's the only reason I'm doing this. So you can see what a mistake you made when you ran out on your wedding."

"When I was with Seth," she said, "there was never any reason to confess about anything, since nothing ever happened."

He glanced sharply at her. "You expect me to believe that?"

"Believe what you want. Oh, Tony, there," she called out. "I see it. It's all lit up."

He let out a big dramatic sigh, which Kate was sure he had done for effect, and nothing more. They navigated the streets, making a few wrong turns, but following the lighted steeple, they reached the church.

He leaned over her and pulled the door handle. Her door swung open. "Go. And hurry."

She held out her hand.

"What?"

"Keys, please."

"Aren't you over that yet?"

"It's not that I don't trust you... I do. I really do. But still..." She wiggled her fingers.

"I'm not giving you my keys."

"Well then, I'm not going in."

"Fine." He turned the key, the motor roared, he gunned the accelerator. When the Suburban jerked forward, Kate reached over, threw the car into Park and turned the key so fast he didn't know it had happened until the machine came to a grinding halt. She pulled the keys out of the ignition, crossed herself and said, "Please forgive me, Lord, I know exactly what I'm doing."

His jaw dropped. "I can't believe you did that."

She looked at him, as if begging him to understand. "I had to."

Before he could answer, she had jumped down onto the concrete, and without even one glance backward, went into the church.

Even though it was late in the evening, and the church was empty, the door was still open, inviting anyone to enter and worship.

The walls and floor were stone, the pews simple wood, without the benefit of cushions. She walked towards the altar, her footsteps echoing in the cavernous sanctuary.

There were a few candles still burning on the table in front of the altar. Kate didn't want to light a candle. She headed straight for the confessional.

She was alone, and even though the priest wasn't there, she could still, as far as she was concerned, confess. After all, she was in church, and God heard all confessions and prayers. "Forgive me, Father, for I have sinned."

She lowered her voice, and asked, "What have you done, my child?"

In her own voice once again, she said, "I have made one man very unhappy, because I was selfish and didn't love him. Although, in my mind, I was doing him a favor."

In a low voice, she said, "My child, you did a very courageous deed."

"But I've had lusty thoughts about Tony, the best man, and he's engaged. That's a terrible thing. That's why I'm here, too."

"Have you done anything?" her low voice asked.

"No. I've restrained myself. But it hasn't been easy."

"Then you are good. You are forgiven."

It was a good confession, even if it was between herself and herself. She felt cleansed. Ready to forge ahead.

When she opened the car door and climbed inside the passenger seat, he asked, "Do you feel better now?"

"I feel great. Maybe you should confess, too."

"There's no reason for me to confess."

He reached over to Kate, taking a piece of her blond hair and twirling it around his finger. "Nice hair. Is that your natural color?"

"What kind of question is that?" She looked at him, her mouth twisted in a frown. Only by his expression she had to wonder if that was the real question he had wanted to ask her, or was it something else?

"Just a legitimate question."

"There's only one way to find out, you know," she teased.

He cleared his throat and dropped his hand back to the steering wheel. "I should never have touched your hair. That was wrong."

"But it felt so right."

He looked at her sharply, a frown across his beautiful mouth. She had done something terrible, she knew she had. No sooner did she utter the words that never should have left her mouth, than she made a dash out of the car and back into the church.

8

WHEN TONY WAS ONE hundred miles east of Houston, the urgent need to get to his restaurant hit him full force. He had a house, but the bistro was his home. The restaurant had everything his home life didn't. The warm feeling of friends and the sense of accomplishment at having succeeded at what he loved doing being two of the most important.

He decided not to stop at the house first. Dropping off the baggage and getting Kate settled could wait. He had to drive straight to Donetti's. He didn't quite understand why he was so eager to show Kate, or why her opinion even mattered. Only, somehow, it did.

Still, as much as he wanted Kate to see the restaurant, he was even more impatient to see how everyone who worked there had fared, how good business had been while he had been away. Despite the multitude of phone calls back and forth between him and his managers, he couldn't help but worry. Donetti's was his baby.

He drove the Suburban up to the front entrance and stopped, leaving it running. Immediately one of the valets, dressed in a uniform that coordinated with the decor of the restaurant, opened Kate's door and gave her a hand to help her down.

A second valet opened Tony's, greeting him with a wide grin. "Did you have a good trip?" He slipped a glance over at Kate standing on the other side of the car.

Tony said, "It was okay, Roger. Not quite what I expected. How's everything been here?"

"Fine, sir," he said. "Busy."

Tony nodded. Roger and the rest of the valets were kids from the local high schools. Tips were good, and so were the working conditions. Tony had no trouble retaining his workforce, except when one of his workforce was having a baby, like Letty did.

He walked around the car to where Kate was waiting, and introduced her around. Then he took her arm, but before they went inside, he pointed up to the sign, and watched Kate's face as she read his name in lights.

Donetti's Irish Pub and Sushi Bar.

Kate thought the sign itself could be considered by anybody's standard as upscale and extremely classy. It was shaped like an ancient Irish coat of arms, complete with roaring lions that flanked either side, protecting the name of the restaurant. The wood had been painted a deep forest green, the same color as the valet uniforms. The lettering, gold leaf in old English script. The sign itself was magnificent.

She liked the sign, and she told him so. But there was something odd happening all around the sign. Bright lime green neon lights strung over the top of the sign from one side of the lions all the way over to the other side. If it had been the neon lights by themselves, it would have been bad enough, but not as bad as it was now. Little leaping leprechauns that did an Irish jig, even though there was no music being piped in, and the flashing shamrocks that bobbled all over the coat of arms, now they were tacky at its finest.

"Isn't it great?" he asked. He held her arm with one hand and had his thumb looped through a belt loop with the other. A hopeful, boyish expression shone from his face.

His anticipation of her approval was evident in his stance. She had no choice. "Great," she said, nodding her head in agreement. "I've never seen anything like it. Not at Disney World. Not even in the movies. Nowhere. It's so original." She didn't think he had to worry about anyone copying his idea.

His body relaxed, his smile deepened, his eyes seemed to sparkle. "I knew you'd feel that way."

He believed her. He really did. She couldn't believe it.

"The sign is one of the most talked about features of Donetti's."

"I bet it is." And she meant that. Men! Were they all so gullible, or was it that they only heard what they wanted to hear? She'd never understand where they were coming from or how their thought processes worked. Because, to Kate's way of thinking, in a purely scientific way, of course, they, the men, did not draw on the same conclusions when she and they were given the same set of facts. That sign was completely tasteless. Maybe even tawdry and if he didn't see the tackiness, then he must need glasses.

A young woman held open the door to Donetti's. She wore a Kelly green suit and a beret, the feminine version of what the valets wore.

Tony introduced the hostess to Kate, and, without letting go of her arm, brought her inside. They walked through a large reception area and into an enormous room that he called the pub. The pub was home to the biggest circular bar she'd ever seen. It extended from one side of the room to the other, with the bartenders in the middle.

Customers filled the room. They stood three deep at the bar, or they sat if a stool was available. Others were standing around chest-high square tables that either sat two or four. Some people sat eight to ten in a circle around the small table, sitting on chairs they'd pulled away from other tables.

The old fashioned wood-planked floor matched the ceiling, except the floor was covered with sawdust.

Tiffany laps shed a soft glow throughout the area. People were helping themselves to appetizer-type food like shrimp, cabbage rolls and hot pastries which had been laid out, buffet style along one wall. Beer foam flew as glass mugs clanked together in rowdy toasts.

She'd been to Ireland once, a long time ago, on a research project through the university. She had been to several pubs there, and Donetti's was just as loud, just as boisterous, and the customers seemed to be having just as much fun. Lively Irish music, the music that wasn't heard outside where the neon leprechauns danced, was playing through the speakers. People everywhere were laughing and seemed to be having an all around good time.

"What do you think?" he asked. Again, that hopeful, expectant look of anticipation covered his face.

"It's beautiful." She took her time looking at the room, wanting to enjoy all the nuances of the area. "This place is really, really beautiful." Unlike when he asked her about the leaping leprechauns outside, this time when she said she liked the pub, she meant each and every word.

Tony walked her around the circumference of the bar. He greeted most of the customers by name, and introduced her to so many people she knew she'd never remember anyone's name.

When they left the pub area, he walked her down a picture-lined hallway and into the main dining area. There, like in the pub, the dining room was filled to capacity. While the atmosphere was more subdued than the bar, it was still pretty lively.

Once again, he gave her a tour of the whole area, stopping to talk to customers as if they were old friends. Kate's heart warmed by the way people treated him, and how he treated others. It wasn't like that where she was from, or maybe it was, she just never noticed.

She could see the kitchen through a lattice-worked wall. "Who was your decorator?" she asked as he lead her toward the kitchen. Her new place of employment.

"I'd been to Ireland several times, and knew what I wanted. A local company found the furniture and furnished to my specifications." He grinned at her, proud and looking a bit sheepish at being so proud. He was adorable. The more time she spent with him, the more she thought so, too.

"It's lovely," she told him. And Donetti's was. "Except for one thing."

He chuckled, tweaking her chin. "Why did I somehow know there would be an 'except' from you?"

She shrugged innocently, trying not dwell on how her skin felt when he touched her. "I can't imagine. But anyway, it's the name. I see the Irish pub, but where does the sushi bar come into this? Your bar looks like a pub."

They were standing at the entrance of the kitchen, and he pointed to the far north corner.

"The sushi bar is in an alcove over there. The appetizers come with the meal, or they can order off the main menu for an entrée."

"Sushi? People from Texas really eat that?" She raised an eyebrow.

He found himself mesmerized by the one eyebrow. How did she do that without any of the other muscles on her face moving? Just one eyebrow and that was it. "Why wouldn't people from Texas eat sushi?"

"I can see California people, but here? It's so unsanitary."

There! She did it again. Only this time she was giving him some kind of look. The same kind of looks she gave him in the car driving back to Texas. The one that he preferred to think meant he was a sexy guy, not a stupid jerk who couldn't see what she was implying, because she didn't come right out and say the words. What did she mean by saying, "sushi" with a question mark at the end of it and a raised eyebrow anyway? Why would she think Californians were the only people in the country with sophisticated taste buds?

"I don't get what you're implying."

"Why not Italian? It would seem to go with who you are," she asked.

"I'm allergic to tomatoes."

There went her eyebrow again. The eyebrow did more talking than she did, and that was a lot of talking. "Okay," he said, "go ahead and laugh."

"I'm not going to laugh. I didn't know Italians were allowed to be allergic to tomatoes. Isn't that against your culture?" She teased him, giving him a poke in the ribs.

"That's what my mother says, too. She still doesn't believe me, and thinks I've been faking those hives all these years."

"Why did you do Irish pub and sushi bar?"

"My favorite types of food."

"Sushi?" There she went with the eyebrow again. He wanted to run his finger across the shape and for a brief moment wished he could read her mind. Then he changed his. No way would he want to read her mind. He'd get too confused in there.

"I love sushi." He smacked his lips for emphasis.

"That's terrible. Simply terrible."

He laughed. She had to be putting him on. "If I do say so myself—and this isn't bragging—Donetti's makes the best sushi anywhere."

"I would never eat sushi." She adopted a very superior attitude.

"Never say never, baby. You haven't had sushi from Donetti's."

The eyebrow shot up again. "I never will either."

She said that with such self-assurance. Yet, Donetti's was filled to capacity with people eating the sushi. "I know if you taste it, you'll love it."

"It won't happen."

"Everyone raves about Donetti's sushi." His words came out in a loud whisper, through clenched teeth.

"Then everyone is flat-out stupid."

"I can't believe you're saying this. You don't know what you're talking about."

She adopted that superior woman attitude again, and he wasn't going to let her get away with it. "People come from miles around to sample it, gorge on it." He swung out his arm to take in the dining area. "Hataki, my head sushi chef, has a reputation for excellence that's world renowned."

"You're heading for a lawsuit."

"What in the world are you talking about?" The people at the tables closest to them were glancing their way.

"A wrongful death lawsuit."

"You're nuts."

"Oh, really? Did you ever think about the parasites that live in saltwater. I'm talking about the mercury content in the fish."

"Our fish is safe." He gave her a reassuring smile. "The proof is in the clients that keep coming back. They're not sick. They're not lighting up with mercury. They're all right here, eating sushi and lovin' it." He patted her arm. Her skin seemed to heat up beneath his fingertips. If he wasn't mistaken, he could almost imagine he felt her tremble with desire for him. But that would be ridiculous.

If anything, she was trembling with anger. Served her right.

"Raw fish carries bacteria." She wouldn't let it go.

"Not my fish," He had to argue with her because the customers closest to the kitchen were listening, and what she said was a flat-out fabrication.

She gave him a sweet smile. Her blond hair hadn't seen a brush, unless a person considered finger-combing the same thing, since she ran out on her wedding. On her, it looked good, that rumpled, tumbled look. He could imagine her falling out of his bed looking like that. No. He couldn't. He couldn't imagine her anywhere near his bed. He closed his eyes, and replaced Kate's face with Cara's.

Yes. That was better. Much better. Cara's face was kind of blurred, but he chalked that up to the two thousand miles between them. Long distance tends to blur the picture so to speak.

"Okay, Tony, but don't say I didn't warn you about death by sushi."

"Come on," he groaned. "Let's get into the kitchen, so I can show you your sink."

Kate didn't mind that Tony took her arm and led the way. People had started to stare at them. Still, she hoped the ones who had heard would heed her warning. For their own health if nothing else.

Once she got to know Tony a little bit better, she'd try and convince him to get rid of the sushi, and turn the Irish Pub and Sushi Bar into something more like Irish Pub and Fresh Vegetable Juice Bar. Now that would be healthy. All those fresh vitamins and minerals did wonders for the health of one's body.

They walked through the right side of the swinging double doors. The left side was for exiting, and that was one area in which Tony seemed very strict, probably for good reason. Collisions of wait staff holding trays of food and other waiting staff carrying trays of dirty dishes would be a catastrophe.

The kitchen was huge. She tried to take everything in, so foreign was it to her, since all she knew were laboratories. She listened, and she tried to absorb. "The kitchen is divided into sections for salads, vegetables, meats, poultry and fish."

"It's very clean," Kate noted. And it was. She had always thought restaurant kitchens were dark and danky with food scattered all over the floor and counters. She didn't know why she had thought that, but she had.

Tony's kitchen blew away the stereotype she had been harboring of restaurant kitchens. This one was organized and very brightly lit. The walls were tiled in white, countertops in stainless steel, everything about it was spotless, including the people who were working there.

"Come on, let me introduce you to your new co-workers."

He took her by the hand, and she followed. There

wasn't any way she would remember everyone's name here either. Not on the first go around, except for Hataki's. The head sushi chef. There wasn't any way she would or could ever forget him.

"Hey, wuz happ'n'in', cupcake?" He held his hand out in a fist. At first Kate didn't know what to do, then instinct told her to make a fist and he slid his against hers.

"Good lookin' chickie, boss man," Hataki told Tony.

"She's all right," Tony said. "If you're into blondes."

"Excuse me! I'm not invisible," Kate said.

"No, cupcake, you ain't." Hataki took her by the arm and lead her over to the raw fish. "Look at these beautiful babies. Have you ever seen anything like them? Their skin so pink and supple. Kinda like you, chickie-poo."

Kate did whatever she could not to hold her nose or gag. The fish were flat-out gross. "Do you know how dangerous it is to eat that fish?" she asked him.

Tony rolled his eyes and moaned. "Not again."

"Ooh, baby, tell me all," Hataki said. "Would you like some saki to help make palatable all this raw shit?"

"Hataki," Tony's voice boomed. "What the hell are you saying?"

"'ey, boss man, don't get your boxers in a wad. This girl is cute." He wiggled practically nonexistent eyebrows. "She can say whatever she wants. I'll follow her anywhere." He started to pant. "Like Lassie."

"She's your new dishwasher."

"I want to be her towel."

Tony grimaced. He grabbed Kate by the arm and said, "Let's get you to the house."

Kate looked back at the sushi chef as Tony was tugging her out of the kitchen, and waved. Hataki kissed his fingertips and threw them at her.

Tony pushed the wrong door open and almost had a collision with a girl holding a tray stacked high with dirty china.

"Now, Tony," Kate tried to reason. "Don't be upset. I liked Hataki."

For some reason she didn't quite understand, Tony growled.

9

TONY HAD A LOT OF MIXED feelings about Kate staying with him. There wasn't any real reason she shouldn't. It would be stupid for him to rent her an apartment or even a hotel room for the time she was staying in Houston. He didn't think she'd be here that long before she'd come to her senses and wanted to go back.

He had plenty of room. In fact, there were some who considered his house to be cavernous. Too big for him.

It was almost a year ago that Seth had called to tell Tony that he was getting married and to ask if Tony would be the best man. Tony would always remember that day because it was the day he told his realtor that he wanted to buy this house.

When he told Seth about what he had done, and gave him all the details, his friend had said, "What does a single guy need with a six-thousand square foot house?"

It was a legitimate question, and Tony answered, "Because it's there and I can." It was a cavalier answer, but that didn't bother Tony one bit. He'd worked his butt off to get where he was, and he wasn't about to apologize, or to downsize because of what people might think.

Besides, he wasn't blind. He'd known when he'd bought it that it was too big for him, and he liked it that way just fine.

"Hey, Tony, you'll get married," Jack, one of the three managers he employed at Donetti's, had said. "And then you'll fill up the house." Jack had wanted every man to get married, since he'd tied the knot himself a few months before. "Until then, why don't we trade? You take my apartment, and Lydia and I can move into your house?"

Jack had laughed, but Tony had a sneaking suspicion that his friend was half serious, so he set him straight. "I'm not getting married. Not now, not anytime in the future. It's not for me." And he had meant it at the time. Of course, that was before he went to Erie, before he had walked in the door of his parents' house and found his mother and Cara's mother waiting in ambush. Before he and Cara had agreed to be ambushed, by deciding that marriage might not be a bad thing.

When Tony signed the mortgage papers for 24 Riverbend in the exclusive Riverview section of Houston, he had only one thought on his mind. In fact it was the one driving force in his life, so he always had it on his mind. The need to prove himself to his parents. Which was stupid, he knew. He was a grown man who shouldn't need to do that.

Yet, between child and parent, he would always be a child, no matter how old he got.

Maybe it was a good thing though, that driving force that pushed him to succeed. It got him through high school at St. Agnes, it got him where he was today.

The only problem, it wasn't easy to impress his own mother.

When he got out of high school he'd told her he had wanted to go into the restaurant business. He had all the plans in his head. The problem with Teresa Donetti was that she didn't see the same vision in her head as he saw in his. All she saw in her mind was Tony slinging burgers in some corner dive.

No amount of talking, explaining and going over his plans could convince her otherwise. "If all you want to do is cook, and not even good Italian food at that, then you'll never amount to anything."

"I'm allergic to tomatoes, Mom."

"It's all in your head," she countered. "If you didn't want to be allergic to tomatoes you could talk yourself out of it."

The prospect of showing his parents his house, his restaurant, his life, had filled him with the kind of egotistical pride he knew he shouldn't feel, yet couldn't stop himself from having.

All the abstract thoughts he had about his mother arriving in Houston, about her having the sudden revelation that her son had made it, about giving her the opportunity to share in his accomplishments and to benefit from them, came to nothing. All because Teresa Donetti refused to board an airplane and come down to Houston and visit him. Not three days ago he had asked her again, "Ma, come to visit. I bought you the ticket." He threw it on the counter.

She had stood in her kitchen, pointing a wooden spoon covered in tomato sauce at him, ignoring the ticket, and said, "I'll visit you when I have grandchildren. That's a reason to visit. To see a restaurant, we have restaurants in Erie."

Tony suddenly realized why he had done what he had done when he agreed to marry Cara. "Damn, I'm an idiot," he said out loud, slapping his palm on the side of his head. "A fool. A jerk."

He only hoped he'd be able to fix the damage. He had to talk to Cara. Soon. Real soon.

He opened the front door and let Kate enter first. He watched the expression on her face as she saw the inside of his house for the first time. Wide-eyed, mouth open, all she said was, "My God."

"What do you think?" he asked.

"They do grow them bigger in Texas, don't they?"

Not quite the reaction he'd hoped for. Where was the awe, the adulation, the complete wonder that a guy like Tony could get this far?

Then he remembered that Kate only just met him, so she didn't know just how far he'd come. "Come on," he said. "Let me show you your room." He walked to the circular staircase.

"Where are you going to sleep?"

"The master bedroom is on the first floor. You'll be on the second. In fact, you'll have that floor completely to yourself."

Kate climbed the staircase behind Tony. She couldn't believe this house. Nothing at all like what she expected, and now that she thought about it, she really hadn't expected much of anything. His house was massive, beautifully decorated and extremely model house-like, but not home-like. When they got to the first landing, she looked down into the foyer. "You can fit my whole apartment into that space," she told him.

"It's a pretty big house." He wasn't bragging, just stating a fact.

It was big, but from everything she'd seen so far, it wasn't a home. Just a house. Nothing of any personal nature was anywhere. No family pictures, no souvenirs, not even a drawer cracked open. Everything was in its place, as if put there by a decorator and not touched since.

The guest room was like the rest of what she'd seen. Perfectly decorated, but with no warmth. "It's very nice," she told him, and he beamed.

"Come on," he said after she had a chance to look around the room and properly ooh and aah to his satisfaction. "I'm going to take you shopping."

"I can't let you buy me anything, Tony. That wouldn't be right."

"You need clothes."

"I'll go shopping after my first paycheck."

"And how do you intend to dress for work in order to earn that paycheck?" He gazed at her from the too-large T-shirt, the too-large jeans, the white wedding shoes. Everywhere his glance touched, she felt as if his fingers and hands were doing the touching. More fuel to feed her fantasies, as if she needed any more fuel. Those fantasies were doing fine without being fed extra.

"I'll wear what I'm wearing now. I'll wash them every night."

"Even that underwear?" His face went kind of pale.

She had to smile. "Oh, those crotchless things. You remember them?"

She was teasing him. He gulped. His body went rigid and Kate was taking absolute delight at the reaction he was having. She was finding out a lot about herself these last two days. Like that she must be a very, very wicked girl. "Tony?"

He looked up at her, and sort of croaked, "What?"

"Do you need to go to confession?"

"Don't be ridiculous," he growled. "You need to get some clothes and decent underwear."

"But, Tony—"

"Do not under any circumstances bring up to me

again that I had to help you that afternoon, do you understand?'' His voice was stern, brooking no argument.

"But, Tony—"

"It was only one time, and I only touched you once, and I didn't mean to, it just happened, and I don't ever want to have that mentioned again."

He lifted his fingers to his nose, and sniffed as if trying to see if her scent was embedded in his skin. Which, of course, it wasn't. She knew it was an unconscious act and she reveled in the very idea that she had that kind of effect on him. She had never known that she could affect any man that way. She never had over Seth.

"I'll never say a word." She made the promise. Still, she watched his body's reaction to him sniffing his fingers. She couldn't help herself, the words just came out, she didn't know where they had come from. "I know you washed your hands. Do you want to touch again?" she asked very sweetly.

He grabbed her arm, and pulled her out of the bedroom. "Don't tease me. I'm only a man, not a monk."

"Okay," she promised.

"I'll advance you money from your first paycheck. You're getting some clothes. And underwear. Those big, white ones grandmas wear."

"It's late. The stores are closed."

"The discount stores are open twenty-four hours.

Or I can call the manager at one of the department stores and tell them to open up.''

She batted her eyelashes at him, which, since they were moving down the stairs at a pretty fast pace, and since batting eyelashes was a totally new thing for her, wasn't very easy. She said in the most feminine voice she could come up with, "Ooh, who am I, to argue with such manly forcefulness?"

They had been bumping into each other, hips against hips, thighs against thighs all the way down, and when they got to the bottom he stopped, so she stopped. "Are you making fun of me?" he asked, his eyebrows slamming together.

"Of course I am," she said with a smile, "not."

He took a deep, exasperated breath, and said, "Let's go." He didn't believe her, and he shouldn't have. He was too much fun to tease, and she hadn't ever had fun before, not teasing a man. It was a whole new part of her personality that she had never known was there. These past two days had been nothing short of a revelation into sides of her which had been closed off until now.

As soon as they came back to the house armed with several bags of womanly essentials, Kate went up to her room and Tony went into the study, closing the door.

It was late, after midnight on eastern time. He didn't know if Cara would still be up, or if she would be sleeping. For knowing someone twenty-nine years, he sure didn't know much about her.

Not the little everyday things, like when she went to sleep at night.

He didn't know her number by heart either, not since she moved out on her own. He didn't even have it in his organizer. He opened the cabinet behind him, and pulled out his old address file, flipping through R until he found her card.

The phone rang about five times before the answering machine picked it up. He left her a message, telling her he made it back all right, and that he had Seth's runaway bride with him. "I have to keep her here until I hear from Seth." He explained to her how he felt he owed his friend, and how he was worried Kate would take off, that she had no money, no identification. Then the sound of the tone cut him off, and the phone went dead.

He thought about the woman who was upstairs in his guest room. She was probably sleeping by now. The sleep of the innocently guilty bride.

He picked up the phone again, and punched in Seth's number. He didn't care if his friend was asleep, he needed to talk to him, and he needed to talk to him now.

"I have her with me," Tony said without preamble when Seth groggily answered the phone.

"Who?"

"Your bride, you idiot. The one that got away."

"I would punch your lights out for calling me an idiot if I were there."

"Whadda mean by asking 'who,' then?"

"I was sleeping. It took me a minute. Anyway, I know you do. I got your message. And then her mother called, and she told me. Then her sister called, and then her father called."

"Are you going to be okay?"

"Eventually. Is she doing all right?"

"Yeah, she's fine. Talks a lot."

"Mary Kathryn? She never talked that much."

He had to laugh. "Maybe Mary Kathryn didn't talk much, but now she goes by the name of Kate, and Kate doesn't ever shut up." Tony looked over at the bookshelf crammed with books. This room was the only part of the house that he could call his own, that he felt comfortable in. It was the only room the decorator hadn't been allowed to touch.

"She goes by Kate?" Seth sounded confused.

"Long story. But yes."

"How odd."

Tony didn't think so, but there was no point arguing. He was tired. Exhausted. Too many emotions going on at the same time. He breathed deeply, almost despondently. It was all too much.

"She had a perfectly good name."

"I know. She's finding herself."

"I didn't know she was lost." Seth sounded a little angry.

"I'm sorry again, Seth. I didn't tell her to do it. I didn't even know she was in the car until I was about two or three hours out of Erie. I was going to put her on a bus going back, only I figured if she were in the mood to run, who knows where she would have ended up. At least this way she's here, and we all know where she is."

"What are you going to do with her?"

"I'm going to put her to work at the restaurant until you two can figure out what you want to do."

"She hurt me, Tony."

"I know."

"I didn't know she wasn't happy."

"Were you happy?" Tony asked. The answer was important to him.

"I thought I was. She's a great woman. She's quiet, smart, pretty. Her and I were working on this research project and we were almost guaranteed tenure."

"I'm sorry, friend."

"Me, too. Will you watch out for her? She's never been on her own."

"I thought she said she had an apartment."

"She did, but it was close to her parents. She's so innocent, and trusting. I feel a lot better knowing she's there with you, and that you'll watch out for her, and make sure nothing happens to her."

"I'll do my best."

"I'm sure she'll eventually come to her senses."

"Sure she will ol' buddy." Tony talked with Seth for a few more minutes, then finally said good-bye. He didn't have the heart to tell him Kate had come to her senses at the wedding, and there wasn't anyway she was going back.

He rubbed his tired eyes. He had known living with Kate wouldn't be easy on his sex drive, because after all, he wasn't blind to her beauty or her charms. Now, with Seth telling him to watch out for her, to take care of her, it was going to be even more difficult. All that added responsibility.

This was just great. Now he had to stay as close to her as possible, while staying as far away from her as he could. Life couldn't get any more complicated.

10

STAYING FAR AWAY FROM Tony wasn't an easy task to accomplish. They drove to the restaurant together every day. They ate breakfast at the kitchen table, usually a bowl of cereal. They ate lunch and dinner together at the restaurant. They went grocery shopping together, which never took long, since buying milk, juice and cereal wasn't something that anyone had to spend a lot of time thinking about.

Kate didn't mind washing dishes either. She was provided with yellow rubber gloves, and all she had to do was rinse off the china and put them into any one of the six massive dishwashers. There were other people who emptied the dishwashers and put the china away.

Rinsing the dishes, listening to the water flow out of the faucets, was relaxing. After all the years of studying, of formulas, experiments, writing papers, teaching and working toward tenure, this mindless act of dishwashing for which she was being paid minimum wage was more therapeutic than spending hundreds of dollars pouring her heart out to a psychiatrist. She liked her job. She liked the people she was working with, and she really enjoyed Hataki.

Hataki didn't like her washing dishes. "Letty had that baby, and I miss her."

"That's so sweet," Kate told him. "I can't imagine liking somebody I work with so much that I would miss them." Which told her how cold the environment she had worked in the past had been.

"'ay, cutie pie, I only miss her 'cause she was my right-hand man. She was my assistant chef to end all chefs. She knew how to mix the fish, choppy the meats, roll the seaweed, spice the dice, know what I mean, my little soybean?"

"I guess." Kate really liked being called soybean. It was so much healthier than being called a pie.

"You cook?"

She had a hard time concentrating on his question, because he was juggling three carving knives. One false move, and fingers could be flying. Kate stepped back, out of his way. "I know how to cook, but not how to fix raw fish."

"Oh, baby, I can teach you. Let's go talk to Mister Tony the Tigerman and tell him to find another dishwasher."

Tony didn't mind if Kate worked with Hataki, but he wasn't going to put her there if she showed no talent in the culinary way of life.

"Why don't you let me prove my abilities as a cook? Hataki needs an assistant and I can do the job." She gave him the sweetest smile. A smile that told him she had all the confidence in the world in her own abilities, and he should feel the same.

"Sure, prove to me what you can do."

She looked around Donetti's huge kitchen, biting her lip, her forehead furrowed in deep thought. The place was massive, she wouldn't know where to begin.

"Not here, Kate. You can cook at the house, and then we'll see about you apprenticing here with Hataki."

"But, Tony, you don't have any food at your house."

"We'll go get some."

They left the restaurant early, which was almost unheard of for Tony, who practically lived there. He took her to the grocery store and gave her free rein. "I'll wait next door—" he pointed to the coffee shop "—while you go shopping." He handed her two one-hundred-dollar bills. "Have fun."

"Don't you want to follow me around, make sure I don't run away?"

He dangled the car keys, and she smiled at him. The smile made his heart expand about fifty feet. "Now go," he ordered and quickly turned and walked away. Her making dinner, them spending all that time alone, he wasn't sure it was such a good idea. In fact, he knew it was a bad, very bad idea. But, what the hell. He was a man, he could control himself. He didn't have to think sexy thoughts about her, and he wouldn't. He'd just make sure that he didn't look at her the whole night. See, he told himself, turning around his scumbag ways when it came to Kate would be a piece of cake.

"Why are you looking at me like you're a fox and I'm a little chicken and you're ready to eat me for dinner?" Kate asked him several hours later, when she was taking the chicken marsala out of the oven.

His jaw dropped, and when he realized his mouth was hanging open, and with little effort his tongue would come out and he'd start panting, he quickly snapped his jaw shut again. "I don't know what you're talking about."

She had that know-it-all grin again across her lips.

He was going to have to work on this. He couldn't be leering at her. He wasn't even supposed to be looking at her. And he hotly denied he had, and would continue to deny it all through his life and until he died of old age. It was a matter of honor.

"Okay, you weren't leering," Kate conceded, "I stand corrected."

An adorable look of confusion crossed her face. Blue eyes open wide, pretty mouth set in a perfect little pout. Damn how he wanted to lean over and mesh his lips with hers, to do a lip-lock tango. "I may have been looking at you in a purely male sort of way, but why not? I'm a man." It wasn't as if he had to brag about that fact. It should be obvious to her, and any other female that he wasn't just a man, he was *all* man. "I wouldn't be human if I didn't look at you as if you were a little cupcake."

Now that eyebrow shot up again. Damn she was cute. She sure knew how to get his libido going. "Hataki calls me his little soybean."

Tony snorted. "That should make you feel like a woman."

"Soybeans are healthy. And so am I." Again she gave him that cute little smile.

"If you want to eat a soybean. Personally give me a cupcake to nibble on any day and I'm a happy man."

He was satisfied to see the know-it-all superior smile fade, and her lips form an O when she realized just what he meant.

He shut his eyes and thought *Cara* and he had better keep thinking *Cara.*

When he opened them again, Kate was still there holding out two wineglasses, a bright, cheerful smile adorning her face. "Bingo," she said, happy as a clam.

"Do you mind if I ask what you're so cheerful about?"

She held out her arms and he took the glasses. "I wasn't sure I could find them, but now that I did we have all the ingredients for a most perfect dinner."

"You could have asked."

"Do you mean you would know where these were?"

"Of course I'd know. What do you mean by that anyway?"

"You're never here. Someone comes in every day and makes your bed and cleans your house. I thought maybe you wouldn't know, that's all."

He gulped. For only knowing him a week, she was getting to know him too well. Because the sad truth was, she was right. He hadn't known where the wineglasses were. If he were going to have a glass of wine it would have been at the restaurant. The decorator and her staff had put everything away and he hadn't been through half the cabinets and drawers. A sorry commentary on the state of his life, not that he'd admit it.

Tony helped Kate carry the chicken marsala, Caesar salad and spinach soufflé into the dining room. Another room in a house full of rooms he'd never used, hadn't even eaten a meal there.

After they set the food on the table, he pulled out her chair. He waited until she was seated, then took his place across the table from her. Way down at the opposite end, as far away from the magic spell she had circling around her as he could get.

"Tony, this place looks as if no one lives here."

"I'm going to take that as a compliment on the maid service."

She shook her head slowly. "No, that's not it.

I'm not talking about clean, which it is. I mean it looks as if no one has ever been in this room.''

"Kate, I'm not here. I work. I eat at work, I practically live at work."

"How long have you been in the house?"

"About a year. In fact, I bought on the same day Seth called to tell me he was getting married."

"Oh." She took a bite of her chicken. "It's good."

He took a bite, too. "Eatable."

"Is that the restaurant owner talking, who has to decided whether to keep me as a dishwasher or push me up to apprentice chef wages?" She was grinning at him.

"Absolutely. The telling will be in the dessert."

"You're a hard taskmaster, but I'm up for the challenge."

"We'll see." The chicken was pretty special, and he might tell her that someday. After they negotiated her new salary.

"So, now that you've changed the subject, tell me why this place looks so pristine?"

"I told you why."

"It almost reminds me of my parents' home. Sterile. The first thing I did when I moved out of their house was to shop consignment shops and find lived in, comfortable-looking furniture. I didn't want sterile, I wanted to feel like I went home and was being welcomed by old friends. My mother had a fit."

"Why?"

"Because to her, buying used was admitting I lived in the poorhouse. What she didn't understand was that I loved my small apartment. It was cozy and I felt at home there, which I never felt in my parents' house."

She looked around the dining room and Tony followed her gaze, trying to see the room as she might see it. White walls, perfect light oak furniture, dove gray carpet without a pile out of place. Even the china cabinet with its perfectly arranged Far East figurines and blown glass vases were there more for effect than sentimental reasons.

"I could never live here," she told him.

"No one asked you to," he responded.

Her face heated. Embarrassment and anger, a terrible combination, came to the fore. "You didn't ask me to, but I know that you might have, because I can tell you're getting used to me, and so I'm telling you right now, this place is too pristine. It's not a home, it's a house. There's no life in here."

"There's not death either." The house had been decorated by the most expensive interior designer he could afford, and that was a lot.

Now if only his mother would come for a visit, then maybe he could say the money was well spent. But he'd have to have babies to get her out here, and that was turning out to be a high price to pay for parental approval.

He smiled at Kate. "I'm not here enough to make the place looked lived-in."

"Why not? It's a beautiful house. It would just take a few things out of place to make it look like a home. Getting this large house and decorating it like a hospital is just not normal."

"That's not true. It's very normal for a bachelor who has no time to do womanly work like decorating."

Kate did not look happy. "That is so chauvinistic. I really wonder about you. Poor Cara. Stuck with you."

"That's low, Kate. What do you know about it? She's lucky to have me."

"Oh, please. What happens if she cuts her finger and bleeds on the carpet? Are you going to throw her out the door?" She shredded the poor chicken marsala, and chomped it to pieces, then went to work on another piece.

All her slicing and chomping didn't help relieve Tony's frustration at having to look at her, smell her perfume, watch her hair swing freely, her lips move lovingly over the chicken, and know the whole time there wasn't a damn thing he could do about it.

"How long have you known her?"

"My whole life."

"She must be wonderful." She said it grudgingly with a smile pasted on. Fake, but at least genuinely fake. She could tell by the way he looked at her that he believed her. She didn't roll her eyes, but she wanted to. Men were just too gullible. Couldn't he tell how upset she was? Couldn't he tell that the two of them would make beautiful music together? Was he that stupid?

"Cara and I were born the same day. Our mothers were in the same hospital room. Our baby beds were next to each other in the nursery." He had this fond-memory grin, as if he could remember what it was like in the next baby bed when they were hours old. He was disgusting.

"You're giving me a funny look," he said.

"Me? I don't think so."

"You don't think two people who have known each other since birth will have a good life together."

"Sure you will," she said. "If you like boring."

"I wouldn't say she's boring."

"Where's the passion of discovery in a new relationship?" *Like with me, you moron.* "Where's the excitement of kissing someone for the first time?" *Like it would be with me, and you know it.*

"That's the beauty of Cara and me. We've been friends forever and we've never kissed in that passionate kind of way. It will be a discovery."

"Who are you trying to convince? You or me?"

"I don't know what you mean." He got all defensive.

Now that was good. Real good. "So you never kissed her?"

He didn't answer for a moment. "One time."

"How was it?"

"Is that any of your business?"

"Consider this research. You know, I'm going to be searching for a new boyfriend, now that I'm un-attached. And since Seth and I never had any kind of close relationship, no passion in the kissing de-partment, I was wondering how it was to kiss Cara passionately."

She had her elbow on the table, and she looked at him with those big blue eyes. All he wanted to do was a meltdown. Right into her. How could he possibly think about kissing Cara when Kate sat at the other end of the table looking so delicious?

"Who said we kissed passionately? Did I say that?" he asked.

"Well, no. I just assumed, since you didn't say you didn't kiss passionately. I had asked, remem-ber?"

"Don't assume anything. My marriage to Cara is strictly a marriage of convenience."

"I'm not understanding this." She speared the romaine. "What's the convenience? Are you merg-ing two family dynasties?"

"Nothing like that."

"Then like what?"

"I have a big house."

"Okay. A marriage of convenience because you have a big house. That makes sense." Like hell it did. It made no sense at all.

"I'm twenty-nine. Almost thirty."

"Ancient."

"I have to have kids soon. Before my sperm gets too old to have normal children."

"Are you nuts?"

"I've done research."

"You're full of it. Sperm doesn't get too old. Men can beget until they die."

"No kidding?" he asked innocently.

"You're pulling my leg."

"I should have paid more attention in biology class."

"Now I know you're pulling my leg."

"I'm not. And Cara, she's twenty-nine, too, and that means if she doesn't have babies soon, her eggs will be too old to have babies."

"You're talking to a scientist here, Tony. You can't believe that what you're saying is something that I'm going to believe you believe."

"Then there's passion. I know that Cara and I will be passionate someday."

"You sound so sure."

"We're good friends, so whether there's passion or not, there's still the friendship factor, and we can still have babies, and kiss and get married. I love her. Like a good friend. Friends do this all the time. And the love of a friend can turn into passionate love."

"If you say so."

"You don't believe me."

She shrugged. "Who am I to say? It's not as if I've known passionate love either." Couldn't he feel the electric surges going from her body to his body? Couldn't he tell the passion was there? This Cara, she was an obstacle, and while Kate would love to get rid of the obstacle, she had enough respect for the institution of engagement and marriage not to try come in between two engaged people.

He picked up the glass of Chateau La Tour, a fine 1985 Bordeaux. "Kate?"

She glanced up from her intense slicing of chicken. An eyebrow curved upward, her head tilted in an unspoken question. Then, when he didn't say a word, only slightly moved the upraised wineglass, she snapped out of her thoughts and picked up her own glass, raising it to the same level as Tony's.

"This is a toast to you," Tony began.

She smiled at him. "Why, thank you."

"You've made me see the light."

She didn't know what light he was talking about. Again, her eyebrow curved.

"You don't understand?"

"Not really. The light of day? The light of the shining moon? The light is bright in this room and you're just noticing? What light?"

He took a sip of wine. "Excellent."

She took a sip. "Hmm." The wine tasted as if she were drinking nothing. This was not her idea of excellent. She was a sweet, wet wine drinker. A

Chablis kind of wine drinker, if she were going to be drinking wine, which she usually didn't. In fact rarely ever did.

"I thought you'd like it." He nodded in approval.

"From my 'hmm' you decided I thought it was excellent?" she asked.

"How could you not think it was? This is a fine wine. It's ageless."

"That old."

"No, not that old."

"You seem to sound a little put out."

"How can you not think this is wonderful?"

"Because it has no taste."

"What are you talking about." He would have to teach her the art of wine drinking. "It's a full-bodied wine with a rich bouquet. A fine rim and an aftertaste of oaken casks and black fruits. It's a big wine."

"Aftertaste, maybe. There's just no taste when you're actually drinking it."

"Of course, you're not used to such fine wine." He sounded down right superior. "I'll have to teach you before you start working."

"You know, Tony, I have news for you, I don't want you to teach me about wine." She picked up the glass and held it out. "I don't even like wine."

"Wine is part of our heritage."

"No, it's not part of mine. I'm sitting here in this room. I'm a terrible klutz. I'm terrified I'm going to take this fine red wine that's obviously expensive, and spill it on your virgin carpet. This house makes me very, very uncomfortable.''

The telephone started to ring before Tony could answer her. She waited until he left the room before she leaned back and closed her eyes.

He threw the wineglass into the fireplace, never taking his glaze from her face, his expression one of lust and desire. His hands would clench then relax. Finally, seconds passed although it seemed like hours. He stood up, away from the table in a rough gesture, the chair flung back. He seemed not to notice, all his attention focused on her. Her tongue ran a circle around her lips, leaving a ring of moisture, readying for the inevitable, Tony's deep, thrusting kisses. Her breasts heaved in anticipation of his touch. Her nipples hardened with need, the need to be stroked, kissed. By Tony.

Suddenly, he was standing in front of her, shaking her arm, startling her out of her fantasy. ''Are you okay?'' he asked.

She had been holding on to the wineglass and while he shook her arm, it tipped over, spilling on to the carpet.

''Tony, I'm so sorry.'' She grabbed a napkin and started blotting, only she managed to soak it in deeper.

''Hey, it's okay,'' he said. ''Now you can't say the place doesn't looked lived in.''

Kate looked up at him with relief as she gave

herself a mental shake. How could he do this to her? How could he make her feel so vividly the lack of love in her life. Love? Mistake. This wasn't love. It was lust.

"Here," he said handing her the phone. "It's Seth."

Lust fled.

11

SHE HAD ONLY BEEN IN Texas two weeks. Two weeks was not a long period of time, yet she felt as if a lifetime had passed.

She had only talked to Seth that one time, when he had called during her trial dinner. He hadn't said much except to wish her luck and announce that he was going to go off on his own adventure. Seth on an adventure. For Seth that could mean anything from selling *The Guppy* and buying a bigger boat, to changing brands of blue jeans.

She was happy for him though. She was doubly happy she'd done what she had done. And she was triply happy that she was now a Kate, and not a Mary Kathryn. She felt as if she had been Kate forever. Mary Kathryn was a person of the past. A shy, invisible person. Kate was a take-charge, outgoing woman who grabbed life and ran with it.

Of course her parents were still holding her driver's license hostage. They had chosen her lifetime mate, and she had rejected their choice in the most embarrassing, public way. To them it was personal. Her belongings were paying the price, since what they wanted to extract in return for her things was control over her life. That was something she couldn't afford to give away. They took Kate's rebelling as a personal affront.

In the two weeks she had worked at Donetti's, Kate had already gathered more job excitement than all the years she had been teaching and researching. She had met more people, heard more accents, and made more friends than she had in the whole time she lived in Erie, and that had been her whole life.

And Tony. She didn't know what to do about him. Every day she was growing more and more attached to him, and she knew it would be so hard to leave his home, his life.

When she stood near him, electrical forces seemed to draw her closer to him. It was an incredible phenomenon of nature.

On her fifteenth day on the job, Kate had planned on working with Hataki, only Tony had other plans. She was apprenticed to Megan, the Irish food chef. She spent a lot of time peeling potatoes and carrots, and washing lettuce and leeks. Hataki wasn't far away though, and every chance he could, he pulled her over to the raw fish and flipped his knives and showed her why sushi was special. At least, to his way of thinking.

She was getting to love the restaurant. But more than working at the restaurant, she had changed on a deep, personal level. The emotions and feelings that had been surging through her body were like none she had ever known before and probably would never again. She couldn't imagine feeling for any other man the way she felt for Tony.

Kate was smart enough to know that those feelings were okay in fantasies, and okay in her mind, but she had better not even try and act them out. No matter how much she wanted to, yearned to. And she knew that Tony was doing his best to control those same urges he had for her. Which was a good thing. Because if one of them was unable to resist the temptation, she had a feeling the other wouldn't be too far away from giving into temptation either.

She was grateful Tony had let her watch Hataki when she was finished with her vegetables. She had never expected that when the sushi chef had to leave for an afternoon, he would ask her to take over his area.

"I don't think I can," she told him.

"You'll do fine, my little soybean. Just wrap those suckers and make 'em look good."

Oh, she'd make them look good all right. This was going to be her one chance to shine, to make her mark, to prove that she had what it took to be original, and on the cutting edge of culinary technology.

Tony knew something was wrong as soon as Jack came into his office and said, "You better come, and come quick." Tony wasn't overly concerned. This was the restaurant business. Things always can go wrong, and what damage was done, could be undone. Of utmost importance always was that his restaurant's reputation for a great dining experience remain impeccable.

When he walked into the main dining area the first and only person he saw was Kate. He shouldn't be surprised that when she was in a room, everyone else disappeared. She was wearing a chef's hat that kept falling down her forehead and onto her nose. She had to keep pushing it up on her head. She looked adorable and distracting. He made a mental note to get her a hat that fit. And an apron, too. The one she had on was wrapped around her twice, since Letty had used it until the day she left to deliver her baby.

Tony then realized that she wasn't in the kitchen where she was supposed to be, but standing beside the table of one of Donetti's most loyal customers. Tony stepped over to the table. Kate wore a serene smile, the smile that told Tony whoever was the recipient of such a smile had better watch out. That was the smile that said to the world, I know something you don't know. You can say what you want but when you're done, I'll turn you into fish food.

"Your chef—and I use that term loosely—insists this is sushi," Paul Cavanaugh complained.

"You should be thanking me," Kate said. "I've saved you from certain death."

Paul's face turned a sickly shade of red and blew up to twice its size. "This is no damn sushi," he shouted.

Kate just smiled her serene smile. "Someday you'll thank me."

"Th-thank you?" he stuttered.

"Maybe not now. You can't see the good in this, but someday."

"What's going on?" Tony moved his body in front of Kate's, effectively blocking her from the table and out of sight of the man intent on spewing words of rancor.

"Our sushi is the best," Tony said looking down at the plate. "That's not our sushi."

"It is now," Kate whispered in his ear from behind.

He turned to her. "What do you mean?"

"I was going to talk to you about it. I've been practicing all week, in private of course, not wanting to get the rest of your staff excited in case it didn't work out, but Tony, I'm so thrilled I invented the perfect sushi. I cooked the fish and boiled the seaweed because when it comes right down to it, raw seafood is very bad for you and we can't have that in our restaurant." She had her arms folded over her waist and looked so self-righteous.

"Our restaurant?"

She nodded.

"My restaurant. Not ours."

"But, Tony, I heard you say that as long as we're all working together here, what's mine is mine and what's yours is ours. Is that not true?"

He hissed at Kate, "That's to motivate the

troops, not to assign ownership.'' Turning back to Paul, Tony said, ''I apologize. It won't happen again. Ever. We'll make you a new dinner, on the house.''

''Tony.'' Kate was pulling at his sleeve. ''Don't do that. What I made him is good. It may be an acquired taste, but it's good.''

''Let's go.'' He took Kate by the apron strings and pulled her out of the dining area.

''Tony, you don't understand. I'm going to make you famous with the first recipe of cooked sushi in the country.''

''Be quiet, will you?'' he growled.

Kate was smart enough to know that despite the very tightly suppressed feelings they had for each other, he would still have liked to fire her over the sushi question. She didn't understand why, either. All she did was cook it. She couldn't help that the client, whose tastes were obviously plebian, complained. And loudly, at that. He was not a trooper, and she would never cook for him again, that was for sure.

Although why Tony, his cohorts and customers were so unwilling to try new things, she hadn't a clue. Anyone who knew him would have thought Tony was more flexible. And since Kate had a lot of brain power, she thought Tony would not only be flexible, but welcome new ideas.

She couldn't believe she'd been so wrong. That she had misread him to such a great degree. She had no idea he was such a stick in the mud. So unmovable. So inflexible. Now she was going to have to rethink this whole operation. She was going to have to take it in a new direction.

After he had dropped her off at the house—because for some reason, which she didn't understand, he said he needed a cooling off period, cooling off from what she didn't know—she decided to come up with a whole collection of cooked sushi recipes, created by herself, of course.

When he came home that night, Kate was her bright and cheery self. As she always was. But did he appreciate her bouncy, happy personality? Of course not. He handed her a new uniform, now her third since she'd been there, and told her, "You are now a waitress."

"Great!" She smiled. "I could use the extra money in tips so I can pay you off and get out of here as quickly as possible."

"Suits me just fine."

"Suits me finer."

He squinted his eyes at her, and she squinted hers right back.

Of course squinting didn't require much brain work, so her mind took off in another direction, which was mostly remembering what a wonderful host he'd been to her. How he had been very generous, advancing her money so she could buy clothes, letting her live in his home, not minding wine on his carpet. It wasn't his fault he was totally misguided when it came to the health of his patrons. So she softened her voice, and said, "I made you dinner."

His face turned red and she thought he was going to choke. "After all that happened, you expect me to eat what you cooked?"

"Sure," she said. "You know I'm a wonderful cook."

His hands formed fists. He was so cute when he was trying not to let his anger out. Only she didn't know why he was angry. She really didn't.

"I made a wonderful turkey loaf. Would you like to try it?"

"I can't believe you think I'll eat your cooking after what you pulled today."

"There's spinach in the middle." She slowly walked up to him, looked into his face and tried to suppress the urge she had to touch him, to kiss his lips. "Dinner tonight has nothing to do with the sushi this afternoon," she said softly.

The yearning desire she felt was so overwhelming. She swallowed hard, and found her voice. "I know the wonderful, tantalizing scents of the kitchen will make you forget all about this afternoon." She couldn't stop herself from reaching up to and gently running her palm down the side of his cheek, following along the jaw line, outlining his lips, before dropping her hand and stepping back. "Make you want to eat."

Hopefully as much as she wanted to eat him,

starting with his mouth and working her way down. There were no two ways about it. She'd been fantasizing about him since before she knew him. Living in the house with him was the sweetest form of torture she had ever known. But she didn't know how much longer she could do it. It wasn't fair to her, it wasn't fair to him.

They sat across from each other at the kitchen table, sharing a bottle of Chablis she'd brought home from the grocery store, not bothering with the glasses, and eating the turkey loaf right out of the pan so they didn't have to dirty anymore dishes.

"It's not very aesthetically appealing," she said, although what she meant was romantic.

"Good."

She shrugged. It wasn't good. But there was really no other way for it to be. "I know you could have fired me today."

"I know you know."

"And there's really no reason for you not to, except that I'm good at what I do, even if you don't agree with what I do."

He was a man, so he didn't say anything, which was probably for the best under the circumstances.

"You don't have to keep me here anymore. Seth isn't an issue."

"I know. But I have to keep you here anyway."

"Why?"

"Because you haven't paid me back yet for that advance of your salary. Remember? When I bought you the clothes, and the girl doodads, whatever they are.''

''Like deodorant, shampoo and minipads.'' She watched his face and if that wasn't a blush spreading over his cheeks she didn't know what was.

''Yeah, that stuff,'' he mumbled, stuffing more turkey loaf down his throat.

''I haven't gotten a paycheck yet.'' She looked down, because if she kept looking at him she was afraid she'd lean over and nibble on his neck, his chin, his wonderful mouth.

''You'll get one on the last day of the month.''

''How much do I owe you?''

''I don't know. Don't worry about it.''

''You just said—''

''Forget what I said until you get paid.''

''Okay, suits me just fine. Pass the bottle, please.''

He took another long swallow before he handed her the wine. She took a sip, tasting him on the lips of the bottle. It was probably the closest she would get to tasting the lips on his face.

Kate didn't mind being a waitress. She knew the tips were good from listening to the wait staff talk about what they were earning. Some of them took in three to four hundred dollars a night in tips.

What Kate really admired about the staff though was that their unwritten policy was that at the end of the night they'd put their tips together. They withdrew ten percent and divided that among the

busboys and other minimum-wage workers, like
Giovanni who swept the floors, and Violet, who
kept the bathrooms clean. Even she had benefited
when she was still washing dishes. The remainder
of the money they split equally among themselves,
and there was always a lot of money to split. No
one went home empty-handed or disappointed.

Even during what most other restaurants would
consider off-peak, Donetti's always had a crowd.
Kate was looking forward to her new job as a waitress. She was really excited when Tony drove her
to work the next day.

Customers came at a steady flow, and the Donetti's management was savvy enough to buddy her
up with Josie, another waitress, until she learned
the ropes.

For the first day, Kate tagged along beside Josie,
wrote out the orders, helped deliver them, and tried
not to gag when the majority of customers ordered
that awful raw fish.

That night when Tony drove her home, instead
of going back to the restaurant, as he was prone to
do, he came inside.

"Sit down," he ordered, after he ushered her into
the kitchen.

He filled a big plastic tub with hot water and put
it on the floor in front of the chair she was sitting
in. "Go ahead," he said. "Soak."

He didn't touch her. He didn't rub her feet. He
only waited until she had taken off her shoes and

stockings and had her feet in the water. Then he threw her a towel, and left.

By Friday, Kate was on her own. She was given tables to serve, and serve them she did. And she wasn't doing too badly, if she said so herself. After all, this was all new to her.

She was enjoying herself, too, except for that sushi which was driving her crazy. So was the ceviche and, worst of all, was the sashimi. She didn't understand how anyone could eat those big slabs of raw fish sitting on top of piles of rice and walk out of Donetti's instead of being carried out on a stretcher.

Finally, she couldn't take it anymore. When her next customer ordered a yellowfin tuna sushi-sashimi combination plate for everyone at his table, and she felt it her duty to warn him.

"Sir, you might want to rethink that," Kate said. "Maybe you'd rather have one of our great big fried onions instead?" She bobbed her head enthusiastically. "You don't want that nasty old sushi."

"Yes we do," he told her. "We want the tuna combination plate. With the raw sea urchin sushi." His voice got a little louder and a bit testier.

"The Country Cork Mutton Stew with Irish Brown Bread is fantastic tonight." She put her thumb and index finger together and kissed the spot where they met, just as she had seen a waiter do in a movie once.

The guest got very red in the face. "We don't want the damned Country Cork—"

"Mr. Murdock, is something wrong?" Tony asked, stepping up to the table.

"Nothing's wrong, nothing at all," Kate answered for the customer with a smile.

"If nothing's wrong, Kate, why does Mr. Murdock look as if he's about to blow up?"

"I don't think Mr. Murdock's about to blow up." She looked down at the customer. "Are you Mr. Murdock? In fact, I'm trying to prevent him and his guests from blowing up with gastroenteritis, isn't that right, Mr. Murdock?"

Before Murdock could respond, Tony asked, "What are you talking about, Kate?"

"The toxic substances in the tuna sashimi with the sea urchin sushi. You know, the bacteria, the copper, and all those other toxic elements in raw fish. Things like that, that's what I'm talking about." She smiled when she said all that.

Tony stared at her, the tone of his voice a clear warning. "We've been through this before."

"I know, and I said I was going to help you."

"You're crazy, there's nothing wrong with sushi."

"Not to mention iodine. That's awful." She smacked her lips with utter distaste. "Let's not even get into the parasitic hazards. Or tapeworm. Oh, God, the tapeworm."

"I make my living off sushi." Tony's voice escalated.

"I've been thinking about that." She shook her head slowly.

"Thinking? You've been thinking? That's not possible. If you were thinking, you wouldn't be telling these people about parasites in the food." He turned to address the customers who filled the dining room. "Which there aren't any of, folks. Keep eating. The food is perfectly healthy."

"Well...if you really cared about those you serve, you'd not serve them a Russian roulette game."

"Kate." Tony's hands came up, and he was shaking. "Kate—"

"And while we're on the subject, Tony, what about all the red meat these people guzzle? You should really look at expanding the vegetarian choices on your menu. What about legumes? Or better yet, some nice tofu selections. You don't want to be responsible for your customers' high cholesterol levels? Or heart attacks? And we have no idea what kind of growth hormones and steroids they're injecting into animals these days. Now that I've considered it, maybe we should drop meat right off the menu."

Tony grabbed Kate by the arm and pulled her away from the table. "You're fired," he shouted. Then he turned to his customers and said, "Everything's fine folks. I'm sending her back to the institution tomorrow.''

"How dare you!" Kate yelled back. "That is so rude. I'm trying to prevent you from getting sued, and you're disparaging my reputation!''

"You don't have a reputation, except for being mentally unstable.''

They stood at the front door of Donetti's, yelling at each other, their faces no more than two inches apart.

"You've got to get off this kick of yours," he told her.

"I've made it my mission to educate you." He was gorgeous when he was all fired up. She wanted him so badly.

"You're not a teacher anymore.''

"I'll always be a teacher," she said with confidence.

"You're ruining me.''

"Don't be silly." If she were going to ruin him, it would have been over something personally worthwhile, like enticing him away from his fiancée. Instead she had been perfectly moral and upstanding. "How dare you say I'm ruining you.''

"Silly! You dare tell me I'm silly?''

"If the oven mitt fits," she shrugged.

He pulled her to him, feeling the softness of her skin, the firm muscles in her arm, the desire to have her and strangle her at the same time. "I don't have to listen to you because you don't work for me anymore," he shouted.

"You can't fire me."

"Why the hell not?"

"Because it would ruin your reputation." Tony's staff was so well hired that no one quit and no one was ever fired.

"I don't care about my reputation." His voice shook in anger.

Kate laughed. "That's for sure. If you did, you wouldn't be serving raw fish."

"That does it." He grabbed her hand and pulled her behind him, leaving the restaurant. He bypassed the valet and went directly to the key box where he pulled the Suburban's keys off the hook.

People were arriving for dinner and drinks. There was a line of cars waiting for the valets. Kate kept a smile on her face and made sure she had a love-struck dreamy look in her eyes as Tony pulled her behind him. To anyone looking at the two of them, they would think: lovers who can't wait to get to the nearest bed. They would be wrong, much to Kate's sorrow. She wished it could be different. "Tony?" She didn't want him angry at her.

"Get in," he ordered.

She climbed inside the Suburban and didn't say anything. She could have said a lot, but she was smart enough to know when silence would say more than any word. And through her silence he would understand her to mean that he hadn't yet recognized how right she was.

Kate had a good fifteen minute ride ahead of her. Fifteen long minutes to contemplate things of equal importance to the sushi issue. Things like how to control her out of control longings for Tony. How to stop dreaming and fantasizing about how he would look naked. If he would hang left or right. If it would be long or short, thick or thin. She glanced at his hands, and wondered if it were true a man's fingers were an indicator of other body parts. He had nice, long thick fingers. She closed her eyes.

He laid her on the bed, not gently, but not rough either. His hands, rough from work, were soft in all the right places. He touched her, right under the shell of her ear, and let his finger slide downward, over the blue vein in her neck, and across the collarbone. He leaned his face in the hollow of her neck, his lips following the path of his finger, down, across the fullness of her breast. Her nipple hardened through cotton and silk when he tugged and pulled, making a singed line from breast to belly. Moisture pooled at her core, wanting and needing his touch, to be filled with him, to have him enter her and make her his. She opened for him, a purring sound coming from deep within her throat, as she helped him unzip…

"Hey." He tugged on Kate's arm. He hated when she did that, got that look on her face like a cat who ate too much cream. Then she made these sounds and it sounded too sexual. Not that he minded her sounding sexual, what he minded was how he reacted to her sexual sounds. "Wake up, will you? We're almost at the house."

This was not good. Not for him. Not for her. Not for his future with Cara. Something had to be done. He was going to have to talk to Kate about moving out. He'd help her find somewhere else to live. He'd advance her the money to move and for rent. But she was going to have to go.

Having Kate around him 24/7 was too much for a guy like him. His thoughts about her had started out innocently enough—okay maybe not so innocently—but now they were getting pretty graphic. In his mind, they always ended up in his bed. Playing out different ways in which they'd kiss, and hug and talk. And make love. Over and over again. Because he knew if it were him and Kate, it wouldn't be a one-time deal. It would be a many time odyssey.

He was getting to the point where he had to make some decisions. Either get out of his engagement, or get out of the situation he was in with Kate.

He liked Kate. He may even be in love with her. But he wouldn't hurt Cara. He could never do that. He knew he would have to call it off. He wanted Kate and he wanted her forever. This anger he felt, he knew it was sexual frustration at its worst.

Then again, she did deserve it. Yelling about how

bad his sushi was to a restaurant full of people. She would have to learn. And she would learn. With a little prodding and a lot of psychoanalysis.

God, he wanted her.

He was one sick man.

He parked the Suburban under the porte cochere and ordered her into the house.

He leapt out of the car, slammed the door and marched toward the house. Kate on the other hand, because the seats were so high, had to slide gently down until her feet hit the concrete. He was fuming, and she was humming some stupid ditty that didn't make any sense whatsoever. He was tapping his shoe impatiently, telling her to move it, and she smiled at him, ignoring his anger, and taking her sweet old time of it.

Finally, she reached him by the front door. "Are we having a problem today?" she asked sweetly, all the while ready to throttle his stupid hide.

He opened the front door and ordered her in.

"Of course, Tony, I wouldn't go out when I just got here would I." He was so handsome. She wanted to be able to stare at him for a little while, to let the moment, even if he was angry, last a little longer. Time seemed to be getting away from her.

"You are trying my patience, woman. I've had it with you."

She faced him, hands on her hips. "You haven't had anything with me and you know it."

"That's not what I'm talking about. You're out to sabotage my business."

"I am not." She would have to find the words to calm him down. To make him less angry. "You stupid, stupid man. I'm trying to protect you…"

"You're out to ruin me."

Okay, maybe calling him stupid wasn't the right thing to say. "Some day, when you're on trial for murder by sushi, you'll be sorry you didn't listen to me."

"You're a friggin' fruitcake, that's what you are." Tony didn't know what to do about her. He wanted to kiss her, and eat her up. He wanted to make love to her, and tame her. He wanted to punish her and reward her. He just damn wanted her. What the hell was wrong with him? What was he going to do?

"You take that back," she ordered.

"I won't."

"You will."

"…Tony?"

A soft feminine voice broke through their heated words. A voice Kate didn't recognize. She snapped her head in the direction of where it had come from. Standing in the doorway that lead from the hallway to the back of the house where the kitchen was, holding two wooden spoons dripping in what looked like tomato sauce was of the prettiest women she had ever seen.

"Cara." Tony, arms outstretched moved toward his fiancée. "What a surprise."

12

TONY FINALLY REACHED his fiancée and gave her a bone-crushing hug.

That was Cara? Tony's Cara? Oh, no. Kate thought she would die right there. She wanted to crawl into a hole and never come out. Her hands went to her face. She knew guilt had to be written all over it. She wondered if Cara could tell she'd been thinking naughty, lusty thoughts about her man.

Of course she'd never done anything, and she never gave any indication to Tony that she had felt that way. She shouldn't feel guilty. But she did.

No she didn't. She had nothing to feel guilty about.

She straightened her shoulders and held her head up high. She had absolutely nothing to be ashamed of, and nothing to hide. Nothing except she had fallen in love, and now reality hit her in the face. She could already feel her heart breaking into thousands of tiny shards.

"Tony, what's going on? Why are you screaming at this poor woman?" She left Tony standing alone. "You must be Kate." She smiled, holding out her arms, ignoring the drippings falling off the spoons and splattering on the marble floor.

"So, this is Cara." Kate tried to smile. She tried to act as if everything was wonderful and meeting Tony's fiancée in the flesh was the most natural thing in the world. Only her hands were cold, chills traveled up her arms and deadweight settled in her stomach. Having Cara here, standing right in front of her, made everything so real. Too real.

Cara bypassed the handshake and gave her a warm hug instead. More sauce splattered. His house was getting to look more and more like a home. Now that Cara was here.

Tony thought he'd have a heart attack when he saw Cara. She was the last person in the world he ever expected to see here. He felt cold inside. Probably from guilt. She must know that he had been thinking about Kate in ways that were more than inappropriate for an engaged man.

Hell, he had nothing to be ashamed of. He hadn't done anything. No one should get in trouble for thoughts that were never expressed, that never had any hope of coming true.

He had been trying to figure out a way to break the engagement, and now she was here. Cooking. Making herself completely at home.

Cara, his wonderful friend. She was the exact opposite of Kate in every way. And the woman he wanted was Kate.

Cara, Kate thought. She was small-boned, yet

strikingly voluptuous, with a beautiful, creamy olive complexion and long, thick dark hair that skimmed her waistline. Her coffee-colored eyes were huge, her eyelashes long, and the smile on her face friendly. She made Kate feel tall and gangly by comparison.

Tony said, "Welcome to Texas. What a surprise."

"You don't know how much of a surprise. I hope you don't mind."

"Why should I mind? How did you get in the house?"

"Your sister gave me your key. Come on, let's go in the kitchen. My sauce is going to burn if I don't stir it. And I want to tell you everything."

They followed Cara, as if she were the owner and they were the guests.

"What are you making?" Tony asked.

"Your favorite, according to your mother. Ziti with marinara sauce." Her smile was huge. "Why, she had me over at her house at least four times, maybe five, until I got the sauce right."

Kate jumped in. "He's allergic to tomatoes. You should know that."

Cara smiled as if she knew a secret the rest of them didn't. "Well, that's what I thought, too. But according to Teresa, it's all in Tony's head."

"It is not. He really is. And if you loved him, you'd know that."

Cara let out a big sigh. "I do love him. And

that's why I'm here." She put the spoons in the pot, turned off the stove and moved the pot to a cold burner. Then she faced them and gestured to the kitchen table. "Let's all sit down a minute, okay?"

"I've been calling you, Cara. Where have you been?" Tony asked.

"I've been here and there."

"Were you screening the calls? You never called back."

"I needed to think, Tony," she said, her voice soft, gentle. "And you can be a bit overwhelming at times."

"What is there to think about?"

Kate cut in. "Let me get something to drink. Would you all like some wine? To celebrate maybe?" She thought she'd throw up.

"Wine will be wonderful," Cara said gratefully.

Kate brought wineglasses to the table, and went back to the wine rack, picking out she had no idea what, and handed the bottle and corkscrew over the Tony. Then she stepped back. Way back. She didn't want her natural tendency to lean into him to rear its ugly head right now. Tony poured and passed out the glasses.

"To the future," he said.

"Whatever it may be," Cara added.

Kate put her glass down without tasting the wine. "Cara," she said through a tight smile and tears she was trying desperately to hold back. "You must be a wonderful woman to have captured Tony's love.''

Cara laughed, only it wasn't a laugh of humor. Even Kate knew that. It was a laugh full of self-deprecation.

"She's wonderful, that is true.'' Tony agreed. "I've loved her like my best friend all my life.''

Cara was nodding in agreement, a sweet smile on her beautiful face.

"We were born on the same day in the same hospital,'' she said nostalgically. "Did you know that?'' She looked at Kate.

"Tony had told me.''

Cara said, "I didn't want to come here. Texas. Ugh! Don't you have alligators in your backyards? Rattlesnakes? Big spiders?''

"Not that I know of,'' Tony said.

"That's not what I had heard. But you know how persuasive parents can be. Especially mothers. Tony, your mom told me alligators don't eat Italian girls. We were too spicy so there was nothing to worry about.''

"The sad thing is,'' Tony said. "She believes it.''

"I know. That was the straw that broke my back, so to speak.''

"What do you mean?''

"Maybe I should go so you two can talk,'' Kate said.

"No, don't go,'' Cara requested. "I have to tell

you, it was you who gave me the courage to come here and talk to Tony. I don't mind if you stay and listen. I don't think this is really private, and I really do admire you.''

''You admire her?'' Tony asked.

''Why are you so surprised?'' Kate scowled at him. ''We girls have to take a stand, and sometimes it's easier if someone else breaks through first.''

Cara smiled, ''Exactly!''

Kate was beginning to relax, and Tony, who at first looked uneasy, started to loosen up his strained muscles a little bit, too.

''What are you talking about?''

''Marriage, Tony. Our marriage.''

''What about it?''

''Tony, having children is very important to me. I'm a kindergarten teacher,'' she explained to Kate. ''I'm around children and their parents all the time. So I have had many opportunities to observe parental behavior and how it affects the child.''

Kate was nodding and Tony looked perplexed.

Cara turned her attention to the man who didn't quite have a clue as to what she was trying to tell him and that made Kate smile.

''Tony,'' Cara started, ''your mother is crazy.''

''Tell me about it.''

''I don't have to, you already know. I mean the woman is positively loony.'' She turned to Kate. ''I love Teresa, she's been like a second mother to me. She even gave me the airplane ticket to fly down here to see Tony. But she also insisted on me making you every kind of sauce that can be made with tomatoes.'' She looked back at Tony. ''I don't think she wants to kill you. But still, the thought is in my mind that the genes that our children would have might be a little off-kilter.''

''What are you saying?'' he asked.

''I can't take the chance. I want perfect children. I can't have babies with you if your mother is trying to kill you.''

''She's not trying to kill me.''

Kate interrupted. ''How do you know, Tony? I wanted to kill you this afternoon, and if I've only known you a few weeks, imagine what your mother must be feeling.''

Cara got up and gave Kate a big hug. ''Exactly. I knew you'd understand. We're kindred spirits.''

''Exactly,'' Kate said.

''So you're breaking the engagement?'' he asked. He wasn't going to fight about it. It was what he wanted anyway and it fell right into his lap.

''Well, not exactly,'' Cara said. ''I can't go home and tell our mothers that I broke the engagement. I have to live in Erie.''

''Then what?''

''I'm going to tell them *you* broke it. Then I'll look like the innocent party, and since you're down here, away from the poison darts they're sure to throw, you'll be safe.''

He took a second to respond. Not because he

needed a second, but because it was the right thing for a man who got dumped to do. He wanted to look at Kate so badly, but he wouldn't. Not until Cara was gone. Because even if this was what he wanted, he would never hurt his friend by letting her know he had been on the verge of breaking it off anyway.

"Okay, Cara," he said. "I'll take the responsibility."

"Thank you, Tony." Cara finger-combed through her hair and she chuckled. "All my mother talks about, all your mother talks about, is becoming grandparents and the wedding, and in that order, too. They were talking about it, planning it, before they even brought it up to you and me."

"Did we get suckered?"

"Maybe in a way. But now it's over. They'll have to live with their disappointment and stop being so meddling. It can ruin lives. Many lives." She glanced at Kate. As if she knew. "You two should think about getting together."

"Oh, no, that's not possible," Kate said. "He's so Italian."

"It's not me. You're the one who's so Irish. She can't even cook right. She tried to cook the sushi. She's practically ruined my restaurant in two weeks."

"I know, bad idea."

"Bad," he said. "I'm surprised I'm still in business after having her work there."

"It's worse than bad, working for a man who has no vision," Kate agreed.

But he looked over at Kate, and Kate saw the look. She knew that what he felt for her was romance that had grown in a few weeks, and that it wouldn't have happened with Cara. It was written all over his face, the softness in the hard lines, the love in his eyes as he watched her smile at him. This was the kind of romance that happened once in a lifetime, and it wasn't something that should be thrown away, tossed aside. It should be cherished and valued. And for once, he wasn't hiding his feelings.

Kate went to Cara and gave her a hug. "I'm glad you came here," she said. "I'm so glad to finally have met you."

"Come on Cara, let me show you my house. The house that my mother refuses to see. Tell her how great it is, okay?"

"Sure, I will."

"When do you have to go back?"

"I'm going back tomorrow. Might as well face the firing squad head-on. Even if it's directed at you in absenteeism."

THE NEXT MORNING Kate waited by the window, watching for Tony's almost SUV to drive up the driveway. She didn't go with him to the airport although they both had asked her. She couldn't. Her stomach was tied in knots.

Kate liked Cara. It was impossible not to like her. And Cara really did love Tony, only not the way that Kate did, which was a very good thing indeed.

Still, everything Kate felt for Tony was all mixed up inside her, half reality, half fantasy, and she wasn't even sure if any of it was real.

When she saw him drive up, her stomach knotted. For the first time she was scared. Because now she'd find out if they had a future, or if the last few weeks were all in her imagination and overactive lusty desire for him.

No more were there barriers like fiancées or leftover grooms. It was only the two of them, and without the protection of those barriers, she'd soon know.

He came in through the back door, and it slammed shut. She heard his footsteps on the marble floor, and when he got to the carpeted area, the walls around her were vibrating from his rapid, heavy walk.

When he saw her in the living room, he went over to her, grabbed her by the shoulders and moved her backward until she was pressed against the wall. His body crushed hers, they were so close. His hands were under her shirt, on her waist, his thumbs skimming her ribs.

She lifted her head up so she could see his face, only his lips descended on hers. He kissed her, opening her mouth with the pressure of his lips, his tongue entered her, explored her teeth, stroked her tongue, the roof of her mouth, circling, caressing. His hands held her tight, his body kept her against the wall. She could feel every part of him, the hardness of his erection, the fullness. He was pressed against her tight and she wanted more.

She heard the sounds of yearning pouring from her throat, and he took heed.

His thumbs moved higher up her waist, until he reached the underside of her breasts.

She moaned deep in his mouth, and relaxed her body. He moved closer to her, her breasts crushed against his chest. Finally, he moved his lips from her mouth and began to kiss under her chin and down her neck. Until he rested his head on her shoulder, and with a deep sigh, said, "Kate."

She moved her arms around his shoulders, massaging the back of his neck. He sighed deeper and pressed his mouth into her breasts, through her bra, pulling at her nipple, pulling at some part of her so deep inside that not even her fantasies had reached.

Finally she placed both hands on his cheeks and gently tilted his face upward so she could see him. She circled his cheeks with her thumbs and looked into his eyes. "Tony. What are we doing?"

"I know what I'm doing, and I plan on doing more."

"I was planning to move on. You fired me."

"Of course I did. How can I have you working at the restaurant? You'll bankrupt me with your ideas. We have to have a means of support you know."

"Support?"

"A future."

"Tony, realistically, we don't know each other."

"I know. But what we feel, it only comes along once in a lifetime."

"Don't you want to wait. To question, to see?"

"Are you kidding? If we wait, then you'll have to have a job to support yourself, and you'll want to work at Donetti's because everyone who has ever worked there has loved it and never leaves."

She nodded. "That might be true."

"So not only am I going to fulfill every desire I've ever had for you, but I'm also going to save you from having the humiliation of being fired for the second time."

"I'm so grateful."

"Don't be sarcastic. Of course you are. And you should be."

"Tony?" Kate wanted him. He had been the object of every fantasy she had ever had. The only fantasies she had ever had. "You do make me very happy, even when you're being very closed-minded about certain things."

He took his finger and put it over her lips. "Woman, don't you know there's a time to talk and a time to keep quiet?" He took his finger away and replaced it with his lips.

He lowered her to the carpet. He had waited forever it seemed. He was a man of steel, a man of many wants. All of them centering around her.

He took her shirt off which was easy since she was helping him along. Her skin was soft and smelled so sweet. He wanted to take it slow. He wanted the moment to last forever. Only Kate was grabbing at his shirt and tugging, and saying things like, "Hurry, hurry. What's taking you so long?"

"What's your rush?"

"I've waited forever," she said.

"I haven't known you that long."

"For as long as you've known me, it's been forever."

His hands and lips moved painfully slow, down her throat, across her shoulder blades. Even when she told him to hurry, like everything else he did, Tony took his sweet time. He did it his way.

His kisses intoxicated her. She was so wet. She wanted him with such an urgency she thought she'd go crazy. She couldn't hold still. Finally, finally she touched him. She felt his hardness through the soft cotton of his khakis. She touched him gently, feeling each ridge as her fingers traveled down the length of him. She could feel him grow even larger with her touch, his length and circumference expanding because of what she did, the way she made him feel. He was the one moaning now, he was the one pulling down her panties, he was the one telling her he wanted to hurry.

And she was in ecstasy because of the power she

felt she had over him. The power to make him hard and weak. The power to spread her legs, to guide him inside her.

Only he held back, placing his fingers inside her mound, and rubbing her numb, making her moan and ride in rhythm. "Please," she was begging. "Please."

Finally he listened and entered her, filling her. She grabbed his buttocks and kept up with him, thrust for thrust, until he couldn't hold back any longer. She had waited for this, and it was better than any fantasy she ever could have dreamed up.

He laid on top of her, using his elbows on the floor as a brace to hold himself up. "I'm not finished with you," he said.

He lowered his mouth to her breasts, and lavished each nipple until they came to painful peaks. Then he kissed her down her ribs, and her stomach, and finally he began to kiss her womanhood, using his lips and fingers to bring her to completion.

"I have to go to confession, Tony," she said after her heart slowed down to an almost normal beat.

"Why? Have you sinned again?" The floor was hard, so he pulled her over the top of him. He liked the way she felt naked lying there. He could do this all day.

"Yes, we just sinned."

"This is good."

"I know. Anything this good has to be a sin."

"You're right." He rolled her back over on her back, then stood up. Extending a hand out to her, he waited until she took it, then pulled her into a standing position. "You look damn good naked." She blushed. He liked her blushing, too. Her whole body had turned a rosy pink. "In fact, maybe I'll have everyone at work dress naked. That would save a lot of dry-cleaning bills."

She punched him gently on the shoulder. "You're so silly."

"Maybe." He took her by the hand and led her out of the living room. "You make me happy. Now go get dressed, and meet me down here in ten minutes."

"Where are we going?" Kate asked twenty minutes later when he brought her outside and held open the car door for her.

"I'm going to take you someplace to ensure our future together."

Kate closed her eyes. This couldn't be true. He was going to make it permanent. He meant it.

"Where are we going?" City Hall. Blood tests. Marriage license. "Do I need to change clothes."

"I just want to make sure you're going to be mine forever," Tony said, kissing the tip of her nose.

"I will be, I promise."

"I bet you said that to Seth, too. Hey, I saw that movie, *The Runaway Bride*. I know all about what women like you do. You say you love me, you say you're going to marry me, and then—'' he snapped his fingers ''—you take off. Gone. Well, lady, that's not going to happen to me.''

"But, Tony, I would never leave you." She wanted him in her bed, right now. Or the floor. That was a wonderful place. Couldn't he see that?

"That's why we're going to get you a Texas driver's license. Then there's no way you can get away ever again. Once a Texan always a Texan."

"No, Tony, you're wrong." She placed her hand on his jaw, and outlined the strong lines of his face, then lowered her lips onto his, and gave him a deep, soulful kiss, almost equal to the one he had given her in the house. "Once Tony's woman, always Tony's woman."

His smile faded. He gazed into her face with an intensity that sent tingles up and down her spine. "I love you, Kate. I probably had since the moment I saw you at the rehearsal dinner. I'm not sure if you hadn't run away, that I might not have said something when the priest asked if anyone knew any reason this couple shouldn't marry, or whatever they say."

"Really?"

"Really. The moment I saw you, I knew I had to have you. But it all got so complicated."

"You've got that right."

"It'll work out."

"What will your mother say?"

"What will your mother say?"

"I think we should fly to Las Vegas and elope, and then no one can say anything."

He closed the car door and got in on the other side. "Let's go."

"To get my driver's license?"

"No, baby, I'm going to take you for a ride in the sky, and then a little chapel in the desert. Then I'm going to make love to you like there's no tomorrow."

"Tony, what about confession?"

"What about it?"

"I have to go. I have to thank God for answering all my prayers, Tony. I have to thank him for you."

"We can't leave for the airport until you go?"

She shook her head.

Tony headed the car toward the nearest steeple. This time, he went inside with her. Together they sat in a back pew, and held hands. Neither said a word for several moments.

"I do love you, Kate."

"I love you, too."

"Thank you," Tony whispered.

Kate smiled. He put his arm around her shoulders and tucked her close to him. She rested her head on his shoulder.

"I don't know if it's luck, or what, but I'm so glad to have found you," he said kissing her temple.

She knew then that no matter what, all would be right with their world. "Tony, did you know that if a person has a fantasy, and if they wish really hard, that the fantasy can come true.''

''I didn't know that.''

''You do now, and you have to promise to remember that. Because a fantasy is a terrible thing to waste.''

How To Catch
a Groom

Holly Jacobs

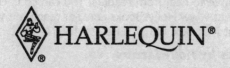

HARLEQUIN®

TORONTO • NEW YORK • LONDON
AMSTERDAM • PARIS • SYDNEY • HAMBURG
STOCKHOLM • ATHENS • TOKYO • MILAN • MADRID
PRAGUE • WARSAW • BUDAPEST • AUCKLAND

Dear Reader,

Have you ever met a stranger and known that you'd
met a kindred spirit? I was at my very first conference,
participating in a large book signing, and somehow
I ended up sitting with authors Rita Clay Estrada,
Jan Freed, Heather MacAllister and Rita Gallagher.
I was in awe as I talked to these wonderful ladies
who so graciously treated me like a "real writer"—
something I didn't feel like at all. And there seemed
to be a common refrain among them: "She has to
meet Bonnie." Later they introduced me to their
Bonnie—Bonnie Tucker. There was an instant feeling
of camaraderie. Here was a kindred spirit who got
my jokes (and liked me anyway). To be able to work
on this book with her was a special kind of thrill. I'd
like to especially thank Rita, Rita, Heather and Jan for
introducing us.

It seems appropriate that this is a story about kindred
spirits, even if they don't recognize that "kindredness"
at first: Seth, a man who lives by logic, and Desi, a true
romantic. They might seem like an odd pairing, but I'm
sure you'll agree that they're meant for each other.

I hope you enjoy Desi and Seth's story, and Bonnie's
story featuring Kate and Tony.

Holly

P.S. I love to hear from readers! You can contact me
online at www.HollysBooks.com, or reach me via snail
mail at P.O. Box 11102, Erie, PA 16514-1102.

Books by Holly Jacobs

HARLEQUIN DUETS
43—I WAXED MY LEGS FOR *THIS?*
67—READY, WILLING AND...ABEL?
67—RAISING CAIN

To Bonnie Tucker,
one of my favorite authors,
a great friend and a true kindred spirit!

Prologue

"SIZE MATTERS. Size always matters." Mrs. O'Malley, the mother of the bride-to-be, gave a little *humph* for emphasis. "And my daughter won't put up with something inferior."

"Ma'am, I've seen it myself, and it's big enough. Plenty big," Desi Smith soothed.

Soothing was part of her job as the wedding coordinator, but she feared it would take a double-strength shot of a strong sedative to truly soothe this woman.

"Seth, there you are," Mrs. O'Malley cried, looking past Desi to the blond groom-to-be. "Help me out here, will you?"

"Sure, if I can, ma'am."

"Mom. I've told you, call me Mom. Not that I look old enough to be your mother," she hastily added, patting her perfectly coifed brunette hair. "Now, I want you to tell this girl that size does matter. It matters a lot. Mary Kathryn needs it big. If it's too small she'll be disappointed. And I don't want her disappointed by something that is inferior."

Seth Rutherford's eyes widened and he cleared his throat before he replied slowly, "Uh…just what are we talking about here?"

Desi tried not to smile as she realized how their conversation might be misconstrued. "We're talking about the wedding cake. Mrs. O'Malley is afraid it's not big enough for all the guests. I've been reassuring her that it is."

"Oh, *the cake*." Seth looked relieved.

"Well, I'm going to go find Mary Kathryn. I think you're both wrong and she'll be disappointed tomorrow." Mrs. O'Malley made her way to the opposite end of The Bayside's banquet room. Mrs. O'Malley had insisted on only the very best for her daughter's rehearsal dinner, and Bayside was the best Erie, Pennsylvania, had to offer.

Desi was sure she hadn't heard the end of the cake issue, but was grateful for the reprieve.

"Do I know you?" Seth asked unexpectedly.

"Pardon?" Desi asked.

"I said, do I know you? You look familiar, but I haven't been able to place where I might know you from."

Desi smiled. "I was wondering if you'd remember. We went to high school together. I was in the gifted program, too, though I was a few years behind you."

What she didn't add was that she'd spent a great portion of her sophomore year fantasizing about the sandy-haired senior. Or that she'd cut his picture from the newspaper when he'd won the science fair and hung it by her vanity mirror.

Heck, she'd even doodled his name and hers together.

He shook his head. "I'm sorry, I don't remember you."

"I've changed a lot. Back then I had braces, was painfully skinny and had horribly frizzy hair."

Thankfully, as she'd let her hair grow out, the frizziness had abated, she'd foregone glasses in favor of contacts and, of course, what was skinny in high school was slender and in vogue as an adult. She certainly wasn't gorgeous, but she felt she'd improved with age.

Seth studied her a moment, and finally said, "Sorry. Still drawing a blank."

"The science fair? My table was next to yours and—"

"That was you? That's why you look familiar. I was so nervous. I spent the better part of three months working on that project, and when I discovered the missing transistor, I figured I'd lost the competition for sure. But then you handed me one and said it was a spare." He stared at her for a moment, and then added slowly, "Only it wasn't spare at all, was it? I didn't find out until later you took it off your own project."

"The science fair didn't mean that much to me."

Desi shrugged. "It was more for my Mom and Dad. Anyway, it was no biggie."

"It was very big to me. That scholarship helped me get through college. I've always wished I could repay you."

"I didn't do it because I wanted your gratitude."

"Why did you do it?" he asked.

Desi wasn't about to answer that particular question, after all, he hadn't known about her crush in high school, so why give it away now?

She just smiled and said, "I really should get back and check on things in the kitchen."

Before she could turn and make her retreat, Seth said, "I never would have known you, even though you looked familiar. You don't look anything like you did then."

Desi smiled. "And for that I'm eternally grateful. High school definitely ranks as my awkward phase."

"Awkward?" He laughed. "I never quite outgrew that phase. I'm still awkward. I tripped at the rehearsal when I walked Mary Kathryn down the aisle, and I've already spilled wine, and dinner hasn't even started. I can't wait until its over. I hate social functions."

"That's why I'm here. To make this as easy on you as possible."

"If you can simply keep me from making a fool of myself, I'll be eternally grateful."

"I'll do my best."

He smiled.

That smile had given her tingles when she was in her teens. Now there was a different sort of tingle that she'd never experienced before. Seth's smile still had a lot of power, even after all these years.

Mary Kathryn, the bride-to-be, gave a little wave from across the room, and Desi pulled herself back to the present. "I think your bride wants you."

He turned and waved back to Mary Kathryn. "See you tomorrow," he called over his shoulder.

Desi watched as her first official crush walked across the room to his bride-to-be and best man. He remembered the transistor she'd given him after all these years.

Her small gesture had helped him get a scholarship. She'd rescued him. The thought warmed her.

Once upon a time, she'd dreamed about being at Seth's wedding—only then she'd been the bride, not the wedding planner.

Desi smiled at the memory. She'd long since outgrown childhood dreams. She had a job to do, and couldn't wait until the wedding tomorrow. She had a feeling it was going to be something to remember....

1

"SHE'S HOT TO TROT."

Desi silently agreed with Phil's assessment. The *she* in question was going to trot right out of her own wedding. The bride was about to bolt before the "I do's" were said.

"Want me to tackle her?" he asked.

Desi turned and couldn't help form a small smile at the hopeful look on the photographer-working-as-her-assistant's face.

"I don't think that will work." There wasn't a thing either of them could do. They'd watched as the ceremony began, and Desi had felt nervous right from the beginning. The bride-to-be wasn't behaving right. Nervous was one thing, terrified was another. She watched helplessly as the bride ran right down the long aisle and out the door.

"Now what?" Phil muttered.

Desi wished she knew. She'd been coordinating weddings for the last five years and had never had a runaway bride before. She wasn't quite sure what the protocol was for something like that.

"I guess we thank everyone for coming?" she

halfway asked. She remembered her promise to Seth the night before and added, "And we try to keep the groom from looking foolish."

"There's no *we* about it, babe. I just snap the pictures and follow orders, you're the one in charge."

She raked her fingers through her long hair, more out of frustration than to push it out of her face.

Desi discreetly fought through the crowd pressed around the groom. She'd made a promise to Seth and she was bound and determined to keep it. "Seth, do you want me to just send everyone home?"

"The reception's paid for, right?" Shannon, the maid of honor, sister of the bride, asked.

"Everything's paid for and ready."

"Everything's ready but the bride, I guess," Seth said.

"No use wasting it, Seth," the almost-sister-in-law said.

"I don't want—"

"Listen, let's just show everyone how much class you've got," Shannon pressed.

"Seth?" Desi asked.

She didn't want him to be pushed into anything he didn't want to do. His back was ramrod straight and tension radiated from his very stance. His expression didn't give away any of his feelings, but his eyes…there she could see his pain and confusion in those deep blue eyes and wanted nothing more than to make both disappear.

He shrugged. "Let's party."

SETH RUTHERFORD FELT foolish.

He'd been comforted by just about everyone at the reception, and it hadn't helped him feel better, it had simply made him more uncomfortable. His mother was so upset that his father had taken her home about fifteen minutes ago.

Seth didn't know how to deal with such free-flowing feelings. His parents wore their emotions like garments, changing them at the slightest provocation. He'd never known how to be like that and, truth be told, had never really wanted to. Such wild emotional ups and downs made him nervous. He was the type to think things through, though obviously he hadn't thought enough about his relationship with Mary Kathryn.

He took a long swig of beer and grimaced. He didn't really like the taste, but he was getting used to it tonight.

He glanced at his watch. He'd lasted two hours at his almost-reception. It was one hour and fifty-nine minutes too long in his opinion.

He'd done his bit, played the good sport, but he was ready to go. He snuck quietly from the hall into the parking lot.

Half of Erie seemed to have come to the reception. Who knew he and Mary Kathryn knew so many people? They lived quiet lives. They weren't exactly people people.

People people? The term made him want to laugh, but he wasn't sure why. Maybe he'd had a few beers too many…

What was he thinking about?

Oh, Mary Kathryn and how he'd always felt at home with her. Since she'd first joined the faculty at the university, he'd felt a connection. He'd invited her to work on his research project, and when she'd said yes, that connection had grown. Balancing his teaching schedule and research interests didn't leave much time for a social life, even if he'd wanted one. But Seth had always been more comfortable with books and microscopes than with people.

Until Mary Kathryn.

She had a brilliant mind, and yes, he was comfortable with her. It's one of the reasons he'd decided to marry her—they were a good fit. Common interests, common goals. They should be the perfect couple.

But she was gone.

He took a healthy swig of his beer. He wasn't a *drinking* man, but tonight he was going to make an exception. In fact, although he'd been drinking for the last two hours, it wasn't enough to numb his feelings, whatever they were.

How did he feel about Mary Kathryn? That was the question that had plagued him since she'd left. He loved her…of course he'd loved her. He'd asked her to marry him, hadn't he?

Or had he?

It was just sort of an assumption that they'd marry. Come to think of it, he couldn't even remember picking out a day. However he couldn't seem to focus on much right now. He felt sort of thick and fuzzy, but not quite numb.

Well, thick and fuzzy was preferable to sharp and hurting. With two spare cans of beer tucked in his tux pockets, he started looking around the parking lot for his car. If he was lucky no one would notice he was gone until he was gone.

The thought seemed sort of convoluted, but Seth didn't let it bother him. He was beyond being bothered tonight.

He was going to just take his thick and fuzzy self home and forget his almost-wedding. He was going to forget women, period.

He didn't need a woman messing up his well-ordered life.

"Seth, can I help you?"

He jumped at the sound of a voice and turned. Ah, the wedding coordinator. Little Desi Smith. Only she wasn't little any more. Oh, she wasn't tall, but she was definitely all grown up.

"Seth? Let me help," she said.

He realized he hadn't responded. "If I hadn't sworn off women, I might consider letting you help me, but as it is, I think I'm better off on my own."

Even if he was forgetting about women, he could still admire their assets, and the tiny brunette standing in front of him had some worth admiring.

After last night, he'd gone and pulled out his yearbook and found her. Desdemona Smith. If she hadn't told him, he would have never connected her with his *transistor* girl of so many years ago.

Gone was the awkward-looking teenager from the picture. The adult version was a real looker. Short, but well packaged. She had miles of dark brown hair. He wondered what it would feel like to run his fingers through it. It looked silky.

He was more than a little loaded if he was thinking about Desi Smith's hair. Seth was an intellectual. He didn't notice things like that. That he was noticing things about this practical stranger just went to prove he had to get out of here.

"Do you know where my car is?"

"Seth, you can't drive," she said.

"Sure I can. Oh, that was the only test I ever flunked, but I passed it the second time around and have been driving all these years without even one accident. Not even a ticket."

She shook her head and that long, brown, silky hair rippled against her shoulders. He started to reach out for it, but wasn't quiet drunk enough to do it. Instead he stuffed his hand in his pocket, feeling a spare beer, cold and moist within it.

"That's not what I meant," she said. "I'm afraid you've had too much to drink to be driving tonight."

"Oh, no, I haven't had nearly enough. I'm thick and fuzzy, but not quite numb." No, if he'd had enough, he'd have forgotten about his almost-wedding and he'd be running his fingers through this woman's hair.

"Well, you've had too much to drive."

"I have to leave. I'm afraid if I don't, I'll make a bigger fool of myself."

"Well, I think you've handled yourself admirably. Everyone does. But why don't you let me drive you," she said softly.

"I—"

"You might as well say yes because there's no way I'm letting you get behind the wheel of a car."

"You're a bossy lady." Seth didn't like bossy ladies. He liked quiet women. Partners. Not someone who thought she had to run the show.

"My friend says I only hired him so he has to listen to me. He says I'm a control freak. A bossy, control freak."

"Mary Kathryn was never bossy."

"I'm not Mary Kathryn," Desi reminded him as she started directing him toward her car.

"I'm glad you're not. She left me. You'd think

that was why I was drinking, but the sad truth of it is, she was right.''

''Seth, I'm so sorry—''

''Don't be. I owe you for getting me out of here.''

Desi led him to a small VW Beetle that had ''Engaging Styles'' painted across the front hood.

''Just climb in.'' She unlocked the passenger door.

Seth peeked in and backed out. ''Oh, no. I take back owing you. That car's a mess. It's a health hazard. I'm not going to get in there. I'll catch some disease or something.''

''It's not that bad,'' Desi said.

''Well, I'm not going to fit anyway. I'm bigger than a tiny little elf like you and there's no way I'm going to fit in there.''

He sat on the seat and tried to squeeze his legs in. He couldn't seem to get them to bend enough to fit, so he didn't make much progress.

''The physical universe is very specific about its laws,'' he continued, ''and guys as big as me don't fit in spaces this small. It's a matter of mass. I could make an equation for you. Hmm, would you say I was a cube, or a sphere? If I'm a sphere you just take a cube of my radius and times it by pi and then by four-thirds and…''

Seth realized that Desi didn't seem interested in the equation. As a matter of fact, she didn't say a word as she leaned over, bent his knees for him and crammed his legs into the car.

Seth was surprised he fit.

"If I'd done that equation I would have figured out I could fit with the proper force. See, I remembered mass, but forgot what force can do. I don't normally forget things. So maybe the alcohol is working after all and I'll forget this day."

He paused a moment. "Nope, I remember."

"You are definitely more of a cube than a sphere. But either way, buckle up."

He did what he was told, but muttered the entire time as the woman shut the door and got in the driver's seat. He was right, she was bossy.

That he was right lightened his mood. He'd been wrong about Mary Kathryn, but he was right about this bossy woman.

"Where to?"

"Twenty-seven Winston Lane," he said as he tossed the empty beer can into the back.

"Hey, you don't have to make a mess."

"Of course I do. This car expects it. I'm surprised you could get a passenger in here, what with all the junk you haul around."

"It's not junk. It's stuff I might need. I do a lot of my work out of this car and I like to be prepared."

"Like a Girl Scout." She didn't look like any

scout he'd ever seen. He popped the top of another can as he chuckled.

"It's not that funny," she said. "And why don't you lay off the beer."

"It *is* funny, and I don't want to." So there. He'd told her.

They were both silent as the Bug delivered them through downtown Erie and toward his street on the westside of town.

Bug.

It was an appropriate term for this vehicle. The car was little and dirty, just like a bug. Okay, not dirty, but cluttered.

If bugs had compartments, he bet they'd be as cluttered as this car was. Seth would never have cluttered compartments. He liked things neat and orderly. That's why marrying Mary Kathryn had made perfect sense. But now he wasn't marrying her, he discovered that made even more sense, which boggled his mind. After all, two diametrically opposite courses of action shouldn't both make sense.

"Which one?" Desi asked as they made their way up the quiet side street.

"The white one," Seth said.

He'd made it. He was home. All he wanted to do was crawl in his house and forget this day had ever happened. He wasn't going to try to make sense out of what made sense and what didn't. See, he couldn't even make a coherent thought, so how did he expect to make sense?

He was going to just forget about women and marriage and get on with his life. It was summer vacation and he didn't have any classes to teach until next fall. He did have his cat and his research. Who needed anything more than that?

Anxious to start forgetting, he tried to open the Bug's door, but couldn't seem to find the handle, and when he did, the door still wouldn't open.

"Did you lock me in?" he asked. "It would be just like a bossy woman to lock a man in her car. Bossy women like to be in control and if a man can't get out of her car, then she's totally in control. I bet you think I owe you for driving me home."

Even in his alcohol-muddled mind he realized that he probably did.

"It's all part of the job."

"Driving the jilted groom home? I don't think so. I guess I do owe you."

Desi got out of the car without saying a word. She walked around the front end and opened the passenger door. "There you go."

"Oh. Thanks." He tried to get out, but couldn't seem to budge from the seat. "See, I told you your car was too small. I'm stuck. Now you're going to have to call 911, and they'll have to pry me out of here. Oh, that's just great. Just one more humilia-tion to add to today. Being pried from a flower-child, sixties-flashback, rainbow-painted, messy, little Bug. Well, I can take it. I'm a man.''

He popped the top of his last beer. If he was going to be humiliated again, he wanted to be prepared this time.

Desi didn't say a word, she just leaned into the car.

''What are you doing?'' he yelled. She was in the way and he couldn't get his can of beer to his lips. And he needed that beer. He wasn't numb enough yet.

And even worse, her *assets* brushed against him. They weren't huge, but they weren't too small. They were big enough for him to have noticed them before and big enough to stick out and graze him as she leaned over him.

The thought *more than a handful's a waste* seemed stuck dead center in his brain, just like Desi's assets seemed stuck in front of him.

''I don't remember you having breasts in high school. Especially not perky little ones. Where did they come from?''

''You're a scientist, figure it out,'' Desi said, annoyance tingeing her voice.

She moved out of the car and waited. Seth stumbled to his feet and then right into her. She caught him—just.

''You're stronger than you look.'' He paused, concentrating on drinking his beer while moving his feet toward the house. Maybe he was drunker than he thought?

He might be, but Seth wasn't so drunk that he couldn't pick up on Desi's exasperation. But he was drunk enough to think annoying her was sort of fun.

DESI CONCENTRATED ON keeping Seth upright as she practically pulled him up the front stairs. He was a big guy. Okay, five foot eight wasn't huge, but it was big to her five feet and three inches.

"I don't need help," Seth mumbled.

"I know."

He paused and said, "Maybe I do a little. Maybe you could help by telling me why Mary Kathryn left me? We were perfect together."

Desi gritted her teeth as they attempted each of the five stairs that led to Seth's porch. She had felt sorry for the deserted groom until she had to halfway carry the drunken ox. He was heavy.

"Sometimes perfection is highly overrated," she said, still struggling with the weight of him.

"But that's not logical. One should always stribe...strite...*try* for perfection." It took him two tries to move to the final step.

"Whoever said love is logical?" Desi asked. She might not be a scientist, but she knew for a fact that love and logic were totally opposite conditions."

"Love? Who said anything about love?"

Desi tried to catch her breath as she practically

heaved him onto the porch. "You didn't love Mary Kathryn?"

"Well, certainly I do…did, but not in some romanticized context. We were friends, colleagues and perfectly suited. Marriage was the next logical step."

Rather than feeling triumphant at having got her drunken charge up to the porch, Desi felt disgusted. "And you have to ask why she ran out?"

"But—"

She cut him off, too angry to listen to his crazy explanation. "Where's the key?"

"Key?"

"To the house."

Slowly, hoping to penetrate his beer-fogged brain she asked, "Where are your house keys?"

"In my pocket." He vaguely gestured with his beer toward his hips.

"Could you get them out?" she asked.

Seth shook his head. "I might spill my beer if I try. You get them out."

"I'm not reaching in your pant's pocket."

No way was she sticking her hand down this drunken, jilted groom's pants. Why on earth had she wasted her high school years mooning over Seth Rutherford?

Back then, she'd put him on a pedestal. But today, she was a little disappointed in him—disappointed that he'd been willing to marry for less than true love.

Desi might be a romantic, but she believed that love mattered.

She put aside thoughts of disappointment and love, and simply concentrated on the task at hand— to get to Seth's keys and get him safely in his house.

Engaging Styles might use There's Nothing We Can't Handle for a company motto, but when she'd come up with the idea she'd never imagined a situation quite like this. Catching the groom before he fell over was enough of a challenge. She wasn't pocket surfing for keys, too.

"You've got a dirty mind, Desi. Dirty-minded Desi. Dainty, dirty-minded Desi. D—"

"Get the keys," she said.

"They're in my jacket pocket." He jiggled his left shoulder.

"Oh." Desi retrieved the keys from his jacket. Anything to get him in the house.

She unlocked the door and Seth didn't wait for her to help him, he practically bounded into the house.

Drunken men would do well to remember that thresholds were not level with porches, she thought as his bound turned into a fall, right onto the slate entryway floor, and right onto a rather irate cat. His beer splatted against the slate, hitting both Seth and the cat.

"Mreow," the cat cried and started hissing at Seth's prostrate form.

"Sorry, Schrödinger," Seth muttered.

Schrödinger, the cat, stalked from the room, apparently not willing to accept Seth's apology.

Desi stared at the crumpled mass on the floor. The only thing that kept her from kicking him was a sense of pity, despite what she'd said. A man whose bride had run out on the wedding deserved at least a bit of compassion.

"Come on, Seth, let's get you to bed," she said.

"I can't go to bed with you, even if you have totally waste-free breasts. I'm not that kind of a guy." With that, he simply lay on the floor and closed his eyes.

"Seth, come on. You can't sleep here."

"Sure I can." He curled into a little ball, and pillowed his head on his elbow.

"You've got to get up." Desi tried to pull him, but he didn't budge. She dropped his arm. She wasn't going to be able to get this guy on his feet until he wanted to get on his feet. And it didn't appear he wanted to.

Darn. Now what?

Desi sank on the floor across from Seth's prostrate form. She glanced through the doorway into his living room. There wasn't much to look at. It was functional and orderly. She doubted she'd find even a stray crumb in his couch cushions.

The room was illuminated by the foyer light. It wasn't enough to tell if there was any color on his walls, but she doubted it. It was probably plain, neutral white. No imagination, or passion anywhere.

Seth's cat crept cautiously onto her lap. She stroked the ugly tabby's damp fur.

"You okay, Schrödinger?" She couldn't resist smiling at the cat's name.

There was a twentieth-century physicist who'd come up with a theory called Schrödinger's Cat. Okay, so it was an odd sort of humor. Certainly not something most people outside the field of science would get. But she got it and she liked it.

Desi wasn't sure why Seth's quiet sense of humor pleased her, but it did.

She looked at him. His blond hair—which would be more at home on a beach boy than a stodgy professor—spilled over his forehead. Gently, she pushed a stray lock back in place.

She hated leaving him lying on the floor, but Seth Rutherford wasn't her concern. She'd seen to it that he made it home safe and her job was officially done.

She could leave now and forget all about him.

THERE WAS ONLY ONE RULE for Wednesday night dinners at Hazard's. No, make that two. Rule one—all diets were off. Rule two—all men must be ogled.

Desi took a large bite of her four-cheese lasagna, savoring every fat-producing calorie.

"Oh, look at that one." Pam Steele pointed to a particularly well-sculpted man in tight jeans. He wore a clingy cotton shirt that left no doubt in any woman's mind about the rippled abdomen that lay hidden beneath it. "He's definitely commando."

All three women looked at him and murmured their appreciation.

Mary Jo Mills, Pam Steele and Desi met at Hazard's down on the bay every Wednesday night for dinner. The food was out of this world, and the restaurant's deck was situated right on the bayfront walkway, which meant there were a lot of men to ogle.

Business men. Jock-ish men. Boy-toys. Tall, dark and oh-so dangerous men. It didn't matter to them. They were equal-opportunity oglers.

Mary Jo, Pam and Desi. They'd been friends since high school. Actually, they'd been more than friends, they'd been sisters.

Mary Jo was the girl Desi's parents had always wished she was. A professional and a mother. She worked as a chemist and balanced four kids and a husband.

Pam taught music and was as single as Desi. She said music was easier to figure out than men…but that didn't stop her from trying.

Their interests were different, but their friendship was strong, even after all these years.

"So, how was last weekend's wedding?" Mary Jo asked.

"The wedding was a disaster," Desi moaned.

"Oh, no. What happened?" Pam glanced a man in a business suit and whispered, "Silk boxers at three o'clock."

Mary Jo and Desi both stole a glance at the James Bond wanna-be and nodded agreement.

Desi answered, "A runaway bride. I've never lost a bride before. Phil wanted to tackle her, but I wasn't quite sure what to do."

"I'm assuming she ran before the 'I do's'?" Mary Jo asked as she sipped on her margarita.

"Oh, yeah. Left the groom standing there all alone. She seemed nice enough when I worked with her planning the wedding… Well, I didn't exactly plan it with her, but with her mother and sister.

They seemed to run the show. But she still seemed nice. Maybe she was a little more nervous than most brides. But no matter what, running out on the wedding? No one should be left at the altar like that. Part of me wanted to let Phil tackle her. I felt so bad for the groom.''

"Oh, the poor man. Was he cute? Maybe you should introduce us and I can comfort him," Pam said.

The idea of Pam comforting Seth didn't sit well.

"Cute?" Desi repeated.

She knew she could rhapsodize on just how cute he was. She'd done it often enough in high school. This was the perfect opportunity to mention the groom was Seth Rutherford. Given the intensity of her schoolgirl crush, she was pretty sure Pam and Mary Jo would remember him.

But Desi didn't mention knowing him or her schoolgirl crush. She knew Pam and Mary Jo would make a big deal about it, would want every tiny detail. And she could imagine what they'd say about her driving him home. No, if she didn't want to think about Seth Rutherford, she certainly didn't want to talk about him. And since there was nothing to tell, mentioning him would be unnecessary.

So, instead of telling them the groom was Seth, she spotted a middle-aged man sporting a earring and wearing clothes that would look more at home on a twenty-year-old. "Silk bikini underwear. He's trying to prove something."

"It's not working," Pam said with a laugh. "I like guys who are more comfortable with who they are. Who don't have anything to prove." She scanned the crowd and pointed to a thirtyish man wearing jeans and a rugby shirt. "Now, take Mr. Rugby for instance. He looks very comfortable with who he is."

"Boxers," Desi said. "Cotton boxers. Bet he has some funny ones in his drawer. Heck, a guy like that would even wear the kind with little pink hearts on them. To him, they're just underwear."

"Dare me to ask what he has on tonight?" Pam asked.

"Pam, behave," Mary Jo scolded in a mommish voice.

"There was a time you'd have been the one asking him," Pam said.

"But that was before I got married. Happily married to a perfect man. Speaking of men—" Mary Jo started.

Pam interrupted. "That does seem to be what we talk about the most on Wednesdays, have you noticed? Talking about them, watching them… What is it about men that makes for such fascinating discussions? Your deserted groom, for instance, Desi. I could spend an entire evening talking about him.

My heart goes out to him. Tell us more. What did you do after the bride left? What did he do?''

"There's not much to tell. He was a good sport and invited everyone to the reception since it was paid for.''

"That's classy," Pam said. "I like classy.''

"So how was your week?'' Desi asked Mary Jo. She was anxious to turn the conversation from Seth.

"My week? It was hellish enough to make my mother feel vindicated that her curse—you know, the one where she said, 'Someday I hope you have kids who behave just like you'—worked," Mary Jo said picking up the conversation, just like Desi had hoped she would.

"The kids were in rare form,'' she continued. "I swear to Pete, one of these days someone is going to turn us in for breaking some sort of noise ordinance. Let's see, the injuries of the week included one human bite, one bruised knee and a brush burn. But the big news is Paulie got a call from a girl. He…''

Mary Jo started entertaining Pam and Desi with her kids' exploits, and though Desi made an attempt to follow the conversation, she couldn't help but think about Seth.

She'd spent a great deal of time thinking about him since Saturday. She wasn't sure why, other than she felt bad for him.

Mary Jo talked about her son's call from a girl

and Desi couldn't help but remember that one time she'd called Seth's house. Thank goodness it had been before the days of caller ID.

She'd dialed, fully intending to ask Seth to the Spring Fling dance. His mother had answered. "Hello?"

Desi had sat there, trying to catch her rapidly fleeing breath. Inhale, exhale. Inhale, exhale.

"Well, I never. How dare you call and breathe in my ear!" Seth's mother had exclaimed right before she hung up on Desi.

Desi lost her nerve and didn't call back.

What would have happened if she'd found the courage to ask for him and asked him out?

She'd never know and that was probably a good thing. Some things were better left in the realm of fantasy. She had a feeling her girlhood crush on Seth Rutherford was one of them.

"...but Paulie's phone call wasn't the highlight of the week. My flowers were."

"Flowers?" Pam asked.

"A dozen roses." Mary Jo looked a little misty as she took a sip of her drink. "The card said, 'You're beautiful.' Isn't that the most romantic thing?"

Mary Jo and her husband, Paul, were Desi's relationship role models. They worked together in the same lab. They shared a family, and still had an incredible, romantic passion for each other. Why, he even sent her flowers saying he still thought she was beautiful. That was romantic. It made Desi's heart melt a little, thinking of their true fairy-tale romance.

That's what Desi wanted. A man who would still send her flowers and think she was beautiful after years of marriage. A man who shared her passion and whose passion she could share. A true, enduring romance.

A Prince Charming sort of guy who would carry her off into the sunset and wake up next to her for the rest of her sunrises.

"Oh, my gosh," Pam whispered pointing at a man who'd taken a seat at the bar. "I don't think it matters what sort of underwear that one chooses. He's the type who only makes me wonder one thing…how long would it take to get him out of his underwear?"

Mary Jo snorted margarita out her nose as she laughed.

Desi looked at the man. Sure he was hot, but not as hot as Seth.

She stifled a groan, not wanting to alert her friends.

She had to stop thinking about Seth.

She shook her head and forced herself to study the man at the bar. "Thong. Definitely a thong underwear. If he doesn't wear one, he should."

Mary Jo and Pam tore their gazes away from Mr. Thong, took one look at Desi and all three women started laughing.

Desi forced herself to concentrate on dinner. She wasn't going to think about Seth Rutherford any more.

She'd outgrown her girlhood infatuation years ago.

There was a question that kept niggling at her thoughts, though. Could she outgrow her adult attraction to him as well?

"FORGET IT, PHIL. You can't just walk out."

Desi glanced at her watch. It was already after three on Friday afternoon. There was no time left to find someone to replace Phil before the Mentz wedding this evening, and there was no way she alone could handle the thousand and one details that needed to be handled.

Phil wasn't full-time. During the weekdays she was on her own, but at the actual weddings, she needed someone to help coordinate all the details.

No way was he walking out on her now. She was going to tell him so. She was going to put her foot down and insist he live up to his obligations.

"Phil, you just can't—"

"Desi, this is the job I've been waiting for. The one in Atlanta."

Atlanta.

That magic word that stopped any further protests.

Desi's heart turned to mush, right then and there. Atlanta.

Anywhere else in the world and she would have continued her fight with Phil. She'd berate him for leaving her in a lurch and insist he stay until she could find a replacement.

But she couldn't fight against Atlanta.

"Does she know?" Desi asked.

The *she* in question was Phil's ex-girlfriend—the girlfriend who'd accepted a job in Atlanta just three months ago after some big, mysterious fight they'd had. He wouldn't talk about it, but Desi knew he hadn't stopped thinking about it—about her.

"Not yet, but she will. My flight leaves at six. I'll have the weekend to get acclimated, then I start work, both at the paper and on Debbie. I'm going to get her back."

How could Debbie resist a man who loved her enough to follow her?

How could Desi put up a fight against that kind of love?

She couldn't.

Desi understood chasing dreams and damning the consequences. She'd started this business against all her parents' dire warnings. The only problem was, this time she was a consequence.

"Listen, Des," he said. "I'm really sorry. I appreciate everything you've done for me, but I can't pass up this opportunity."

"You're right," she said. "You can't. You

should go after Debbie and make her see that the two of you are meant to be together."

Phil was a good friend, in addition to being a great assistant. But no matter how good an assistant he was, he was a greater guy. Debbie didn't realize how lucky she was. She had a man who'd give up everything to be with her.

"Go pack," she said. "Call or e-mail me next week and let me know how it's going."

She could hear his sigh of relief over the phone line. "I will. Thanks for understanding, Des."

"No problem." At least it wasn't a problem for him. "I'll figure something out."

Desi hung up the phone and stared at her small, cluttered office. There was a neater office just beyond that door—soft colors and fabrics, huge overstuffed furniture that lent the room a romantic feel, she thought with more than a little bit of pride. But that was just for show, for clients. This was where she worked. It wasn't much more than a glorified broom closet, but it suited her. Desi worked best in the midst of chaos.

And she'd need to work her best to figure this out.

What was she going to do? It was late Friday afternoon and the wedding started in just an hour—she should be leaving for it right now. The reception was right after it until nine. How on earth was she going to find a replacement for Phil?

She flipped through the names in her phone book. Her parents would never lower themselves to helping at a wedding. They'd never approved of her starting this business.

Desi could have talked Mary Jo into it, but Paul was out of town this weekend. That meant Mary Jo was dealing with the four kids on her own.

She paused on a page. Maybe Pam?

She dialed her friend's number.

"Hello?"

"Oh, Pam, you're there. I need you."

"Sure. Anything, you know that. What's up?"

"Any chance that you have this weekend free?"

"Well, in terms of hot dates, yes. But the students have that concert for their parents tonight— I'm on my way out now. Then it's open to the public tomorrow afternoon, remember? I mentioned it Wednesday. But what do you need? Maybe I can swing it."

But. There it was. Desi felt like the butt of some cosmic joke. "No big deal. I was a little short for a couple weddings and thought of you. You have fun at the concerts, I'll figure something out."

"You know, if it was anything but my kids…"

"I know you'd help me if you could. That's why I called. But don't worry about it. I've got other ideas. I'll see you next Wednesday."

She hung up and stared morosely at the phone.

She couldn't think of another soul who she might be able to convince to help her out in a pinch. Some favor she could collect on.

And then it hit her.

He owed her. He'd said so. Giving him a transistor all those years ago might be a rather weak debt, but it was all she had. That and the fact she'd driven him home last week. Why, she'd practically saved his life. Maybe, just maybe, he'd meant what he said.

And actually, it would be almost therapy. An after-you've-been-thrown-from-a-horse-you-need-to-climb-back-on, sort of thing.

Why, asking for help was almost a good deed. She flipped her phone book and dialed the number.

"Hello?"

Desi knew it was him. She'd recognize that voice anywhere.

She put on her professional chipper voice. "Hi, Seth. This is Desi." When he didn't say anything she added, "Desdemona Smith."

"Desi," He didn't sound overly enthusiastic. "Is something wrong?"

"It's been almost a week since…well, it's been a week. I just wanted to call and see how you were." She tapped her pen against a sheet of paper and started to doodle little circles, one on top of another.

"My life's been a comedy of errors. First Mary Kathryn left, then she called. I still don't understand, but she says we would have been miserable married, that it takes more than logic to make a marriage work. I don't know about that, but if she wouldn't have been happy, then it's a good thing we didn't go through with it. I think we're still friends. But she's not coming back to work. That might have been okay, but then our research assistant broke his arm in a freak bathtub accident and..." His voice trailed off a moment and then he said, with a sigh, "There's just so much to do."

Bathtub accident, freak or otherwise? Desi would have asked if she didn't have more pressing questions.

"I didn't mean with work, I meant, how are *you* doing?" She doodled a sketch that looked like a man's torso. A *naked* man's torso.

She took the doodle lower and realized how anatomically correct she'd just made it. Diddling with a doodle was poor form.

She scratched it out and found herself blushing. She was thankful Seth was on the other end of a phone line and not looking over her shoulder.

"I'm okay. And I'm glad you called," he said. "I want to thank you again for...well, for bringing me home before I made a total fool of myself. You promised at the rehearsal dinner that you wouldn't let me do that and you didn't. It seems every time we meet you rescue me, whether it's transistors or rides home. I'm grateful."

"I wish I could have got you into bed—" She stopped short, realizing how that sounded. "I mean, get you off the floor, but you were too heavy."

"But you covered me. That was probably more than I deserved. I'm swearing off alcohol. The whole night is pretty much a blur."

"Um, Seth. You just said you were *grateful*. I'd

like to know if you're appreciative enough to reciprocate and help me out.''

"Help you out?'' Seth asked.

"Well, I need somebody today. I need someone desperately.'' There was the faintest hint of pleading in her voice, but she didn't care. Desi knew she did need Seth Rutherford and she needed him desperately.

SETH GULPED CONVULSIVELY.

Desi couldn't mean what he thought she meant. She didn't need him like *that,* so he didn't tell her that one of the most vivid recollections he had from his almost-wedding night was Desi's *assets* rubbing against him in the car.

He wasn't sure why they were rubbing against him, and he certainly wasn't about to ask, but he distinctly remembered her breasts and that led to quite a bit of *need* on his part, too.

"Desperately?'' he simply asked, waiting for her to clarify what it was she needed because he knew it wasn't him. He didn't seem to inspire that sort of need in women…at least not Mary Kathryn, and probably not Desi either.

"Oh, you don't know the half of it. I couldn't think of anyone who would do it but you.''

Seth didn't want to tell her that he'd been thinking of her as well. That didn't seem like what a jilted groom should be thinking about, after all. "Uh, maybe we should talk about this *need.*''

"Oh, there's no time to talk. It's really just a

matter of being able to follow directions. And since you're into science, I'm sure you can follow along.''

''You're going to direct me?''

''Of course. I mean, I'm sure you shine in the lab and even in the classroom, but I don't think you're as experienced as I am at this kind of stuff.''

Had he, in his drunkenness, told her that he and Mary Kathryn had never made love?

If he told her, he hoped he'd explained that he was more than capable of making love.

He hoped he'd told her that it was just that Mary Kathryn had always seemed like a friend—just a friend—and it was especially hard to get all hot and bothered by a goggle-wearing, lab-sharing friend. He just figured he'd get hot and bothered after the wedding.

But he'd reassessed that postulate since the almost-wedding. Chemistry alone might not be enough to base a relationship on—he still believed common interests and goals were the most important ingredients—but hot and bothered should be *part* of a relationship.

Maybe if he and Mary Kathryn had experienced more elemental reactions to each other, she wouldn't have left.

But now there was no wedding and no marriage, so he didn't have to worry about getting hot and bothered in the least by Mary Kathryn.

But Desi…now that was another story all together.

Not that he was hot and bothered. Maybe he suspected he could get hot and bothered about her, not that he would. He was swearing off women.

"Seth, I know it's asking a lot, but I truly do need you. You said your research assistant was injured and you're swamped. Well, I'll even help you out in return if you like, sort of a tit-for-tat thing."

Her phrasing reminded him of his need and left him grateful she was a phone line away at the moment, and not near enough to notice that she wasn't the only needy person in this conversation.

"I know you're not used to being bossed around," she continued, "so I promise I'll be gentle."

"I'll do it!" he exclaimed, though he wasn't sure what he was agreeing to and was even less sure why he was agreeing to it in the first place.

"You will? Great. I'll explain everything when you get there. St. John's on East Twenty-sixth Street. I need you there in an hour."

"We're going to do it in a church?"

"Of course. I admit, I've done it other places. Some of them were almost bizarre. I mean, the beach makes sense, but there was one time we did it in the middle of the mall. Why would anyone want to do it there?"

"In the mall?" He gulped convulsively. "In the middle of the mall?"

"I'll tell you all my stories, if you like. Just be at St. John's in an hour. Oh, and do you own a tux?"

"A tux?" he asked.

"Never mind, I'll take care of it. Thanks, Seth. I owe you. Bye."

Seth sat, feeling shell-shocked, as he listened to the dial tone buzzing in his ear. What on earth had he just agreed to?

It had to have something to do with her job. She worked in churches. He was sure he hadn't agreed to what he thought he'd agreed to. And maybe he felt a little disappointed that he hadn't. Because if he had agreed to what he originally thought he was agreeing to, he'd be the one who'd owe Desi.

He'd owe her big.

3

DESI WAS IN BIG TROUBLE if Seth didn't arrive soon.

She glanced out the church door for the hundredth time. Where was he?

Maybe Seth had reconsidered and wasn't going to show.

She groaned at the thought. Well, she'd just have to muddle through the wedding without an assistant, if that was the case. She'd just have to figure out how to be in two places at once.

No problem. She could handle it.

She looked at her watch again. She'd wait another couple minutes, and then she'd have to get started without him.

A neon-yellow sports car shot passed the church and parked down the block. A man climbed out of it.

A man with sandy blond hair who looked like Seth from a distance. But it couldn't be Seth. Seth was a stodgy, professorly sort who should drive a practical car, not a sporty, neon-yellow two-seated babe-magnet.

No, Seth wasn't some blond boy-toy driving a car guaranteed to make women drool.

The boy-toy came closer.

It *was* Seth.

Desi let out a long breath she hadn't realized she'd been holding.

"Hi," he called as he started up the long flight of stairs that led to the front doors of the old church.

"Seth." Desi couldn't remember when she'd been so happy to see someone. She was only happy to see him though because she needed his help, not for any other reason. "Nice car."

"Do you like it?" he asked.

"Of course. What's not to like?"

She could almost imagine sitting in the passenger seat, the wind blowing through her hair, the car's engine purring as they rode down the interstate going somewhere, anywhere.

"It's a great car," she said, though she was still rather caught up in her mental picture of riding in the car.

"I bought it this week. I wanted to do something wild. Something out of character. This was the best I could come up with." He smiled a lopsided smile.

Desi suddenly realized that in her fantasy ride, Seth was the one driving.

She had to get control of herself. Despite the awesome car and the lopsided grin with accompanying dimple, Seth wasn't Desi's type.

Or was he?

She wasn't precisely sure what her type was, come to think of it. It wasn't as if she wasn't looking, but she never seemed to find her Prince Charming, and Desi wasn't going to settle for less than her perfect man. And she certainly wasn't going to settle for less than love.

She glanced up at Seth and for a moment tried to imagine he was the prince she'd been waiting for. She imagined him climbing off his pearly white steed, wearing a regal looking cloak and crown as he whispered the sweet words she'd waited her whole life to hear—

The mental image popped like a balloon, and instead of a prince, her imaginary Seth was wearing a lab coat and shaking a finger in her face as he said, *"Love isn't logical, and I like logic."*

Desi shook her head, trying to clear the daydream.

"Come on, we need to hurry," she said as she led Seth into the church and down the stairs to the restroom.

No more fantasies today. She had a wedding to run.

"Here—" she handed him the tux "—go change in the bathroom. It might be a little off, but I think I came close on the size."

"You never told me exactly why I was here. I mean, we're not getting married, are we? You remember the last time I tried that. It didn't go so well.'' He paused a moment, and added, ''You didn't say just what you needed me for.''

''My assistant quit, and I need someone to help me.''

''Help you with…?''

''The wedding. The Mentz wedding.'' She gave him a little shove into the bathroom. ''Hurry up and change. It's already started, and I like to watch.''

A few minutes later he came out wearing the tux. It fit as if it had been made for him. He held out the tie. ''Would you mind?''

Desi *did* mind.

She minded a lot. She didn't want to get any closer to Seth than she had to. She wasn't sure what to make of this man who one minute was throwing beer on his cat and the next minute he was driving a sports car and looking yummy in a tux. She didn't want to get any closer to this man who invaded her fantasies.

She glanced at her watch and knew there was nothing to do but tie his tie. So she took it from him and quivered as her fingers brushed his.

The church must be drafty. That was the reason for the chills that ran up her spine, she assured herself as she took a step closer, and wrapped the tie around his neck.

She ignored the fact that Seth smelled good. Not

in a I-used-half-a-bottle-of-cologne sort of way but in a I-smell-like-a-man sort of way.

She held her breath and tried not to notice, as she made short work of tying the tie. She took a step back, exhaled and inhaled deeply, and admired her handiwork.

"You'll do," she said. "Let's go. We're running late."

She led him back up the stairs and they snuck quietly into the sanctuary of the church. "We'll sit back here until just before the end of the service."

"Then what?" he whispered.

"Don't you worry, all you have to do is follow directions."

SETH HAD BEEN RIGHT WHEN he'd known he was wrong. On the drive over to the church he figured whatever Desi needed him for had to do with a wedding.

She was a wedding coordinator and needed him at a church.

Yes, it didn't take a keen intellect to reach the conclusion that she needed him for something wedding-ish, but that didn't stop the idea of her needing *something more* from crossing his mind.

That he wished Desi wanted him in a carnal way instead of a business way confused him. After all, his entire relationship with Mary Kathryn had been built on common work interests as well as mutual admiration and respect. It wasn't this chemical sort of attraction he felt for Desi.

The idea of Desi merely wanting him was an appealing thing on some basic level, but basic was all it was. It wasn't as if he really knew her. This attraction was a hormonal thing. Women weren't the only ones who were sometimes at the mercy of them. It was perfectly natural to be attracted to a gorgeous woman.

Gorgeous. Oh, yeah, that was the right word to describe Desi.

He glanced at her, sitting next to him but not touching him. She was wearing a navy blue dress. Not too businessy, but not overly dressy. It hung to her knees and was...*demure,* that was a good word for it. It was sort of shimmery and soft looking. He didn't know much about fabrics, but he bet it was silk.

Her hair fascinated him. As soft and silky looking as the dress. He had an urge to reach out and just run his fingers through it. He wanted to do something more wild and out of character than buying a sports car—and specifically, he wanted to do it with this woman. But his kept his hands firmly in his lap.

Yes, Desi was gorgeous, but that being said, he didn't really know her. Oh, he knew she was generous. All those years ago she'd proven that by helping him win the science fair. She'd proved it again by helping him home. But beautiful and generous weren't enough to form an attraction, at least not for him.

He wanted a partner, someone who shared his interests, not just someone to share his bed.

And yet...

As he studied her, Desi sniffed, pulling his attention from shimmery dresses to the tissue she dabbed her eyes.

"You're crying," he whispered.

"I cry at everything from commercials to sad country songs," she whispered back, and punctuated the sentence with another sniff. "I cried when you won that science award. And as much as other things make me cry, weddings are the worst. I always end up bawling."

"Why?"

"Because they're *so* romantic. They're two people standing in front of their friends and family and declaring that they're going to spend the rest of their lives loving each other."

"If you believe that, then why are you crying? That shouldn't make you sad."

"I'm not sad, I'm happy. Happy they're going to have happily-ever-after, and happy that I had a hand in making this a special day."

"That's a lot of happys for something that probably won't last. Marriages needed to be based on more than emotional nonsense."

He thought of his mother and father's relation-ship, full of emotions run amuck. Volatile, that was the word for it. They fought with as much passion as they loved. And they wore those feelings on their sleeves—bubbling, fuming, fighting, loving.

Something a little less capricious would be pref-erable.

"Look at the statistics," he continued. "If love did indeed mean fairy-tale endings, then there wouldn't be so many divorces. Logic. Compatibil-ity. Common goals. Those are things that a mar-riage should be based on. Those are things that will make a relationship work long after the initial emo-tional, chemical response has faded into a distant memory."

He'd based his relationship with Mary Kathryn on that premise. It was a sound theory.

Then why didn't it work out?

He hadn't made it beyond the engagement. But why?

That was the question no amount of scientific research could answer.

Desi just shot him a dirty look, and then turned her attention to the ceremony.

"I'd like to introduce Mr. and Mrs. Mark Mentz," the priest said as the ceremony ended. The guests stood and applauded.

"Come on," Desi said. She led him into the church's foyer.

"What now?" he asked, wondering why he'd said yes in the first place.

"Remind me to debate what marriages should be based on later. Right now, we're on. I'm going to stay here and take care of the reception line, and then get the pictures started."

She dug through her briefcase and handed a couple sheets of crumpled paper to Seth. "Here. Do you know where the Siebenbuerger Club is?"

Seth took the mangled looking papers. "What are these?"

"That one's the seating chart, this one—" she indicated an even rattier looking sheet of paper "—is the checklist. I need you to head over to the club. Make sure they have everything set up, that the candles are lit and…well, it's all there. Then, as people come in, help them find their table. I know you can follow the chart. I'll join you as soon as possible."

"I need a clipboard," he muttered. He needed to put her messy notes into some order. He smoothed them, but it didn't help.

How could she work like this? He thought of his own orderly system. Desi could use some pointers on neat, orderly charts.

"Pardon?" she asked.

"I need a clipboard, something to organize all this. I need to get it all straight so I can think."

"Think about what?"

"About…just get me a clipboard. I can't work like this," he said, turning over the crumbled mass of paper in his hands.

"Seth, I don't have time to get you a clipboard. I just need you to take care of this. It's all written down. No problem."

"But—"

"It's all on the lists," she said, her voice tinged with exasperation. It didn't take a scientist to analyze her frustration level. "You don't need a clipboard. How hard can it be?"

How hard could it be?

Seth looked at the mangled papers Desi had thrust at him. How hard could it be to fold a paper in half, neatly and evenly? Obviously too hard for Desi.

"Fine," he said. He could meet this challenge. He'd not only meet it, he'd surpass it. He'd show her how to be organized. "I'll take care of everything. You won't be long?"

"I'll be there as soon as I can."

THE SIEBENBUERGER CLUB was only a few blocks from St. John's, so Seth arrived within minutes. He parked his car in the lot across the street and walked toward the brick building wondering just how he'd become an assistant—a wedding coordinator's assistant.

Another wedding reception.

How had it happened? The only good thing was that this time he wasn't the jilted groom, but the gofer.

He plodded into the club, wishing he was anywhere but here. A doorman was checking in guests.

"I'm with the Mentz wedding," Seth said. "I'm Desi Smith's assistant. If you could show me—"

"Oh, thank goodness," the gray-haired man said. "The staff is going crazy. It seems the cake didn't arrive and they're not sure what to do."

Seth didn't know what to do about a nonexistent cake either, but before he could tell the man so, he found himself hustled down a hall to a small office.

"Are you from the Mentz wedding?" a rather frazzled looking dark-haired woman asked.

"Yes," Seth said, tentatively.

"Here—" she handed him the phone "—it's the bakery. Dealing with cakes isn't my job. I'm just the caterer."

It wasn't his job either. What did he know about wedding cakes, other than his almost-mother-in-law had thought his was too small last week?

Seth longed for his quiet office. Books and mussels. Heck, though the science was more his thing than the classes, he'd even prefer a lecture hall full of college kids right now.

At 8:00 a.m.

On a Monday morning.

But since he knew nothing was going to save him

at this point, he put the phone to his ear. "Now, what's the problem?"

"THERE IS NO PROBLEM I can't handle."

Desi murmured the phrase over and over. It was her own private mantra.

She was going to kill Seth Rutherford, Ph.D.

Pretty Hideously Dead. That's what the abbreviation should stand for. A slow, agonizing death, that's what he was in for when she found him.

He taught science, for pity's sake. Surely he could follow simple instructions? She'd written everything down for him. And yet, as she walked into the reception hall, the candles weren't lit, there were no hors d'oeuvres set out, and there was no Seth pointing guests to their tables.

There was no Seth period.

She watched people mill around, reading name plates, looking for their seats.

As she rushed into action making sure the caterer started serving, that the bartender was ready, that somebody lit the candles, and that people found their tables, she thought of new, horrible ways to torture the fink.

She would—

"You're here!" Seth, the man doomed to die a painful death as soon as this reception was over, said as he rushed into the room. His tux rumpled and smeared with dirt. There was something in his hair.

Not only was he late, he was a mess. She was going to have to pay extra to get that tux cleaned.

"I'm here, but where were you?" Desi said sharply and then continued without allowing him time to answer. "Nothing's ready. The bridal party will be here in a few minutes and nothing's done. I called you today because I was desperate, I needed you and—"

He interrupted her. "You also needed a cake."

"Pardon?"

"The cake wasn't here. The bakery's van broke down on I-90 and the tow truck was coming, so I shot out of here to get it. If I hadn't, it would have been too late by the time the bakery driver arranged other transportation. You'd have had a reception and no cake."

"Oh, Seth, I take back every wicked thing I thought about you. I'm so sorry. I—"

"Uh, don't be too thankful just yet. It's a big cake. There were five boxes, and then there was all the little fountain and column stuff, and, well you saw my new car, it's only got two seats and not much of a trunk."

"So you don't have it?"

"Oh, the cake is fine. It's the bride and groom. I was driving uncharacteristically fast, and I'm afraid they're gone."

"The bride and groom?" He'd hit her newly married couple? Desi turned ready to rush to the parking lot and save her clients, but Seth caught her.

"Not the real bride and groom. The cake bride and groom. They're somewhere on Old French Road. I filled up the trunk with the columns and the fountain. Then I took down the top of the car, and stacked everything. I sort of belted all the boxes in place in the passenger seat, and they were pretty secure.

"Generally I drive slow, but I knew that you needed me here, so I was going a little faster than I should have. So when this truck in front of me slammed on his brakes, so did I. The bride and groom were riding on the top of the boxes and they flew out of the car. I spent fifteen minutes looking for them, but it was on the part of Old French with the steep incline, and I think they're in the creek and half way to Lake Erie by now. I'm sorry."

"I—"

Whatever she was going to say was cut short by the videographer interrupting them. "Desi, where's Phil? I need his help with this—" He held his camcorder out. "It's—"

"Listen, Desi, you've got your hands full. I'll figure out putting the cake together. Trust me," Seth said.

Certain that she was going to regret it later, Desi gave a small nod. "Okay, but don't ruin it."

4

RUINED.

Well and truly wrecked.

Her career was over.

Desi Smith knew the truth when it stared her in the face. In one short evening Seth Rutherford had completely obliterated her business reputation. She'd never get another job. She'd be forced to work for someone else.

Another thought occurred to her.

It was horrible.

If her parents found out that Engaging Styles had failed, they'd renew their efforts to get her into a *real* job. A professional job. A nine-to-five job.

She hiccupped again.

She'd been hiccupping ever since Seth had destroyed her business. Not just ordinary hiccups.

No.

Her's were body-wracking hiccups. Everyone dealt with stress in their own way. Though she'd never have chosen it, given her druthers, her way was hiccuping.

Last time she'd got them this bad she'd just stood

up to her parents—finally refusing to go to grad school. She'd told them about her dream job and they hadn't taken it well. The resulting confrontation had led to hiccups that were so bad she'd had to go to the doctor's for a shot.

When she got them like this they could last for days. The shots cleared them up, but she hated shots. Thinking about getting one made her even more nervous and she let out a long string of hiccups.

"I'm so sorry about everything," Seth said for at least the hundredth time.

He'd insisted on driving her to her apartment, and Desi hadn't been able to put together enough words between the hiccuping to argue.

Hiccup, was her only response. Her diaphragm was already aching.

"At least the cake turned out nice," he said. "Well, until I sat in it."

Nice? Seth had obviously not seen many elaborate tiered wedding cakes. His finished product resembled the Leaning Tower of Pisa.

Or closer to the point, a Salvador Dali painting. Surreal and leaning every which way.

Hiccup.

"And the bride and groom. They were pure inspiration," he said, trying to cheer her up.

"They were...*hiccup*...Barbie dolls, Seth."

"But getting the bride's niece to lend them to

me, well, it cost me five bucks. And then she said I ruined them at the end so that was another thirty dollars to replace them. Though I don't think frosting ruins dolls. And I'm going to check and see if Barbies really cost that much. I think I got suckered.''

''I know you…*hiccup*…were trying to… *hiccup*…help, and the cake…*hiccup*…problems weren't really your fault…*hiccup*…and the dolls were sort of cute. But…'' She let the sentence trail off and had a loud series of hiccups.

''I know, I know, I shouldn't have lectured that lady about sexual harassment, but come on, Desi, she pinched my butt.''

''That's not what I…*hiccup*…was talking about either…*hiccup*…and you know it.'' She hiccuped and said, ''I'm ruined. Done in…*hiccup*…by a mad scientist and a wedding cake.''

Seth glanced her way, and the wind caught his blond hair, messing it slightly. He gave her an apologetic look. ''You're right. I know what you're talking about. It's just that there it was, that garter, flying right at me, and the last thing in the world I want is another wedding, so I backed away, hoping that kid with the glasses would catch it and I forgot about the cake.''

''No one else…*hiccup*…ever will. I'm ruined.''

She'd worked so hard for the last few years.

She'd defied her parents and followed her dream. Engaging Styles was that dream and because of Seth it had now turned into a nightmare.

"Desi, I don't think it's the end of your career. After all, you didn't sit in the wedding cake. I did."

"You were working for me." She hiccuped again. "I should have driven myself home. I'm perfectly... *hiccup*...capable...*hiccup*...of...*hiccup*...driving."

"Desi, you'd end up in an accident. You're upset and it's my fault," he said, and then added, "Plus I owed you a ride. Friends don't let friends drive drunk, or while under the influence of near-terminal hiccups."

He pulled up to the address she'd given him and parked in the lot. "Come on, let me take you in."

"I can...*hiccup*...get in myself."

He opened his door, walked around the car and opened hers. "Still, I'm going to see you to your door. It's dark and I'm not letting you go up yourself."

He offered her his hand, but Desi ignored it. "Fine."

They took the elevator to the second floor and Desi morosely led Seth to her apartment.

"Desi," came a cry. And Desi didn't have to be a scientist to know that Murphy's Law was being applied in full force tonight.

Her parents were here. Standing in the hall. Waiting.

Oh, no, they found out about the date with Stanley...or rather the date she'd broken with him.

Stanley, an up-and-coming banker who her parents thought would be perfect for her.

And he would be...if she was looking for a man who couldn't pass a mirror without preening. A man who left a fifteen-percent-to-the-penny tip for the waiter at their one-and-only dinner. She just couldn't face going out with him again, and after breaking a second date, she'd dodged his calls, but obviously couldn't dodge her parents, since they were standing right outside her apartment door.

"Mom and Dad...*hiccup*. What's up?" she asked, playing innocent.

Desi looked at her parents, and tried to see them through Seth's eyes.

They looked harmless enough.

Her mother, Barbara, was petite, her dark hair highlighted with striking streaks of gray, and vivid blue eyes that defied age. Her father, Verle, was much taller, taller than Seth. His hair was completely gray with no signs of thinning at all.

"Your mother wanted to talk to you about Stanley. He called, upset that you'd broken your date. He'd been so excited about your first date and says he hasn't been able to get a hold of you to reschedule the second one. We said we'd help and were just about to let ourselves into the apartment to wait for you. And who is this?'' Her father eyed Seth suspiciously.

''Seth. Seth Rutherford.'' He held out his hand and the men shook. ''I'm filling in as Desi's assistant tonight.''

Desi unlocked the apartment door and let in all her uninvited guests.

''Hiccup.'' She led them into her living room with its rose-colored walls, lace curtains, floral printed fabrics. Normally walking into her living room was the biggest pleasure of her day. She loved the room. But today all she wanted was to walk straight through her living room and into her bedroom where she could climb beneath the covers and hide for the next week or so.

She glanced at her three uninvited guests and knew there was no escape.

''Mom, Dad, this is Seth—we went to school together—and Seth, this is my mother and father, Verle and Barbara Smith.'' An uncontrollable series of hiccups punctuated her introductions.

Rather than address Seth with social pleasantries, her mother turned to Desi and asked, ''Where's Phil?''

Desi couldn't seem to get a word out between

the hiccups, and finally Seth answered, "I volunteered to fill in for him."

"So you're not a wedding consultant by trade and not Desi's date?" Her mother was staring at Seth as if he were a specimen under her microscope.

Don't say it, Desi willed. *Please don't say it.* She'd forgive him for ruining her career if only he didn't tell them—

"No to both. I'm a professor of biology at the university, and Desi and I are just friends."

He said it. A professional. A real profession.

He could have said male escort or tarot card reader. How about rodeo rider? Anything but a professional.

Darn.

Her mother was eyeing Seth up in a most uncomfortable way, even as her father said, "If Seth is just a friend, then there's no reason you can't go out with Stanley again."

No reason except he had the personality of a parsnip. No, make that a mushroom. Fungus. That was how she'd describe Stanley Stall. Her parents had just *happened* to invite him to dinner last week on the same night they happened to invite Desi. She'd gone out with him once after that, and once was enough.

"You broke your dinner date with him Tuesday, then he asked you to go to a movie on Wednesday and that you *said* you were busy.'' Her mother placed just enough emphasis on the said part that Desi knew that her mother knew she'd lied to Stanley.

"Sorry, Mom. You know, I always have dinner with Mary Jo and Pam on Wednesdays. And I don't really have any nights open soon. With Phil gone I'm going to be busier than usual.'' And unlikely to get un-busy, at least for Stanley.

Her parents acted as a unit. They used to push her toward a career worthy of her intellect, both acting in tandem. They dreamed of Nobel Prizes and academic honors. When that didn't work, they started pushing her toward men.

Suitable men.

Unfortunately their idea of a man who would suit Desi was about as accurate at their opinion of a career that would suit her.

Desi might not know what she was looking for in a man, but it obviously wasn't what her parents were looking for.

Her mother shot Desi a look that said they weren't finished discussing Stanley, then turned to Seth and said, "So tell us, Seth, what you do.''

"I'm studying the impact of foreign invaders on the lake's ecosystem—''

"I'm going to change,'' Desi said, though her parents didn't even hear her. Seth did. He looked at her helplessly as her mother led him toward the couch.

Desi walked toward her bedroom, but could hear her mother grilling him about his teaching and his research. She took off her dress, stripping down to her lacy underwear, then pulled on jeans and a T-shirt over her hiccup-tender chest.

Desi had been stressed before her parents arrived, but now? She might not ever recover.

She hurried back out to the living room.

"...and Desi's in Mensa. Did you know that? She was in the gifted program in school. She got a full academic scholarship to college. And what is she doing with her life? Planning weddings, that's what."

Seth said, "I don't know—"

"Neither do I," her mother said. "Why look how she broke the date off with Stanley. He's a perfectly respectable, successful man. I love my daughter, but I don't understand her."

"I think you're missing the big picture here," Seth said. "Desi isn't wasting her talents at all. She's very talented at what she does. I've got letters behind my name, but I couldn't do what she does. I ruined everything she worked so hard at in just one short evening."

"But she could be anything she wanted," her mother insisted.

"And that's just what she's doing. Finding something you love doing, something you're good at doing and then doing it…that's a success in my book."

Desi heard the words and realized that she hadn't hiccupped once as she blatantly eavesdropped. Seth had just stood up to her mother on her behalf.

He was a hero.

Suddenly Desi forgot his every mishap.

"Well, I guess I never thought about it that way," her mother said slowly.

"You should. I wish I could find a way for all my students to discover what it is they would love to do with their lives. I know I'm a better researcher than an instructor, but teaching is part of the package and I do my best to inspire them to do just what your daughter has done. I encourage them to find their passion."

He paused a moment and said, "Watching Desi in action I learned that she handles a million different details flawlessly, and seemingly effortlessly. It isn't as easy as she makes it seem. I lost the bride and groom, got groped by a number of women, and I knocked over a stack of dishes, stepped on the bride's train, and the final icing for the evening was when I sat in the cake. I'm a total wedding disaster."

Desi's hiccups were gone for good, she realized. And she realized something else, something new about Seth Rutherford—he understood her. At least, he understood her love for what she did. And that was more than her parents had ever done.

She forgave him for his wedding disaster-itis and cleared her throat as she walked into the room.

"Desi, are you feeling better, dear?" her mother asked.

Desi would have sworn there was something different in her mother's tone. Something that said she was finally beginning to understand her.

"Seth was just telling us that he doesn't think you're going to offer him a permanent job as you assistant," her father said.

Desi chuckled. "That would be an understatement. But he did try. He helped me out of a bind, and even if there were a few accidents—"

Seth openly choked at her new, kinder version of his assistance.

"—I know he did his best. Did he tell you there wouldn't have even been a cake if he hadn't gone and rescued it?"

"Seth told us everything we needed to hear," her father said.

Desi shot Seth a look of gratitude.

Seth stood. "I just wanted to be sure you made it home. And now that—" Suddenly he broke off his sentence and said, "Hey, you haven't hiccupped since you came back in here."

"Like I said, I'm feeling much better."

"But I ruined your career."

"I'm sure you didn't. I'll make it up to the new Mr. and Mrs. Mentz somehow."

"You know, Desdemona, you could have called us, if you were desperate for help," her mother interjected.

"Not that we'd be any better at receptions than Seth here, but we would have helped you," her father added.

"You would have?" she asked, praying her jaw wasn't dragging the floor.

"Desi," her mother said, her voice uncharacteristically soft, "we might not understand why you chose this profession, and we might have, maybe, been a little disappointed thinking you weren't making the most of your intellect, but Seth here reminded us that you are following your heart and that you are good at what you do. And both your father and I respect that. But whatever you do, whatever our feelings about it, you are our daughter, and if you need us, we'd be there."

Desi's eyes misted up. She wanted to say something, but couldn't seem to find any words. "I—"

"Why don't you see Seth out," her mother said. "He's looking very uncomfortable with our little family discussion."

Wordlessly, she stood and took Seth's arm as she led him to the door.

She was touching him, she realized. She dropped

his arm and stammered, "Seth, I don't know how to thank you."

She opened the door, waiting for him to leave, but he didn't. Instead, he asked, "You have another wedding tomorrow, too, don't you?"

"Yes."

"Since you couldn't have replaced Phil yet, do you still need me? I mean, if you get through this weekend, you can use next week to find someone more permanent, right?"

"Right."

"Well, I'm volunteering. Unless you'd rather ask your parents."

"I can't tell you how much their offer meant, but I suspect Mom and Dad would be less capable at assisting than you are. They're much better at running the show or giving orders."

That much was true. But what she wasn't going to say was that she wanted to see Seth again, and if he helped her she knew she would.

"Fine. What time?"

Desi stared at him. If she'd followed her parents' wishes and become a scientist, Seth Rutherford would make an interesting specimen. She wasn't sure what to make of him and maybe studying him would help.

No. She took that back, she didn't want to figure him out.

Desi knew what she wanted in life—a successful

career, and a happily-ever-after of her own. She wanted romance. Someone who loved her to distraction and would prove it in a romance-worthy way.

She couldn't imagine Seth ever waxing poetic about his love for anyone.

No, Seth might have rescued her from her parents tonight, but he wasn't a romance hero. Add to that he was on the rebound in a big way and you had the most unsuitable man in the whole world. She would have better luck chasing after Stanley than chasing the man her girlhood dreams had turned into.

But that didn't stop Seth from being one of the most attractive men she'd seen in a long time.

The thought made her sigh.

"Is that a 'Yes, Seth, I really need you' sigh?" he asked. "Or is it a, 'I'm between a rock and a hard place, so I guess I don't have a choice' sigh?"

"You're sure you want to volunteer?" she asked, hoping he'd change his mind and back out.

"I guess I am. That is, if you're not afraid to give me another try."

"Well, you didn't pass your driver's test first time, but you've managed to drive all these years without an accident, so maybe it will be the same with the wedding assistance."

"Great." He grinned.

It almost looked as if he was pleased to be helping.

"What time?"

She'd let Seth help this one last time, and that would be that. They'd be even and she'd get back to normal. "Meet me at the Lutheran Church in Wesleyville about eleven, okay?"

"Why don't I pick you up a little before that and we can go together?"

"Okay."

She shut the door behind him. One more day working with Seth Rutherford and that would be it. She'd find a new assistant and get back to her life.

"Desi?" her mother called.

Speaking of getting back to, there was still the matter of Stanley to take care of.

"Coming," she called.

She glanced at the closed door.

One more day of dealing with Seth Rutherford and she'd say goodbye to the object of her teenage crush for good.

That would *really* be it.

5

THAT WAS IT.

Desi admitted defeat.

She couldn't sleep.

She'd tossed and turned all night long. The sun hadn't risen and she finally gave up the pretense, turned on her bedside lamp and picked up her book, *Her Perfect Man.*

Generally, reading—especially reading a good romance—soothed her. But this morning, non-soothing phrases kept catching her eye as she flew through the pages.

"They had everything in common."

Seth thought love should be a partnership of the minds; she thought love should be a partnership of the heart.

Not that it mattered.

It wasn't as if she was considering a relationship with Seth, she told herself sternly. What she felt for him was simply a remnant of a girlhood crush.

"Romero and Cassandra fit together like two pieces of a puzzle."

Her attraction to Seth was puzzling, but she

wouldn't say they fit together. She was a read-romances-in-bed sort of girl, he was a clipboard-obsessed sort of guy.

"He'd spent his whole life looking for her."

Seth might have looked at her, but hadn't even noticed her in high school. Maybe he noticed a little now, but he was on the rebound, which meant that even if he was looking, he wouldn't look long. Rebound relationships never lasted.

"Romero sent Cassandra chocolate…dark, rich chocolate that spoke of passion and pleasure. It was her favorite. But that came as no surprise. Romero seemed to have a sixth sense about her, as if he knew her every thought and fantasy."

Seth's idea of a fantasy was…

Desi didn't have a clue what it was. Her fantasy man would be one who knew her inside out. Even armed with a clipboard, she doubted Seth would ever figure her out.

"Romero—every woman's dream man—admitted he dreamed of her and only her."

Desi snorted. Seth probably dreamed of periodic tables.

Not that she wanted Seth to dream of her. It wasn't as if she dreamed of him. No, in order to dream she'd have to sleep, and all she'd done was toss and turn.

Finally, she couldn't stand reading another word

about Romero. He was perfect. Perfect for Cassandra.

No, more than that, he was just plain perfect. Nauseatingly perfect. Heck, he'd even folded his clothes before getting into bed. He probably never left the toilet seat up and the story made no mention of him snoring.

Yeah, Desi would have liked him more if he snored. But instead, Romero was a saint.

That should make her swoon for him, instead she tossed the book on the nightstand in disgust and glanced at the clock. She needed to get ready anyway.

She took a quick shower and got ready for the day, then made her way into the kitchen for a cup of coffee. It was stupid getting so worked up over a book and Romero. He was exactly the kind of hero she was looking for, after all.

A man who shared her interests, who was romantic, who anticipated her needs and desires. A man who loved her and would do anything for her.

She put a filter in the coffeemaker, then scooped heaping teaspoons of coffee into it.

Yeah, Romero was everything she was looking for in a man. A true Prince Charming.

She wasn't sure why that thought distressed her, but it did.

As she filled the carafe with water and then transfered it to the coffeemaker Seth flashed through her mind. Just a quick image of him climbing out of his banana-colored sports car.

Seth was the antithesis of what she was looking for. He was a man on the rebound, a man who didn't believe in love so much as compatibility. A man...

Oh, she had to forget about Seth Rutherford.

She should have said no last night when he offered to help at today's wedding. But she hadn't and she refused to wonder why she hadn't.

Well, she'd get through today, and then she was putting all thoughts of Seth out of her mind. She was going to forget about him if it was the last thing she did.

She went to get the paper. She'd needed a heavy dose of reality after that saccharine-coated Romero. She opened the door, bent to get paper, and found herself staring at shoes...well-polished, black shoes.

She looked up and there was Seth, decked out in his tux, looking totally hot.

How could she start forgetting if he looked so darned good?

"Seth?" she asked in a morning croak.

"I'm early. It's a habit. I hate to be late, so I'm always a little early. Of course if we were in the Atlantic time zone, I'd be right on time."

"I was just making coffee. I need it to jump-start my morning, especially my early-afternoon-wedding Saturdays. Come on in. I'll share. A quick cup and then we'll get going."

"That would be great. Are you sure you want me to help today? I mean, after yesterday…" He left the sentence hang there as he trailed after her into the kitchen.

Desi nodded at a stool, indicating he should be seated. "Sure I'm sure. I really need the help."

What was she saying?

She'd just wondered why she'd agreed to Seth's assistance today. This was the perfect opportunity to change her mind. But instead of telling him to go, she said, "You just had a few mishaps. Perfectly understandable. This is a difficult job."

She poured two cups of coffee and handed one to him, then took a seat across from him.

"You're right. This is nothing like research. Step one is always followed by step two, which is followed by three and then so on and so on. From what I can tell there is no order to running a wedding."

"That's because weddings are days built around emotions. And there's no telling where those emotions will take you. I mean, people passing out, overindulging, fighting." She took a long sip and felt the caffeine surge through her system. "That's just the people stuff. Then there are wedding dresses that don't fit and you have to sew the bride into them, and missing wedding cakes—"

"Sat-in wedding cakes," he added.

Desi smiled. "Yes and the sat-in ones. It's always something. Something new, something different and frequently something challenging. It keeps life interesting."

"Interesting is finding that the lake's clarity has increased by three percent. Interesting is following the new applications for fuel cells in automobiles. Interesting is not a plethora of overemotional people collected in one location."

"Seth, people are what makes my job so wonderful. I mean, my parents wanted me to do something…well, like you do. But I wanted the wild emotions, the unpredictability. I wanted to be part of happily-ever-afters on a daily basis."

Seth just shook his head. "I'll help you today, but after this, I plan to go back to my rational, orderly life and forget all about weddings."

Desi looked at Seth and silently agreed. After today it was best he headed back to his lab. And she was determined that when he did she was going to forget about him as easily as he planned on forgetting about weddings.

"FORGET IT."

Desi knew, despite their nice conversation that morning, Seth was going to be difficult. Not that there had been any mishaps today. No, he was just being ornery.

She sometimes wondered if there was some sort of gene attached to the Y chromosome that made men so…mannish. Seth had been so contrite about last night that she'd almost forgotten that he was still all man and bound to be a pain.

"It's all part of the job, Seth. And now that you're working for me—"

"This is the last day," he pointed out with a stubborn look on his face. "Next weekend you'll have a new assistant and I'll be back on the lake looking for samples, or in the lab analyzing them, or—"

"Even if it is your last day, this is part of the job and you'll have to just deal with it."

"I'm not playing stand-in-groom. The idea of being a groom, stand-in or otherwise, gives me hives. I'm not meant to be married, I've proven that. I'm mystified by the whole process of being in love. But I think the idea of smashing cake in each other's face is even more confusing than the idea of marriage."

"It's just a piece of cake." She laughed, though he didn't even crack a smile. That was one of his problems. The man had no sense of humor.

No, she took that back. He did have a small sense of humor—she'd seen it in his cat's name. But not enough to deal with cake smashing.

"Mary Kathryn and I had decided we wouldn't indulge in this arcane, insane practice." He gestured toward the beautiful five tiered cake. "It serves no purpose."

"It's tradition." She took a mini-veil from a bag stashed underneath the cake table.

"Well, it's not a good one."

Desi set the small veil on her head, pinning it in place as she said, "It doesn't matter what you and Mary Kathryn planned, this bride and groom want it. They don't want to tempt the fates by abandoning a tradition, but the bride doesn't want to mess up her makeup, so we're the stand-ins."

"Well, you're standing alone." He crossed his arms across his chest.

"Oh, no, bucko. You said you'd help me out, and this is part of it. You sat in a cake yesterday— How much more degrading could it be to have a little frosting on your face, rather than on your butt?"

She was surprised at how breathy her voice was. What was it about being near Seth that sucked all the oxygen from her body? There must be a scientific explanation, but she wasn't about to ask Seth for it.

"Do you ever let up?" he asked.

"Not when there's something I want."

Want.

She could want this man. And then suddenly it hit her. There was no *could* about it. There was something about Seth Rutherford that sucked up her oxygen, that made her want to tear off his clothes and…

Cakes and weddings.

When this wedding was over she was going to put aside this vestige of her girlhood crush, and she definitely wasn't going to spend another sleepless night.

But first she had to get through this wedding. She had to get her mind out of the gutter and onto the job at hand. That spark of *something* she felt was nothing more than gratitude.

And this? She looked at the man standing next to her, the man who heated her blood. This was nothing more than leftover girlhood daydreams mixed with a smattering of lust.

Cakes and weddings.

"So, is that a yes?" she asked, her mind firmly fixed on the business at hand.

"Yes. But you're going to be the one owing me when this is all said and done."

"Fine." She waved Seth away from the bar, and closer to the table. And tapped on a glass with her knife. "May I have your attention?"

The room quieted. "It's time to cut the cake. Tom and Susan, would you do the honors."

The bride and groom took up their position in front of the elaborate, five tiered cake. No Leaning Tower of Pisa today, no Barbie cake topper, and best of all, no impression of Seth's butt in the center of it.

No, this was a beautiful, traditional, un-sat-in cake. The photographer snapped pictures as Tom and Susan ran their knife through the sweet confection.

The happy couple cut two slices and placed them on a napkin then handed them to Desi, who in turn handed one to Seth.

She smiled and faced the crowd gathered around them. "I know that a modern-day tradition is that the bride and groom would now feed each other a piece of cake. And somewhere along the line, that sweet tradition turned into a smash-fest. But since the bride looks so lovely, we're not going to mess with perfection. My assistant, Seth, and I will play stand-ins for the cake smashing."

The audience clapped loudly.

Desi offered a slice to Seth. "Seth?"

They intertwined their arms and held the cake in front of each other's mouth.

And for a moment, Desi looked into Seth's deep blue eyes and she could almost believe that it was for real…that this was the man she loved and she had just promised to spend the rest of her life with him.

Desi smashed her piece into his face, hoping to break whatever spell he'd cast on her.

Seth grinned through the icing as he pushed his slice into her face with a twist.

"Kiss, kiss, kiss," the guests all chanted.

Desi knew that they were talking about the bride and groom, heard their collective exhale and cheering as the happy couple obliged them and kissed, but she barely noticed it. What she did notice was how cute Seth was with icing all over his face, and he seemed to be coming closer…closer…closer, as if he were going to kiss her as well.

Only he didn't.

No, Seth, took his napkin and wiped part of the icing off her face.

Desi tried to hide her disappointment as she tore the veil from her head and said, "Let's leave the happy couple and go get cleaned up."

Noting that the catering staff had started cutting and serving the cake and that everything else was in order, she led him into the kitchen. She kept wiping at the cake as they walked into the back office where she'd set up her command central for this reception.

She tossed the veil on the desk and turned to her assistant.

"For someone who didn't want to do it, you certainly have a way with smashing cakes."

He was wiping at his cake-covered face.

"Here let me help," she said, moving toward him.

He took a step backward. "I can do it."

"But you've missed some frosting right here." She wiped a bit of frosting from next to his left eye.

"And right here," she said, moving down and toward his nose. "There. Did I get it all off me?"

"Not quite."

"Could you help me?" He took a napkin and slowly, gently dabbed at her face.

He moved closer, studying her. "Did you know your face is asymmetrical?"

"Pardon?"

"It's not quite the same on both sides. Your right eye is just a little larger than your left and…"

The napkin stilled on her face, as Seth stopped speaking.

"And?" she prompted.

"And looking at you makes me want to kiss you."

He was echoing her own thoughts, and rather than make her happy, it made her nervous.

She should simply walk away. After all, Seth Rutherford was on the rebound. He wasn't her type. She wanted a Prince Charming. No, he wasn't her type at all, as a matter of fact, he was her parent's type. He—

He had a cat named Schrödinger, which meant he had a quiet sense of humor.

He forgave his runaway bride, which meant he had a kind and generous heart.

She couldn't wrestle out the whys and nots of kissing Seth, so she simply said, "So why don't you?"

He didn't kiss her, instead, he studied her, looking perplexed as he said, "I hardly know you. I can't stop thinking about you, about touching you. That doesn't mean I should kiss you."

"It doesn't mean you shouldn't."

"But…" Whatever he was going to say was lost as his lips touched hers. Or did her lips touch his?

She wasn't sure, but it didn't matter. What mattered was that their lips were touching. There was no gentle introduction here…just raw, hot need.

Desi was overwhelmed by the taste, the scent, the feel of him. Frosting on his lips. Sweet and strong. An underlying scent of the outdoors, wild and fresh. And the feel…she took a step closer, melding her body to his. There was so much warmth in his embrace and she wanted more of it. She wanted to strip off his clothes as well as her own and remove all the barriers that stood between them.

Even as she toyed with his tie, the memories of those barriers came flooding back.

"Seth," she said, pulling back. "I was wrong, we shouldn't do this."

"What the hell was that?" He stepped back and stared at her.

"Pardon?"

"You kissed me," he said, an accusation in his voice.

"No," she corrected him. "You kissed me."

"Why?"

"I don't know. Why did you kiss me?"

He shook his head and took another step backward. "I don't know, and I don't like it."

"You didn't like my kiss?" Granted, it had been a while since she kissed anyone, but Desi thought she hadn't lost all her skills.

"No—I mean yes. I liked your kiss, but I don't know why I liked it. When I kissed Mary Kathryn it was nice, but…well, this was different than that and I'm not sure why. As a scientist I need to know why. I mean, you've got great assets—I might have been drunk, but I notice when you put them into your car. And I've dreamed about them every night this week. But they're just physical. Physical attraction is…well, it's a chemical, hormonal thing. It's nothing to base a relationship on."

"Who's talking about relationships?" she asked. She needed to remind both of them that this kiss couldn't lead anywhere. "But I kissed you," he said.

Trying to adopt a cavalier attitude, Desi said, "Seth, this is twenty-first century. Kissing me doesn't compromise my virtue. I'm not waiting for a proposal of marriage based on it."

"Good, because I'm not getting married. Ever.

There are just to many variables involved. I could never be sure of it. But I'd like to compromise your virtue. And that's what's got me so confused. I was friends with Mary Kathryn for years, worked with her every day, and I never once wanted to strip her naked in an office.''

"And that's what we need to remember. We're in the office, and there's a wedding out in the hall. A wedding I'm responsible for. You made me forget about it. And though my parents might not think being a wedding coordinator is a lofty career, it's mine and it's important. I don't forget about it.''

Seth didn't say a word. He was staring at her in a rather befuddled fashion.

"Listen, it was just a kiss. Forget it. I'm going to. Let's get back there and see to it this reception goes without a hitch.''

Forget about it?

Seth wished he could forget about that darned kiss yesterday. But he couldn't seem to. He's spent the night definitely not forgetting it.

He remembered every detail of yesterday's wedding in vivid detail. He was relieved he'd done better than the first wedding, that he hadn't destroyed anything or anyone. No, it wasn't the wedding that bothered him, but his reaction to Desi.

Even though he analyzed it, he couldn't figure out what was going on between him and Desi. He'd never felt such primal responses to a woman. If it was just that elemental reaction, he could ignore it. But there was something more going on. He genuinely liked her. He'd showed up early at her apartment yesterday, not because he was always early—he wasn't—but because he couldn't wait another minute to see her again.

"Darn, Schrödinger, what am I going to do?"

"Merp."

"Yeah, that about sums it up. Merp."

He'd watched Desi handle the rest of reception yesterday with grace and a deftness. She seemed to be everywhere at once.

Everywhere but where he was.

She'd kept her distance after they'd smashed the cake and kissed, almost as if he made her nervous.

But that couldn't be. From what he could see, Desdemona Smith was fearless.

She ignored her parents wishes and chased after her dream. He wasn't sure when she'd started Engaging Styles, but from what he could see, she was a success with it. She managed drunken grooms, runaway brides, smashed cakes and even terminal hiccups with grace and style.

She was fearless and good at what she did…and she was avoiding him. When he'd said goodbye, she'd simply given him an absentminded wave and thank-you, but never truly looked at him.

He wanted to talk to her, to discuss their kiss

with her. Maybe she'd have some additional data that would allow him to form a hypothesis, but she obviously was keeping her distance. He couldn't come up with a theory without all the data, and he couldn't get all the data he needed without Desi's help.

It was obvious she wasn't interesting in helping him analyze their almost chemical reaction to each other. She was avoiding him.

But he had an ace up his sleeve.

"Hello, Desi. Remember that tit-for-tat thing you talked about…? Well, you had your tits, now it's time for my tat…"

6

___

SUNDAY MORNINGS WERE meant for long mornings in bed reading the paper. They were meant for brunches and lazing about. They weren't meant for this…for taking life in hand and hitting the open sea—lake.

She'd promised herself she'd forget Seth Rutherford after the wedding, but then he'd called talking about tits for tats and since she owed him, she had to put off her forgetting for one more day.

Desi gulped convulsively, not sure she'd ever manage to forget this trip. She'd be okay if the darned boat stopped rocking so fiercely. Lake Erie seemed bigger from a boat in the water than it did from on shore.

"What kind of assistant has a freak bathtub accident?" she asked between gulps.

Bigger and rougher. Despite the bright afternoon sun, there was a brisk wind kicking up waves. And Seth's boat, *The Guppy*, didn't look big enough to withstand too many waves. It wasn't much more than a rowboat with a motor on it. Oh, there were several seats near the steering wheel, a couple more at the side, facing the water and a some flat deck space, but Desi suspected the boat would be more at home in a tub than on the great lake.

She was sitting next to Seth, who was driving. A debt was a debt—but really this was going to heck with the deal.

"And who names their boat *The Guppy* anyway?" She fought back another wave of nausea that crashed against her fragile stomach like the big waves crashed against the boat's hull.

"My assistant fell in the tub and broke his ankle and as for naming my boat *The Guppy,* it's a joke. You see, when Tony and I were about eleven, we went to swimming lessons together and he was miffed because I was put in the dolphin class and he was back in the guppies."

"Seth?" Desi said, seeing a flash of pain on his face as he finished the swimming story.

"Mary Kathryn's with him. We talked and she said that neither of them wanted to hurt me. I'm not sure about much, but I am sure about that. She's working at Tony's restaurant and she sounded…well, happy. I loved Mary Kathryn. Still do. But I've spent the last week thinking about us and about what went wrong, and I've realized I was never *in love* with her. I don't really know if I'm capable of something that…" He paused, as if he was searching for the correct scientific term.

"Emotional," Desi supplied.

"Yeah, maybe. It seems to me that phrases like 'in love' are bandied around all the time, but judging from the number of divorces, it seems a rather fickle emotion. Tenuous. More of a chemical reaction that dissipates rapidly than any lasting relationship."

"You told me before you weren't in love with Mary Kathryn."

"Kate," he said.

Desi could hear the confusion in his voice.

"She says Tony calls her Kate. She says she always dreamed of being a Kate. I never knew that. To me she was always Mary Kathryn. She's staying in Houston with him where she'll be a Kate full-time. He runs an Irish pub and sushi bar. She said on the phone that he was going to have to cook his sushi because of the contaminants. He was in the background yelling that his sushi isn't contaminated."

"Ah, see, they're already fighting." Desi felt almost gleeful. She'd like to smash Tony "The Guppy" Donetti for hurting Seth.

Seth might be behaving nobly about this whole best friend running away with his fiancée thing, but Desi didn't feel noble at all. She was outraged on his behalf.

He might deny it, might rattle on about not feeling deep emotions, but he must be hurt and confused. She'd do just about anything to fix that.

Why? Why did it matter to her?

Maybe it was a feeling of debt. Maybe it was simply that she liked him. She thought about… thought about his defending her to her parents, about his pitching in and helping, though it was obvious working at weddings wasn't his forte. She even thought about his cat and its silly name.

She liked him and she didn't want to see him hurt.

"No, it wasn't a fight. She started laughing as he hollered. I mean, I've heard her laugh before—once we read this article about Prigogine's theory of self-organization, and Mary Kathryn said I could have been his case study and we both laughed about that—but we never laughed like she and Tony were. It was…well, maybe sensual is a good word. And he was in the background laughing as well. Mary Kathryn, Kate, and I worked together for over a year but never had anything like that. Not that intimate."

He sat a moment, looking as if he was trying to digest the thought of Mary Kathryn, his research partner turning into a sensually laughing Kate.

"Let's face it—the only heat between us was our Bunsen burner. I'm happy she's found someone," he finally said. "I'm happy for her and Tony. I love them both and hope they're happy."

"You're a good man, Seth Rutherford," she said.

She was struck by the accuracy of that statement.

Desi might not know many things, but she knew in every fiber of her being that Seth was a truly good man.

"No. I'm a simple man. I found out just in time that things would never have been simple with Mary Kathryn."

Simply wonderful.

That's how she'd describe Seth at this moment.

He might deny his ability to feel deeply, yet she knew that he meant what he'd just said. He willingly forgave Tony and Kate. He loved them both enough to be happy for their happiness.

Yeah, he was simply wonderful.

"Okay, enough of that. Let's get to work and see what we have."

Desi followed Seth's directions. There was a snakelike tube on the deck of the boat. She helped Seth place it in the water. He used it to collect his samples of the lake's sediment and watched as he examined the contents from the bottom of the lake. In amongst the sand were rocks and all sorts of creepy crawlies shelled things.

Desi hated things that crept.

Smooshy, yucky-looking things.

They gave her the little shivers down her spine.

She'd almost flunked biology in high school because she refused to dissect a worm.

"What a haul. Why, look at that beauty," Seth

murmured as he stared at the sample. A pinky-nail sized shelled thing lay in the center of his palm.

"Zebra mussels aren't native to the Great Lakes. They appeared in the mid-eighties. They've been a mixed blessing. They've helped clean the lake, and yet, they've thrown the entire ecosystem out of whack," he said, slipping into his teacher mode seemingly without any effort. "They stick together and clog up water intake systems and—"

He looked up and stared at her. "Are you okay?"

"No." Desi was desperately trying to keep from screaming like a girl. That creature in Seth's hand gave her the willies.

"What's the matter?"

"I'm just a little seasick, that's all." Seasick sounded better than scared of a glorified slug.

"Oh, well, try to focus on something else. Here. Look at this beauty." He dumped the zebra mussel into her hand.

SETH WAS PREPARED FOR Desi to ooh and aah. Prepared for her to study the specimen.

He wasn't prepared for her shriek, or for the mussel to go flying across the boat. And he especially wasn't prepared to have it land right between his eyes with a nice little thwack.

But Desi obviously wasn't prepared either... wasn't set for the fact that *The Guppy* was a small boat. As she backed up, wiping her hand on her shorts as if she was trying to wipe childhood cooties off her hand, she'd backed right over the side into the churning lake waters.

Seth's heart squeezed into his throat.

"Desi!" he screamed as he raced to the edge.

He saw her safe within her orange life vest, bobbing next to the boat.

"Here, grab my hand." He leaned over the edge and thrust his hand toward her.

She smiled then and reached up.

He pulled.

Desi braced her feet against the side of the boat, but rather than pulling herself up as he expected—as any sane, rational person would do—she pulled him down.

Hard.

Seth went toppling over the side, headfirst into the water as well. He immediately bobbed up to the surface because of his life vest.

"What did you do that for?" he burbled as he choked on the water he'd inhaled on the way down.

"I don't know," she said, laughing.

Laughing hard.

There was something familiar in that laugh. Seth bobbed in the lake, desperately trying to analyze what it was as he studied her.

Then it hit him.

Desi's laugh had the same quality to it as Mary

Kathryn's had when she was on the phone laughing with Tony. Sensual.

It made him think about the kiss they'd shared.

Looking for a diversion, he did the only thing he could think of. He swam for the still laughing Desi and said, ''That wasn't nice,'' just before he dunked her.

She bobbed, in a life-vested induced way, like an apple in a barrel. She came up still laughing as she coughed and sputtered.

At that moment, Seth did something totally out of character.

He laughed.

Not a small chuckle, or a quiet laugh he might make politely at any faculty party when someone made a joke.

No, this was a laugh ripped from the tips of his toes that traveled throughout his body, gaining momentum, until the moment it burst forth and rang out.

It surprised him.

Maybe it surprised Desi, too, because she stopped sputtering and laughing, and simply stared at him a moment, looking at him as if he was something rather foreign and mystifying.

Then, just as suddenly, she was laughing again. ''You think you can take me on and win? Well, you asked for it, Rutherford.''

''Oh, yeah?''

"Yeah. Prepare to be conquered."

Conquered. That's just how he felt as he spent the next half an hour playing in the water. Conquered by a brunette with green eyes and a quick smile. The thought was more alien than his laughter.

To be conquered by a small laughing woman who reminded him that there was more to Lake Erie's water than zebra mussels and gobis, it was…

For once in his life, he refused to overanalyze the situation.

Seth pushed all worries about Desi's effect on him, and instead just allowed himself to relax. They played freely, carelessly. Like overgrown children who didn't have a worry in the world.

There were no runaway brides, no worries about careers.

There was the sun and the waves…

And there was Seth and Desi.

For that moment in time, it just simply was.

And the fact that it *was* was enough for Seth.

"I think I'm as pruned as an eighty-year-old woman." Desi had just dunked him for the umpteenth time, and held up her hand and examined the wrinkled skin.

"Are you ready to get back in the boat?" he asked. He kept his tone light, though the question was tinged with regret.

It was almost as if Lake Erie had mystically

made him forget himself. As soon as he left its dark waters, he knew that the magic would fade. And rather than see the world as magic, he'd once again fade into a logical view.

"Don't make it sound as if us being out here is my fault. You're the one who dunked me," Desi said. "It's your fault I'm all wrinkled."

"You're the one who pulled me into the water," Seth teased back.

"Well, only after you put that slimy thing in my hand."

"It's not a slimy thing. It's a zebra mussel. I've been studying their effects on the lake for the last two years."

"It doesn't matter what you call it, it's still slimy."

Seth knew whose fault it was that he'd just spent part of his afternoon playing instead of working, and he'd have to think of some way to thank her for that. "Come on. Let's get out of here. You first."

The small ladder at the side made getting out of the water easier, but the life vests were bulky, and so it took Desi a few extra minutes to climb up. And Seth spent those extra minutes studying her form. Well, studying all of her form that was visible to him. Her short-covered bottom.

He realized that a cold lake wasn't enough to

chill the heat that raced through his body as he stared at Desi.

She made it onto the boat and put an end to his agony.

No, actually, she made it worse. As he reached the top of the ladder, he realized she'd stripped off her life vest, shorts and T-shirt. She was clad only in a demure tank bathing suit that looked anything but demure. It hugged her body in all the right places as she toweled herself off.

"Gosh, the lake is colder than I thought. I'm freezing."

Her taut nipples showed through the thin material, giving strength to her statement.

Seth stared at the samples on the deck of the boat.

"Here," she said, a towel hit him across the chest. "You'd better dry off, too."

"I'm fine."

He gulped as she sat on the deck of the boat, and turned her face toward the sun. She looked like some Greek goddess.

Like Eve.

Only instead of offering him an apple, she was his apple and he wanted nothing more than to take a bite.

Seth shook his head.

What was with him today? He'd just recently been with a woman who had everything in common with him, a woman who should have been perfect, but wasn't.

How could he be thinking about Desi like this?

"Seth, what on earth is the matter with you? Are you waterlogged, or what?"

"I'm—" He stopped, unable to say another word.

"Sit down before you fall down. I know you're all work, but if this is how playing in the water for a little while affects you, you obviously have a problem."

She reached up, took his hand, and pulled him onto the deck next to her. "Now dry off and warm up."

"I think I'm warm enough."

"You can't be. That water was chilly."

"No. No, I'm not chilly."

She reached over and took his hand. "Hey, you're not."

Seth pulled it back, as if her touch burned.

"What's wrong? Are you mad at me because I pulled you into the water? Really, I was just teasing. I thought you had fun."

"No, I'm not mad. And I did have fun."

"So, what's eating you?"

"You." The word was out before he could stop it.

She was obviously was surprised by his statement as he was to have made it.

"Pardon?" she asked.

"You're not really eating me, I'm simply fantasizing about what you'd taste like."

"Pardon?" she repeated.

"You sound so prim and proper when you say 'pardon'—" he mimicked her inflection "—like that, but I don't think you really are. I think…" He paused, studying her.

Before he could change his mind, he leaned toward her, forgetting everything but the desire to kiss her. And though there was no frosting on them this time, she was still sweet.

Intoxicating.

Addictive.

Seth heard someone groan. Maybe it was him.

He was groaning over Desi?

The thought sobered him and he broke off the kiss.

She reached up and touched her lips, as if their kiss had somehow left a mark. "What did you do that for?"

"I'm not sure." Seth hadn't known what he was doing since the day of his almost-wedding. But maybe it wasn't the almost wedding that had confused things. Maybe it was Desi?

"But maybe I want to do it again?" he added.

"Are you asking me, or telling me?" she asked.

"Telling you. But—" What on earth was he saying?

"Desi, I'm as confused by this as you are. Probably more so. Let's finish up here, then, if you'd like, I want you to come home with me."

"Pardon?" she asked for a third time.

DESI WAS SURE SHE'D heard Seth wrong. She must still have water in her ears from her impromptu trip overboard. She wiggled her index fingers around in them, hoping to clear her hearing before he repeated himself.

"Come home with me," Seth repeated. "I'll make you dinner."

She tried to keep her face neutral, tried not to let him see the way her heart lightened just a bit at his suggestion.

"Are you a good cook?" she asked, instead of saying, *Yes, Seth. I'd love to go home with you. And I'm not worried about your cooking, but about my burning when you're around.*

"Yes," he said, in that serious way of his, as if her question was on of earth-shattering importance, rather than just a joke. "I'm a very good cook. I know how to make a meal that optimizes nutritional values and minimizes calories."

"Uh, Seth are you implying I'm fat?" She teased him, hoping to throw him as off balance as she felt.

"No. You're not fat."

"It sounded as if you were suggesting I might

be.'' At the serious look on his face, she realized that Seth wasn't used to being teased.

He tried again. ''No, you're not fat. I like how you look. I mean, I *really* like how you look. I can't stop thinking about how you look. In fact, I've dreamed about it. And—''

''Burgers,'' she said, interrupting him.

She wasn't sure if she was pleased he found her attractive and had been thinking about her, or just nervous. She was sure that she needed a safer subject.

''What?'' he asked.

''Burgers. Hamburgers. After a day on the lake, I don't want to maximize nutrition and minimize calories. I want burgers. Big, greasy ones with French fries.''

''Do you know what a meal like that does to your cholesterol levels?'' he asked.

''Yep. But sometimes you just have to throw caution to the wind and live on the wild side. Sometimes it's okay to have fun, Seth.'' She paused, watching him take her comment in, and grinned as she added, ''And milk shakes. I like strawberry best. How 'bout you?''

She was ready for more arguments on the health risks associated with fast food, but all he said was, ''Chocolate. Rich, thick chocolate.''

''Let's go then. I'm hungry.''

They changed into dry clothes in the public rest

rooms after they'd docked *The Guppy.* Desi was glad she'd thought to pack some in a bag.

She followed him to the parking lot. Watching him walk. For the first time she noticed that he had an amazingly tight butt for a professor. Actually, for anyone.

Not that it should matter. Seth wasn't her type. He was her parents' type, and that made him as far from her type as you could humanly get. She was just being nice. Friendly.

They drove from the dock, up State Street, the top of Seth's convertible down, the wind blowing through her hair and her mind running in circles.

Yeah, friendly.

Desi was just having dinner with Seth because he was good company. It had nothing to do with the toe-tingling experience of kissing him, not once, but twice. It had nothing to do with the assets she'd been admiring. It didn't even have anything to do with the fact that he was extremely cute when he got all serious and enthusiastic about tiny little slimy slugs.

Nope, not at all.

Desdemona Smith was simply an altruistic, generous human being. That's all.

Ordering burgers at a drive-through window interrupted her inner musings, but soon with grease-laddened burgers in hand she was thinking again.

Seth was a nice guy. But Desi wanted more than nice.

She wanted someone who was madly in love with her.

Someone who couldn't live without her. A passionate, adventurous soul mate.

Someone who would sweep her off her feet and carry her away to a happily-ever-after.

Look at how quickly Seth had recovered from losing Mary Kathryn. That definitely isn't a sign of a deeply passionate sort of man. Add to that, the only carrying away had been her carrying his drunken self up his front stairs.

Of course, he'd defended her to her parents.

That was hero-ish.

But...

She realized the car had stopped and Seth had opened her door for her. "Here we are."

Desi followed him into his house, no closer to sorting out her feelings than when she'd started thinking. She pushed her worries away and took in Seth's place now that she could see it plainly.

It was every bit as organized as she'd imagined a little over a week ago in the murky light. And she'd been right—the walls were white. Dull, institutional white.

Something brushed against her leg. "Hey, Schrödinger."

Desi knelt down and stroked the shabby cat's fur. "How you doing, Dingie?"

"Dingie?" Seth asked, pausing as he carried the food into the kitchen.

"Well, Schrödinger is a bit of a mouthful, don't you think?"

"I named him after—"

"Erwin Schrödinger. A physicist with a theory about a cat in a box being alive and dead at the same time. It's sort of like the question, if a tree falls in the woods and no one is around, does it still make a noise?"

"How did you know that?" he asked, looking confused. He pulled two plates out of the cupboard and loaded their artery-clogging goodies onto them.

Desi took her plate and milk shake over to the small table in the corner. "You mean, how would a wedding coordinator know about a twentieth-century physicist?"

Seth sat next to her. "I didn't mean to—"

"Of course you did. But despite the fact that I'm a *mere wedding coordinator* doesn't mean I don't know things."

She bit into her burger. "Oh, this is heavenly. Try yours."

She swallowed, then said, "Back to Schrödinger. There are subjects I'm not well versed in, but science… Well, my parents wanted to turn me into a Nobel Prize–winning scientist. I mean, instead of summer camp, you know the kind where you ride horses and swim? I went to science camp. It wasn't bad, but it wasn't what I wanted.''

"Parents should respect a child's interests," Seth said, solemnly, then took a bite.

"How about yours?" she asked.

"How about mine, what?"

"Your parents. Did they respect your interest in science?"

"They never really cared. No, that's not quite right. They love me, I know that, and they cared—care. It's just that they were always so wrapped up in each other and their private dramas that I just faded into the background and they never really noticed me."

"I'm sorry," Desi said softly.

"Sorry for what?"

"You deserve to be noticed." In her mind's eye she saw Seth at the reception, standing alone, quietly watching the people.

"I prefer not to be. Really. It was better that they left me alone. They were always so...volatile. I wasn't. I never want that type of relationship. On again, off again. Loud fights, louder reconciliations. That's why I want order. Some sense. I—" He stopped short and then mumbled, "Never mind."

"Listen, let's finish these burgers before they get cold," she said with forced cheerfulness.

She wished Seth wouldn't have stopped.

She suddenly remembered the science fair again. She'd watched as Seth got up to accept his award. Her secret girlhood crush, and she'd found a way to help him. Her ecstatic feeling had threatened to overwhelm her.

He'd looked so good up there on the stage, waiting to accept his award, she could see his pleasure hidden beneath his serious exterior.

She thought of the man he'd grown into. Maybe his parents relationship explained a lot about Seth's willingness to marry someone because she was comfortable.

Desi looked across the table and noticed a small drop of the burger's special sauce on his chin. Without thinking, she reached across the table and wiped it off.

Seth moved back, as if she'd pinched him. "What are you doing?"

Desi let her hand fall back onto her lap. "You had sauce dripping down your chin."

Seth took a napkin.

"I got it all," she assured him.

"You got it all off me maybe, but your sandwich was apparently as drippy as mine."

She reached for a napkin and wiped at her own face, but Seth stopped her. "Allow me."

He reached over and wiped her face for her. It felt more like a caress. Like when he'd wiped the cake from her face at the wedding yesterday.

"Seth." That's all she could think to say, just his name.

He'd confessed he'd thought about her. And right at this minute, she wanted to shout out her own confession as well—that she couldn't get him out of her mind—but she couldn't make the words come out.

Wouldn't let them.

He sat back in his seat. "Maybe we should talk about this."

"*This?*" she asked, her voice little more than a squeak.

"This. Whatever this attraction is that's between us. In my experience—"

"Seth, I don't want to talk about it. I don't want to analyze it. I just want to—"

She didn't know she was going to do it, until she did it.

She leaned toward him and let herself go. His lips felt as if they were frozen, as if they were shocked by her forwardness, but then there was some kind of release, as if something had been set free and he began kissing her back. More than that, he took over.

Hunger.

That's what he felt like. A man who was hungry for what she could give him. The feeling was powerful. Desi was almost high with it.

He pulled her from her chair onto his lap. As his hand threaded through her hair, he groaned.

She'd done that to him. She'd ignited the same turbulent need in him that coursed through her blood. Hot, heavy and growing.

Feeling bold and brazen, Desi kissed him, right there in the middle of his kitchen.

She felt the tension in his body, and as she continued the fascinating exploration of the contours of his mouth, she gently kneaded his shoulders, feeling him begin to relax.

"I still think we should talk about this. I can't seem to keep my hands off you."

He might be analyzing again, but Desi was pleased to note he hadn't released her. He wrapped her in his arms. She liked the way she felt, safe in his embrace.

"Listen, Seth, I think it's obvious that there's something between us, and since we're both consenting adults, there's no reason we can't…" She let the sentence trail off, suddenly not sure what to say.

"I don't know why this keeps happening. I keep trying to figure it out, but end up simply chasing my thoughts in circles. We don't have anything in common."

He looked so cute when he was confused. Desi didn't think he'd appreciate hearing it. "It's not as if that hasn't occurred to me as well. I want romance. I want the prince on his charger carrying me off to his castle—the whole package.''

''And I'm not romantic,'' he said. ''I don't know how to be. I want logic and order. And this isn't…''

''Maybe we could bypass the romance, and forget about logic and…''

''But we should discuss this and weigh all the factors.'' There was a small furrow in his brow, as if scrinching up his forehead would help him figure out the complexities of their mutual cases of lust.

Desi reached up and gently ran a finger through the furrow. ''Seth, I have a confession, I don't want to worry about our differences. I think we've proved we have one overwhelmingly big similarity. I want you so bad it hurts. I want all of you…now.''

7

IT WAS AS IF DESI'S confession freed something in Seth.

"Me, too. I want you that bad."

"Then what are we waiting for?"

"I can't promise the things you said you wanted, but I promise I'll try." He promptly tried to scoop her into his arms. "You're an awkward shape, you know."

"Oh, no. You're not going to start figuring out if I'm a cube or a sphere, are you?" She wasn't sure he remembered that particular conversation in the car, but she did.

"I don't need to calculate mass, in this case. I just need to find a better means of levering you up."

"Seth, I can walk. You're going to hurt something if you carry me."

"You wanted romance, and though I'm no Cyrano, I know carrying a woman into your room to make love is romantic."

"Not if you're going to break your back," she pointed out. "I can walk."

"Okay, so maybe cradling you and standing isn't going to work. We'll adapt."

"Adapt?" she asked, not sure she liked the sounds of that.

"Yeah." He stood up as well, and studied her, a crooked grin on his face. "I think I've got it."

Without waiting for her to say anything, he bent and threw her bodily over his shoulder into a fireman's hold.

"Seth, I don't think this is what the romance novels mean when they say he carried her into his bedroom."

"Ah, but as a scientist I've learned that there are frequently a multitude of solutions to any one problem."

She was laughing as she thumped at his back and she was pretty sure he was as well, judging from the small shake of his shoulders. "Put me down."

"No, I'm carrying you into my room and then…what's the proper romantic word?"

Making love. That's the phrase she wanted to blurt out, but instead, she kept her tone light and said, "Ravish. You're going to ravish me."

"Ravish. Oh, that sounds as if it has potential." He paused mid-stairs. "Dingie, get out of the way."

"Don't you drop me," Desi cried, unable to see where they were going. No, what she could see was a whole new perspective on Seth's behind. Even from that angle, it was a fine-looking backside.

Despite the fact they were laughing her desire was as hot and heavy as before. Maybe even hotter.

She wanted this man. Wanted him more than anything.

She wanted to laugh with him. Wanted to tease him. She wanted to keep the world from hurting him.

She just wanted him.

They reached the top of the stairs, and Seth turned to the left. ''Here we are.''

Desi was suddenly flipped back over his shoulder onto his bed. ''Do you feel romanced?''

There was a smile on his face that said he was joking, the sight caused her heart to constrict.

Seth Rutherford was about to make love to her, to ravish her, and he was joking.

Emotions that Desi was hard-pressed to identify, seemed to squeeze all the oxygen from her body.

''Yes, that was plenty romantic enough,'' she said, trying to keep her tone light.

''Good, because I don't think I could have thought of much more to do than this…''

Seth sat on the bed next to her, and gently leaned down, closer, closer…and kissed her with an intensity that made Desi feel as if she was the most important thing in his universe—that she was the *only* thing in his universe.

Her world focused to just Seth. There was only this...kissing him, touching him. His stomach was firm and tight, and sprinkled with a light dusting of fine, soft hair. She ran her fingers through it even as she explored every contour of his mouth. Warm and inviting, she reveled in the feel of him.

He groaned, the sound a soft rumble against her eager lips.

He tried to pull away, but she reached around him and held him to her. She didn't want to let him go, didn't want to break the new and heady connection.

Desi was bombarded by sensation, almost overloaded with it. The feel of his chest against her palm, the weight of his body, pressed to hers. The scent of him...it was like a summer day on the lake, warm and fresh. And the taste of him. He was everything she ever wanted.

Clothes became an unwanted barrier. And though their lips parted momentarily as they tore off their shirts, it still felt as if the kiss hadn't been broken, the intensity wasn't diminished in the least.

Sweet and intoxicating, their bodies pressed, fusing into one. Hands roaming, touching, teasing. Each stroke seemed to only fuel the fire of her need that showed no signs of ebbing. Desi could feel his desire pressed against her.

Finally, the kiss ended. Desi was breathless with it, and felt a surge of pleasure when she realized he was, too. Calm, cool Professor Rutherford had lost control because of her. She liked the feeling of breaking through his otherwise iron clad control.

"Before we… I mean, before I…" Seth started.

"Before you ravish me?" Desi helped.

"Yes," he said, relief in having a term evident. "I need you to know that it's been a long time since I've been intimate with anyone. I…well, I have protection."

His concern warmed her. Desi wasn't exactly innocent, but might have found a discussion like this uncomfortable under other circumstances. But it didn't take her from the moment at all, as a matter of fact, his regard for her well-being only intensified her feelings.

"Seth, it's been a long time for me as well, just to set your mind at ease."

He got up from the bed and rummaged through his drawer. "I bought…well, they're new, not that I expected you and I…but I wanted to be sure. I haven't been able to get you off my mind and after you kissed me yesterday with that cake, well—"

"Thank you for thinking of me." Desi felt warm and treasured. The thought was a validation. He wanted her and had been considering a moment like this just as she had.

Desi had never felt like this. Never. She'd read a million romances, and even had a few tender relationships before this, but nothing had ever prepared her for the raging fire of need that burned in her body—burned so bright she was consumed by it.

Seth cupped her breasts, lightly tracing her taut nipple with his finger. "I've fantasized about this."

"Me, too," she said, soft and breathy.

"That night when you drove me home, I don't remember much, but I remember thinking, more than a handful's a waste. They're a perfect handful, totally waste-free breasts." He paused. "That didn't come out the way I meant it."

He paused and tried again. "You have the most beautiful breasts I've ever seen. I mean, not that I've seen enough to make an accurate scientific comparison... It's not that I'm checking them out on every woman I meet, that would be piggish, and I'm not—"

"Seth."

"No, I'm going to compliment you right—romantically. Let's try another attribute. I'll concentrate on your eyes."

He pulled back and studied her, staring right into her eyes.

"They're green, no make that jade eyes. Jewels. Beautiful jewels. That's what they are. Shining and—"

He sighed. "See, I might try, but I just can't wax poetic. It just comes out waxing stupid."

"Seth, when you look at me like..."

"Like what?"

"Like you are right now, as if I'm the only thing that matters. As if your entire universe has narrowed until I'm the only thing in it. When you look at me like that, you don't need words and clichés. That's more than poetic, that's perfect."

DESI WAS RIGHT, SETH felt as if his entire world had narrowed until there was only her. He studied her face. She had a light sprinkling of freckles across the bridge of her nose. He'd like to memorize the pattern.

He'd like to memorize every curve and point on her body. He wanted to brand himself on her, so that she'd never notice all the reasons they were wrong for each other, but could only remember him.

He might not be able to offer her all the beautiful words she deserved, that she longed for, but he'd do his best to show her without words.

His hands explored her body, but he held her gaze, watching as her eyelids drooped halfway over her green eyes. He moved his hands lower, exploring every intimate spot, and watched as her head tilted back, and her breathing became shallower. Watching her experience the pleasure he was giving was a powerful aphrodisiac for his own desire.

"Seth," she breathed, a small, half whisper.

The sound of his name sent him over the edge

of control. He'd wanted to wait, to take all night, but he couldn't. He needed her, needed her more than he'd ever needed anything. He wanted her with an emotional intensity that might have shocked him just a few days ago.

Now, all he could think about was bringing them together. He slipped into her moistness, joining with her, fusing two separate organisms into one symbiotic relationship.

Symbiotic. That was the perfect word. He needed what only Desi could provide. She was necessary to his very survival.

She rose to meet his every thrust, her rhythm matching his. They were synchronized. Two people moving as one.

As her head tilted back again, her eyes totally shut, he sensed she was at the edge of satisfaction and he allowed himself to topple over with her.

At that moment, Seth felt as if Desi had branded herself somehow on him. He wasn't sure what the feeling meant, but he knew that somehow this experience had left him altered.

They curled together afterward, Seth cradling her in his arms. He needed to figure out what to do about Desdemona Smith. The last thing he wanted to do was hurt her. He needed to analyze the situation in order to determine how to proceed. But at that moment he was too replete to try. So he simply contented himself with holding her, to living in the moment. He'd worry about the rest tomorrow.

DESI WOKE BEFORE SETH the next morning. She was acutely aware of the heat of his body pressed against her nakedness. Skin to skin. They lay entwined, mingling until it was hard to know where Desi left off and Seth started.

She knew her hair must be a fright. Pieces were plastered across the front of her neck. And she didn't even want to think about her breath. Morning breath was a given.

But instead of worrying, Desi chose to watch Seth. Asleep, his serious expression relaxed. A lock of his beach-blond hair lay across his forehead. She would have liked to move it, to push it back into place, but she didn't want to wake him. So she just lay there, contentedly watching him.

Content.

That's how she felt here, with Seth. Content. Satiated. Happy. Painfully, blissfully happy.

Gradually, he stirred, waking slowly; and he sensed, when he became aware, that he wasn't alone.

His eyes bolted open and he stared at her.

''Um,'' was all he said.

It was a nervous sort of sound that people make when they want to fill up the quiet space, but couldn't really think of anything worthwhile to fill it with.

"Now, that's just what a woman wants to hear after she's spent a night with a man. *'Um.'* Of course, when it's accompanied by that worried look you're currently wearing, it's even more flattering. Are you *umming* me because you're not sure what to do with me? Were you hoping I'd left, so you didn't have to deal with the messy morning-after-itis? Or did I maybe misinterpret your tone and was that a more sexual sort of *um?*"

Teasing obviously wasn't going to help ease the tension. He looked so unbelievably flustered and uncomfortable that Desi put aside her own worries of bedhead and morning breath and tried to think of something to do.

Before she could come up with a plan he said, "Desi, I'm not sure what happened. I mean..."

"Seth," she said gently, "I'm sure with all those science classes you took and have taught, you had at least a smattering of biology."

There, she'd done it. He smiled, and some of the worry dissipated.

"Yes. I think I understand that part." He chuckled. A rich, low, rumbling sound that reverberated throughout Desi's system. No longer satiated, she was hungry for more. More of Seth, more togetherness.

"It's the rest," he said. "I mean, I told you Mary

Kathryn and I never…and I knew her for a long time and was planning to marry her. Yet, she never made me feel the kind of desperation I felt with you last night. Last night, I needed you so much I ached with it.''

She was going to ignore the fact that he'd just brought up his ex-fiancée and concentrate on the fact he'd used the word desperation.

Desperation. That sounded good.

He was desperate for her? Oh, yeah, she liked the sound of that. She'd felt a bit of desperation herself last night. But unlike Seth, didn't feel the need to analyze it this morning.

''And how about this morning?'' she asked. ''Any aches and pains you want to talk about?''

''I just didn't want you to think I'd used you to satisfy some hormone-based lust. It was more than that. It was…''

He left the sentence hang a half a beat too long.

Desi knew he didn't have a clue what it was, and she wasn't insulted, because neither did she. She could list all the reasons why things with Seth would never work out long term. He was on the rebound, they had nothing in common—except maybe this. She reached out and touched his chest.

No, she wasn't about to spend the day trying to figure out whatever this was with him. She didn't want to qualify it, or label it. She had other plans.

''Seth, in those biology classes did anyone ever

mention that females are known to experience a bit of lust, too? Because, if not, let me guarantee you that they do, and I did. I still do. So if there was using going on, it was both of us. A little mutual lust is a good thing, nothing to look so worried about. And if you're willing, I was thinking that last night wasn't enough…I'm not quite as satisfied as I thought. Maybe you'd consider doing some mutual lusting this morning?''

Suddenly all worry and confusion disappeared. In its place was a good dose of the lust they'd been discussing.

''Not quite satisfied?'' Seth asked. ''Well, we can't have that, can we? I think I'm up for the job.''

''Hold that thought and give me two minutes,'' Desi said. She might not be able to do much about the bedhead, but she refused to make love to Seth until she'd brushed her teeth.

She scampered out of bed and into his bathroom. She didn't have a toothbrush, but rubbed his toothpaste around in her mouth with her index finger and tried to smooth down the worst of her hair.

He took a turn in the bathroom when she finished.

She was still trying to de-mess her hair when he came back and climbed into bed.

''You don't have to do that,'' he said.

''Do what?''

"Primp for me." He pulled her into his arms. "Because, I have a confession."

She snuggled closer. "Oh, do tell. I love knowing your deep, dark secrets."

"This one's not so deep and dark. You look lovely."

Desi laughed. "I think you may need glasses, Seth."

"Oh, no." He traced the bridge of her nose with his finger, just a light, casual touch, but it was enough to make her heart rate accelerate. "Would you like a detailed account of your loveliness?"

"Pardon?"

"There you go, being all prim and proper again. I love when you say 'pardon' like that."

He ran his fingers through her hair, taking a section and letting it fall, strand by strand. "And I love the way your hair isn't really just brown. Look— there's light blond and even a few reddish streaks in this. Variegated. That's a good word for your hair. I love looking at it. Yesterday on the lake, when the sun hit it, I was mesmerized. And this morning, it's even more captivating."

His fingers still threaded in her hair, he continued, "And your eyes. They remind me of the lake. Sometimes they're grayish, and sometimes, like right now, they're so a greenish gray. Sometimes there's even a touch of blue green."

"Contacts. I wear those extended-wear contacts."

"Shh. I'm working on collecting scientific data. Now, where was I? Oh, your chin."

She touched her chin, but didn't feel anything exceptional about it. "My chin?"

"Oh, yeah. I like your chin. It's absolutely lovely. It's got the smallest little line in it."

"A cleft." She'd never noticed a cleft in her chin.

"No, not really. Just a little line, a crease maybe is a better word. When you smile, it's noticeable, and I love seeing it."

She'd never had anyone talk to her like this, and felt a little flustered with it.

"Well, thank you," she said to mask her feelings. "I think you're learning this waxing poetic stuff at an accelerated rate. Want to hear what I like about you?"

"No, it's still my turn," he said, and shook his hair. A small section spilled across his forehead. "You see, there's more."

Desi brushed his hair back, and realized what he'd said. "More?"

"Well, I have to confess, there's a lot more. Let's see, I was on your chin. You know how I like to be orderly about things. We'll just work sequentially our way down my list of things I like."

He dropped her hair, and gently caressed her

neck. "I like your neck. It's long, and elegant look-ing. Like a swan. And below your neck…" He cupped her breast. "Oh, below your neck comes two body parts I've become very fond of."

He wiggled his eyebrows and grinned.

A playful Seth was a sight to behold. Desi was enjoying every second. "Do tell, Mr. Rutherford."

"Well, they're a nicely matched pair."

So saying, he leaned down and focused every bit of his considerable concentration on her breasts.

"Seth," she said, her voice all hazy and breathy. Desi hardly recognized the sound of it.

This wasn't some leftover girlhood infatuation. It wasn't simply a hormonal attractions.

What was this man doing to her?

She wasn't sure, but Desi was happy to let him do it some more.

"Seth," she whispered again.

"Yes, Desi?" he asked with a grin.

"Is there any more attributes you enjoy farther down your list."

"Oh, I've got a number that are down lower. Let me see…"

Desi was awash in sensation, reveling in it. She tried to capture and memorize each moment with Seth.

But even as she did, Desi had a feeling that re-membering wasn't going to be a problem at all.

Forgetting was.

8

"DID YOU EVER IMAGINE, all those years ago at the science fair, that we'd end up here?" Seth asked on Monday afternoon.

Desi had never experienced anything like the last twenty-four hours. They'd finally left Seth's bedroom and headed downstairs to get something to eat. And rather than cooking, they'd ended up on his living floor, caught in a need that showed no signs of dimming.

"No, in high school I don't think I had enough imagination to envision something like this. Even last week, I couldn't have imagined something like this. I can't get enough of you. You've turned me into a wild, wanton woman, Professor Rutherford."

Desi lay in the middle of his floor, enveloped in his arms and felt, rather than heard, his chuckle. His chest sort of quivered. She loved making him laugh.

She remembered when she'd driven him home after his almost reception. There'd been no laughter then. He'd been hurt and confused. But now, this minute, she knew that he was happy, and that she'd given him that.

She wanted to give him so much more.

"Listen to that," she whispered.

"To what?"

"The rain tapping against the windows. I love the sound. It's sort of the same feeling as a good snowstorm, when the entire world's shut down and I'm safe and snug in my house, or in your house, as the case may be."

Desi had an idea. She sat up and started to pull on her clothes. "Come on."

Seth raised himself on an elbow, watching her dress. "Where are we going?"

"Out on your porch to watch the rain." She took his hand and pulled upward, though she couldn't budge him.

"Why would we want to do that? It's warm in here and dry."

"Seth, do you do anything for fun, without having a reason for it? I mean, haven't you ever just watched the rain?"

"No. What is the point?" he asked.

"There's no point, that's the point. You just stand and watch it fall, watch the sky grow darker and darker. Watch the small puddles turn into huge lakes of water. Watch the water wash down the street. You smell the rain in the air and it, well it revitalizes you. It's clean and nourishing. And when you stand in it, you're part of something.''

"Stand in it? You're not part of anything but wet," he grumbled, but he did pull his shorts back on.

"Come on, spoilsport." She pulled him out the door and onto the porch. "See, look at all that water washing down the street. You could race a boat in that stream.''

"I don't have a boat," he pointed out.

He wasn't getting her point, not getting it at all. But Desi wasn't giving up. "Okay, so you don't have a boat. You could splash in it.''

"I'd get wet.''

"Seth, sweetheart, you're already all wet. Come on.''

He shook his head. "Desi, I don't think so.''

"Come on," she said, pulling him toward down the stairs.

Seth allowed himself to be pulled onto the sidewalk just to please Desi, not because of any dire need to be rained on.

It wasn't unpleasant. As a matter of fact the rain was warm and steady. He looked at Desi as she laughed and threw up her arms as she tilted her head backward. "Doesn't it feel lovely?''

Lovely.

"Lovely," he murmured.

"Come on, just don't stand there." She was pulling him again, but this time Seth didn't put up any resistance. Resistance around Desi was futile. If she wanted him to play in the rain, he would. Who cared if his neighbors thought he was crazy?

He would do anything to see her smile at him, like she was right now. He'd give anything to hear the tinkle of her laughter and that included standing in an ankle deep puddle like he was right now.

"Come on, Seth, don't just stand there." And she kicked water at him.

Splashing him couldn't get him any wetter than he already was, but he knew it wasn't the wetness, but the playing she wanted. So he obliged.

"My feet are bigger, and therefore have a larger surface area and can displace more water which should mean I can make a more effective splash."

To prove the point, he kicked a huge tidal wave of a splash in her direction.

She kicked back, and like a couple of kids, the battle ensued. There was no winner. But when Seth finally caught her in his arms, holding tight to restrain her from any more splashing, he knew winning didn't have a thing to do with their water battle.

As his lips pressed against hers and as she kissed him back, he knew he had a prize in his hands. He just wasn't sure what to do with it.

"Come on," she said. "I think I saw some

canned soup in your cupboard. I'll cook for you after we dry off.''

She was pulling at him again, leading him into the house and up the stairs.

''I don't think opening a can constitutes cooking,'' he said, just to get a rise out of her.

''I'll have you know I'm the best canned soup cooker around. It's all in the ratio…water to soup. I don't follow the directions. I improvise.''

''No way,'' he said, shaking his head even as he chuckled. ''I mean, Desi doesn't follow directions? I don't believe it. It's so out of character.''

''Don't you dare mock me, Seth Rutherford. I might not follow directions, but I give them pretty good.'' She reached into the bathroom closet and tossed him a towel, and took one for herself.

''Oh, and what are you planning to direct this evening?'' he asked.

''Well, after some dry clothes—aren't we lucky that I brought extras?—and some soup, I was planning on inviting myself to sleep over again… Only I wasn't planning on a lot of sleep.''

He had the towel on his head, drying his hair, and lifted the edge so he could see her. ''Do tell.''

''Oh, yeah…I've got tons of directions to give you tonight.''

''You did tell me that you were good at that when you called me to help at the first wedding.''

Seth remembered being sure then, that first wedding, that she wasn't thinking what he was thinking. And he'd been right. She wasn't. But now she was, and he was right about owing her, too. Oh, he owed her big time. "You also said you'd be gentle with me."

"And I was. I plan to be again tonight. Only not too gentle."

SETH COULDN'T SLEEP. He looked at the woman lying next to him. What was he doing?

Right on the heels of the thought came another—what was wrong with him? Why couldn't he take what life had so graciously tossed in his lap and simply enjoy it?

He couldn't, he realized. At least not until he'd analyzed the situation and came up with some acceptable answers. He needed to understand. He needed to think.

Quietly, he crawled out of bed and went into his office. He shut the door and turned on the light.

Here, order still reigned. His books were all nicely shelved in alphabetical order. His pencils were all sharpened; his pens neatly in their holder. His diplomas and certificates were on the wall.

There was no woman driving him crazy here. No questions he couldn't answer with a little research.

Research.

Maybe that's what he needed.

But in all his trips to the library, he couldn't ever

recall seeing a book called, *There's a Woman in My Bed... Now What Do I Do?* Or even better, *There's a Woman in My Head... How Do I Get Her Out?*

Desi had been on his mind since that first wedding. No, actually, since the rehearsal for his aborted wedding.

What was he going to do about her?

She'd single-handedly shaken his orderly world. He'd allowed her to. More than that, he'd welcomed it. Why?

Seth pulled out a piece of paper, and snapped it into a clipboard.

He drew two columns. ''Desi,'' he wrote as a header.

What to do about Desi and this attraction?

Reasons Why This Infatuation Can't Last, he labeled one column.

He was on the rebound, just left at the altar by a woman he'd thought he'd spend the rest of his life with. A woman who shared his interests and his goals, unlike Desi. Desi was an impractical romantic. She believed in things like love at first sight, and fairy-tale endings. He believed in compatibility, in similar goals and interests.

He scribbled away, filling his Reasons Why This Infatuation Can't Last side with amazing speed.

Then he thought of one thing they had going for

them. *Common ground.* He wrote "Sex" under it. Then crossed it out and wrote "Good sex."

No. He scratched that out as well and wrote "Earth-shattering sex." He put down the paper, and stared at the words. No, that was wrong. What they had was more than sex, good or earth-shattering. Making love with Desi…making love. That was what they did.

Making love with Desi was about as far removed from sex, even earth-shattering sex, as Newtonian physics was from quantum mechanics.

She made him laugh. That was a plus. A huge plus. He didn't write it down, he just leaned back in his chair and let the feelings she inspired wash over him.

He couldn't remember the last time he laughed before Desi. She dragged him into the lake, out into the rain. And yet, when she was around, he felt…happy.

She made him happy.

According to this paper, they had nothing in common. Different goals. Different ideals.

Different.

He'd had everything in common with Mary Kathryn, but she'd never made him laugh, never stirred his blood. He'd never loved her. Oh, he loved her like a friend, with the same feeling of loyalty and comradery he felt for Tony. But he didn't love her deeply. And that's what made it possible for him to get over losing her with absolute pain-free ease.

No, he'd never truly loved Mary Kathryn and wished her luck with Tony. They were as odd a pairing as he was with Desi. And yet, Desi evoked such strong feelings from him. He loved her in a way that he'd never loved Mary Kathryn.

There was the physical side...and oh, the physical side was good. But holding her after they'd made love, the feeling hadn't ebbed. That would leave him to deduct that it was more than physical. That the need he felt for Desi was something deeper, something more.

Love?

It was an emotion impossible to measure. There was no reliable quantitative data on that emotion, and yet love was the most accurate term for what he felt for Desi.

He loved her.

He'd have to tell her, but he wasn't sure how.

She was a woman who'd built a career on romance and he knew absolutely nothing about such a thing. Yet, for Desi's sake, he needed something big, something so romantic she'd forget all the logic that said they shouldn't be together and simply say she loved him, too.

9

THAT WEDNESDAY, Hazard's was busier than usual, but Desi barely registered the overabundance of nice-looking men. She was riding a wave of happiness.

Part of her wanted to tell her friends all about Seth Rutherford. But if she did they'd ask questions about what sort of relationship it was. And the truth was, Desi didn't have a clue. She refused to worry about it. Refused to worry that Seth was on the rebound, that they didn't seem to have any common ground except sex.

She refused to worry and refused to explain, so she didn't say anything to Mary Jo and Pam. She regaled them with her assistant-search woes instead.

"How hard could it be? I just need someone available Friday night and Saturdays." Before Mary Jo or Pam could answer, Desi continued, "Darn hard apparently."

Tonight she was indulging in Pasta Fromage, which was, despite its fancy name, nothing more than macaroni and cheese. Fancy macaroni and cheese. Millions of calories in a bowl.

She took a bite then continued. "Let's see, there was the girl with the nose ring and tattooed forehead. There have been a number of applicants who leave as soon as they find out the job requires they work on prime-dating nights. And then there was this grandfatherly type who seemed perfect until…"

Desi took another huge bite.

"Until what?" Pam asked.

"Until he told me I'd have to talk to his probation officer for him. Seems he just got out of jail."

"What he do?" Mary Jo asked.

"He's a flasher. He guarantees he won't do any flashing at a wedding, but can't you just see it now? The bride and groom are cutting the cake when suddenly—"

Desi stopped short, not because of worry about a flashing assistant, but because talking about cakes made her think of Seth.

Heck, breathing made her think of Seth. She couldn't get him off her mind.

"I don't think I want to see him," Pam said.

For a moment, Desi wondered if Pam read her mind and knew about her torrid affair, but then she realized that Pam was referring to the flasher.

"Me, either, which is why I didn't hire him."

"So did you find anyone? If not, I can help this weekend," Pam offered, then went on, "And speaking of weekends, did I tell you about my date?''

"I may just take you up on that. And no, you didn't tell us about your date," Desi said. She took another huge bite of her calorie-rich dinner as she listened to Pam's happy bubbling monologue.

"...and then he walked around and opened up the car door for me," she practically cooed.

"He didn't think you could manage it yourself?" Desi asked.

"He was just being a gentleman."

"Paul used to hold the door for me, but now I'm just happy if he'll hold a kid now and again, or maybe get a chance to hold my..." Mary Jo paused a pregnant moment and finished "...hand now and again."

"That's not what you were going to say," Pam scolded.

"No, but it's close enough," Mary Jo said with a wicked grin.

"Look," Pam said, pointing to a lovely specimen of manhood standing across the street from the deckside table. "Oh, that's a commando and if he asked, I'd let him hold my—"

"I thought you were dating Mr. Car-door," Desi said.

"Oh, I am, but I don't think it will last."

"Why?" Mary Jo asked. "You and Desi need to be more optimistic. Maybe he's Mr. Right."

Pam snorted. "I don't think so. Even though he's hot—and boy is he hot—and opens doors, he's not the kind of man you'd want to marry. He's got a wandering eye and wandering hands, which have momentarily wandered my way, but I don't expect them to linger long."

"So why are you seeing him?" Desi asked.

Maybe if she could figure out why Pam was in a relationship she doubted would last long, she could figure out why she was with Seth.

"Because sometimes you have to settle for Mr. Right-Now while you keep looking for Mr. Right," Pam said.

"And how will you know Mr. Right when you meet him?" Desi asked.

"I believe I just will. He'll like the same things I do, he'll want to settle down and have a family. He'll like my friends, and my friends will like him. Why?"

Desi shrugged. "Just wondering."

Mr. Right-Now.

That's what Seth was. Even if they could get past their differences, he was on the rebound and would eventually bounce back into his old life…a life that didn't include her.

She was his transitional woman.

The thought didn't cheer her up. She took another sip of wine.

Seth was a man who entered relationships mind-first, not heart-first. Eventually his analytical mind would figure out how many differences stood between them.

She hoped her heart would figure it out as well.

"Oh, silk boxers!" Pam yelled.

Desi murmured her approval and wondered how much longer "right now" was going to be....

THAT SATURDAY AFTERNOON, Desi slumped into the pew next to her new assistant with a sigh.

Not really about the girl she'd hired. She was a college senior and seemed as if she'd fit in well. Actually, she said she was considering a similar career. No, the girl was fine.

Desi was sighing because she was having a hard time keeping her mind on work.

Who was she kidding?

Her thoughts were so far removed from the Feeney wedding, that she was lucky she even knew the happy couple's names. Somehow she'd managed everything, and the ceremony was about to begin at any second. Yet, here she was, sitting at the back of the church ignoring what she needed to do next. Instead, she was fantasizing.

Fantasizing about Seth.

She looked up at the altar and she saw Seth there. But the funny thing was, she didn't see Mary Kathryn. No, the face was fuzzy, and she wasn't about to try and tune it in because she was afraid she knew who it was. And she didn't know if she liked that it was an image of herself standing next to Seth.

She was romanticizing about standing in front of a church and telling the world she…

She what?

How did she feel about Seth?

Love, a little voice inside her head whispered, but Desi tried to ignore it. It was too soon to throw around that word, and even worse, too soon to throw around the emotion connected to the word. And yet, she couldn't shake the whisper.

"Excuse me, is this seat taken?"

"Seth? What are you doing here?"

He sat next to her and the beat of Desi's heart picked up its tempo. After all the times she'd made love to Seth, she would have thought she'd exhausted her desire, but if anything, it had only increased.

He reached out and took her hand and gave it a gentle squeeze. "How could I leave you in a bind?"

"But I thought you had samples to take this weekend?"

"I left right after you did and took them already."

They'd spent every night this week together, either at her place or his. Getting out of bed each morning, leaving the warmth of his arms, was tough, and every day it became just a little bit tougher.

"But you didn't have to—"

"Shh. They're starting the music."

Desi watched the bridesmaids march down the aisle, but any hope of enjoying the Feeney wedding evaporated. Seth had arrived and she couldn't keep her eyes off the man.

Finally, she nudged him and whispered, "Why are you really here?"

"Like I said, I thought you could use the help of someone who knows what they're doing."

Desi shot him a look and Seth grinned and corrected himself, "Okay, someone who *almost* knows what they're doing. I obviously know how tough it is to be the new assistant. And—" he dropped his voice even lower and leaned close to her ear, tickling it as he whispered "—I wanted to be near you, even if it meant working at a wedding."

He paused and added, "By the way you haven't introduced us."

"Seth this is Bambi, my new assistant, Bambi, this is Seth."

"Pleased to meet you," he said, giving the knockout blonde only a cursory nod. His attention was still focused on Desi. "I'm just helping out today until you get the hang of things."

"Don't you have any zebra mussels you need to count, or whatever it is you do to them?" Desi asked. The instant surge of relief she'd felt when he'd sat next to her, scared her. She was starting to count on him. What would she do when they were no longer together?

Pam's phrase, Mr. Right-Now, flitted through her mind.

What would happen when "right now" was over?

"Nope. I'm all yours. Whatever you need me to do, I'm willing." He inflected just the right amount of innuendo into the statement.

Desi couldn't help responding, "That's good to know. I might hold you to that later. But for now, shh, here comes the bride."

The congregation all stood in a fluid motion and watched as the beautiful young woman walked past them.

Desi fought back the tears. Though she always cried at weddings, these tears weren't for the beautiful bride marching down the aisle toward her happily-ever-after.

"Are you crying again?" Seth asked.

"I told you I always cry at weddings. Look how Leonard's staring at Evelyn. It's as if she's the only woman in the world. As a matter of fact, she is the only woman in the world for him, and he's looking at her that way. That's what I want. Romance."

ROMANCE?

Seth sat glumly by Desi's side as the ceremony progressed. He'd spent a lot of time thinking about romance, looking for ways to woo Desi, and didn't feel any more prepared than when he'd begun.

What did he know about romance?

It was abstract. Every woman he'd talked to had a different idea. Every book he read said something different.

He'd started with a dictionary. Romance. A noun. *(1): a love story.*

Gee, that helped.

He'd gone through some of his texts, but mainly came up with either clinical descriptions of sex, or biological explanations.

So he did what he'd always done…he'd gone to the bookstore.

Normally when he visited, he stayed in the nonfiction section; but this time he'd headed toward fiction and found that they had an entire section devoted to romance. An enormous section. A massive section. There had to be more romance books on the shelves than any other genre of fiction.

Not knowing what else to do when presented with such a large array of choices, he'd decided to take a sampling. He randomly drew ten books from the shelves and took them to the register.

"Are these for you?" the clerk asked, with a raised eyebrow.

"Yes."

"Oh, honey, you're going to make some lucky girl very happy."

"What do you mean?" he asked.

"Why, a man who's not afraid to read romance, who's secure enough in his own masculinity, is every woman's dream man."

The clerk thought he was every woman's dream man. Maybe there was hope of convincing Desi he was hers.

With a sense of excitement, Seth had dug in.

The first book he'd read had fairies flitting through its pages, helping the couple come together. He'd been pretty sure he didn't have any fairies hanging around ready to offer him help and advice.

Seth had tossed it aside and started the second book. It was a romantic intrigue, according to the cover. People were shooting at the hero and heroine from page one on. This gave the hero a number of opportunities to be heroic, and prove his love to the heroine.

No one was shooting at Seth and Desi. The most heroic thing he'd done was not fall on her that first night that she'd brought him home.

As Seth watched Desi's latest couple exchange vows, he reflected on the third story. The hero had found a baby on his doorstep and the heroine had helped him care for the infant. As they worked their way through each problem—and Seth had never realized how many problems a baby could cause until he read this story—they became closer.

He didn't see any hope of finding a baby, or a gun-toting madman, or even a handful of fairies on his doorstep. So the question remained—how was he going to romance Desi Smith?

How was he going to make her fall in love with him, because nothing less than that would satisfy him.

He realized that the minister was announcing, "And now, may I present, Evelyn and Leonard, Mr. and Mrs. Feeney."

The crowd stood and clapped as the happy couple walked down the aisle.

"Well, here we go. It's show time," Desi said.

"YOU'VE BEEN VERY QUIET," Desi said.

She'd followed Seth home after the Feeney wedding. She never got to eat at receptions because she was so busy, so they'd eaten a late lunch, or early dinner, depending on your perspective. It was a rather quiet meal. She'd let him chose this time, and instead of greasy burgers, they had a stir-fry. She wasn't going to admit it, but the food was pretty good, despite the fact it was healthy.

"So what's wrong?" she asked. Seth didn't seem mad, but his thoughts were obviously somewhere else tonight.

"Just thinking," Seth said.

"About what?"

"Oh, this and that..."

He was hiding something. Desi could sense it.

"I'm going to take a shower, okay?" he said.

"Sure. Do you mind if I check my e-mail on your computer? My friend, Mary Jo, tends to send me weird little e-mails throughout the day. Things like asking me to save her."

"From what?" he asked.

"Her kids," Desi said with a laugh. "She's got four. They're tough. And Phil was going to e-mail me. The paper is sending him to Hawaii."

She was also hoping for a romance update as well. Phil was still trying to woo Debbie back.

"Tough job," Seth said with a laugh.

Even Seth's laughter seemed forced, she realized with a sinking heart. Could "right now" have ended so fast?

"Yeah, that's what I told him," she said, forcing a smile of her own, trying to keep things light.

"Sure. Go ahead and help yourself to my computer. I'll be out in just a few minutes."

Schrödinger was sitting at her feet, staring at her.

"You are the laziest cat in the world," Desi said as she lifted the giant feline and carried him up the stairs with her. Schrödinger seemed to be of the opinion that there was no need to walk if someone could be coaxed into carrying him.

Desi set him outside the office door. "Are you coming in?" she asked.

"Merp."

She wasn't sure if that was a "yes" merp or a "no" merp, so she left the office door open as she walked in.

She was surprised to see papers sitting out on the desk. Seth was a stickler for filing things right away.

She booted up the computer and tapped on the clipboarded paper.

Her name caught her attention.

Feeling a bit guilty, Desi took a closer look.

Her name topped the paper, and under it was a column labeled, "Reasons Why This Infatuation Can't Last." It was full of scribbled reasons. He was on the rebound, they were different…

Desi read them all, having thought each and every one of them herself at one time or another. Yet, though she'd thought them as well, it hurt to see them listed so methodically in black and white.

The other column, the things they had going for them had "Sex" and "Good sex" scratched out. *Earth-shattering sex.*

Desi stared at the paper in her hand and hiccupped.

Sex. That's all they had going for them, at least according to Seth's list.

Hiccup.

Sex. Earth-shattering sex, maybe, but still, it was just sex.

Hiccup…hiccup…hiccup.

That's all she meant to him.

A roll in the hay.

Mattress bouncing.

Nothing more. Nothing less.

She tried to end the string of violent hiccups by holding her breath, but that only made her feel light-headed.

Hiccup.

Desi had thought they were building a relationship. Maybe they were different, but she thought those differences were turning out to be good differences. He filled in the cracks of her life, and she'd thought maybe she was doing the same for him…helping to give his life some balance.

She remembered the way he'd defended her to her parents. He'd seemed to understand her—understand her so much better in their short time together than her parents had in an entire lifetime.

She thought they'd connected. She'd actually started allowing herself to whisper the word love, at least in the safety of her mind.

Sex.

Hiccup.

That's all he could think in terms of what they had going for them. And look at his list of reasons why they shouldn't be together. It was miles long.

Well, fine.

She walked out of the office, Schrödinger wrapping around her ankles. She reached down to pet the cat. "Sorry, Dingie. *Hiccup.* I've got to go."

"Go?" Seth said, walking out of the bathroom. "I'd sort of hoped I could talk you into spending the night. We could take *The Guppy* out on the lake tomorrow. I have a few samples to gather, but I swear I won't hand you any zebra mussels. Afterward, we could have a picnic or something."

"Sorry. *Hiccup.* No. I…I have plans with Mary Jo and Pam."

"But—" He stopped short and studied her. "What's wrong?"

"Nothing. It's just that I'm busy. *Hiccup.* You're busy. And really, what do we have going for us? Sex. *Hiccup.* That's all. We have nothing in common. I think it's time to nip this in the bud."

"You're upset. Look at you, you're hiccuping again. What happened?" He paused a moment, and added, "What do you mean nip it?"

"Seth, yes, I'm upset. I see that I've been wasting both our time with some girlish fantasy. *Hiccup.* It's always a bit upsetting to see yourself clearly."

She held her breath a long moment, and then, trying not to let him see her pain, said, "Let me see if I can put this in terms you will understand. What we had was a brief, explosive chemical reaction. But now the reaction has fizzled out and all that's left is a less than satisfactory heterogeneous mixture—one part of the composition is different than the other part. *Hiccup*. We can't completely combine no matter how hard we try. We don't have anything in common, we're just sitting in a beaker, each of us on our own side, doing our own thing. There's nothing to base a relationship with. No reason to continue seeing each other.''

"Desi—''

"Goodbye Seth." Hiccups threatened to escape but she held her breath as she walked out the front door—striving to maintain at least that much dignity.

10

WHAT HAD JUST HAPPENED?

Seth tried to analyze the situation. He'd spent the day flawlessly helping at the Feeney wedding, then come home and taken a shower. Desi had seemed happy enough when she'd gone to his office to check her e-mail.

In the time it had taken him to shower she'd had some sudden revelation that they weren't going to work out and left.

It didn't add up. She'd been happy to see him today, he'd have bet on that.

So what had changed? What variable had been added to the mix without his knowing?

He went into his office and sat at his desk. The computer was on, but no programs had been opened.

What had happened?

He glanced at the clipboard on his desk and found the notes he'd scribbled earlier.

Earth-shattering sex.

That's the only good thing he'd written down on his list. Uh-oh.

And Desi had read it.

Damn.

He'd stopped writing as he tried to figure out their relationship. She hadn't got to read all the feelings he'd so painstakingly worked out. She hadn't seen his personal revelation.

She didn't know about the romance books he'd been reading, trying to think of some way to tell her how he felt.

Now what?

Schrödinger sat on the floor staring at him. "Yeah, I know, I know, I blew it."

"Merp."

"So, now what?"

The cat didn't say a word.

That's how it was with cats, they never had anything worthwhile to say when you needed them to.

He called Desi's number. "Des, I know you're not there yet. Call me when you get this. We need to talk."

He hung up and sighed. He glanced at the corner of his office where his stack of romances sat. There were seven left to read. Maybe one of them would have the answer.

He read through several books that night, but was no closer to an answer, and no closer to talking to Desi. It didn't take a rocket scientist to understand that she was avoiding him. He called and talked to her machine repeatedly.

The next day, he sent flowers asking for a chance to explain.

Flowers.

He was proud he'd thought of it. Flowers were supposed to be romantic, but obviously they weren't enough to make Desi listen.

He'd finished all his books by Wednesday and was forced to admit he still didn't have a clue how to win her back—how to make her listen.

He needed help.

He needed to figure out how to apologize for hurting Desi, and how to tell her, in a romantic way, how he really felt. Books weren't the answer.

It galled Seth to reach that conclusion. For as long as he could remember he'd truly believed that all the answers were contained in one book or another. That any problem could be solved when approached methodically and logically.

But he'd yet to find a book that would help figure out Desdemona Smith, no amount of logic would help. She was a woman who knew what she wanted. And he needed to make sure that she knew what she wanted most was him.

He could only think of two people in the whole world who might come close to having the answers he needed. Two people who *lived* their lives, going after what their dreams and grabbing them loudly. Two people he never imagined he wanted to be anything like, but now found himself aching to be able to emulate.

Two people.

He dialed the phone.

"Mom?"

THERE HAD BEEN FLOWERS on Monday.

There'd been repeated calls on her machine ranging from, *I hate this machine,* to, *I know you read my list. Let me explain.*

Explain?

Seth thought they had earth-shattering sex... nothing else. What was there to explain about that?

She'd been a fool to hook up with a guy on the rebound. They had nothing in common. He was right about that much.

Desi, when you get this, call me. We have to talk, that was one of his most frequently repeated messages.

Right.

Desi, I know what you're thinking, but you're wrong.

No, she'd been wrong to think they even stood a chance at anything beyond what they had...sex. She'd been wrong when she thought maybe she loved him.

She was tired of hearing him on her machine and decided to tape a new greeting on her machine. *To-*

day is Wednesday. I work from nine to five. Then
I'm going out to dinner with friends. If you're friend
or family, please leave a message and I'll get back
to you as soon as possible. If this is Seth, you're
neither friend nor family, so don't bother.

She should feel better. But she didn't.

Desi went to the office and had spent the day
nailing down details on upcoming weddings, and
talked to two new clients. Normally a new client
was an exciting thing. She loved being part of the
magic and enthusiasm.

Today, she wondered if they could sense how
fake her smile was.

The thought of going to dinner with Mary Jo and
Pam didn't even cheer her up. She didn't feel the
least bit inclined to ogle anyone. She'd planned on
dumping her feelings on them, telling them about
the entire situation, but didn't know if she could do
it.

They'd tell her that she was lucky, that he was a
louse and she was better off without him. They'd
get mad on her behalf and threaten all kinds of
wicked retribution.

Yeah, Mary Jo and Pam would be sympathetic.
But in the end, she canceled, feeling a bit guilty
that she called and left messages on their machines,
knowing both were still at work.

She didn't want to be cheered up. She didn't
want to see anyone. She just wanted to wallow in

her misery and beat herself up over being such a fool.

After all, could she have picked a more inappropriate guy to fall for? He was on the rebound. He didn't have a romantic bone in his body. His idea of a hot date was digging up slimy critters from the lake. And the only good thing he could think of in regards to their relationship was sex.

Well, he was right, they were wrong for each other. And Desi was going to get over Seth Rutherford in record time. After all, it was just a short fling, nothing more.

Nothing more.

She kept saying the phrase, but it didn't help.

She returned home and checked her answering machine. No blinking light. No messages. Well, of course not. Seth probably gave up.

After all, it wasn't logical to keep chasing after a woman who'd made it clear she didn't want anything to do with you. And Seth Rutherford believed in logic, not love.

The thought made her feel even more morose.

She changed into her ragged flannel pajama bottoms and a tank top. Comfort clothes. She was going to sit in her worst looking outfit, gorge herself on junk food, and give herself this one last night to wallow in despondency. Tomorrow was a new day and—

There was a knock at the door.

Ha! He was here. Her surge of excitement at the thought was simply because if he was here she had a chance to slam the door on his face. Maybe if she was lucky, he'd stick a big fat foot in the way and she could step on it.

"Don't send flowers, don't call—" Desi broke off mid-tirade. She flung open the door. "Mary Jo. What's up?"

"What's up?" Mary Jo repeated as she elbowed her way into the apartment. "I don't know. You canceled dinner at the last minute, so we decided to come here."

"We?"

"Pam's on her way, too. She's just running a little late. You know Pam, she's always burning the candle at both ends. So, what's up? That's my question for you. You can start by telling me and we'll catch Pam up when she gets here."

Mary Jo plopped onto the couch and kicked her feet up onto the coffee table. "Start talking."

"Pardon?" she said, and was immediately reminded how much Seth enjoyed her *prim and proper* question. She quickly changed it to, "I don't know what you mean."

"Sure you do. Don't you think we noticed that there was something you were hiding at our last couple dinners? Why, you hardly noticed all the men…and even though I'm totally in love with my husband, I notice. It's not natural not to. Pam and

I talked yesterday and decided we were going to beat it—whatever it is—out of you tonight and then you cancel. And I call your machine and find a new greeting. Who's Seth, and why don't you want his messages?''

"What did you do with the kids?" Desi asked, hoping she could change the subject. Mary Jo could go on for hours regaling everyone with stories of her children's antics.

"They have a father. He'd planned to watch them while we had dinner, and was rather excited when he got your message, thinking he was off the hook. I simply informed him that even if I just sat on the dock and watched a solitary sunset, he had to deal with homework, bath time, story time and whatnot tonight. He needs to take his turn."

"Listen," Desi said. "You know I love you, but I'm not exactly dressed for going out. I just wasn't feeling up to a restaurant. Nothing's wrong. Just a hectic schedule at work. Lots of weddings."

"We don't need to go anywhere. Anytime I'm out with no kids that's out enough for me. Plus I stopped at the store and bought—" she pulled a carton out of the bag "—ta-da, pecan praline and caramel ice cream. I brought it to use as a bargaining chip. I want the full story."

Desi grabbed a couple spoons from the kitchen and handed one to Mary Jo as she sat next to her on the couch.

"You might not let up, but you've got good taste," Desi said.

"I know," her friend said with an infectious grin.

"What about Pam? She hates being left out of things."

"She's late, so she's on her own. But you're stalling. Tell me about it."

"Not *it, him.*"

"Hims are always so much worse than its, aren't they. Seth. Like I said, I heard your message on your machine. What did this particular *him* do?"

"He said we had earth-shattering sex." Desi took a huge bite of ice cream and let the sweet confection soothe her aching heart.

"He said earth-shattering sex and you're complaining? With four kids running around, I generally count myself lucky to have any sex, much less sex of the earth-shattering variety. Well, there was that other day in the shower—"

Desi cut her off. "Enough details, thank you."

"You've got a strange look in your eyes."

"I don't know what you mean."

"Wow, you've got it bad." Mary Jo took a huge bite of ice cream.

"What? What do I have?"

"You're in love."

"I am not."

She might have had a tiny thought in that direction, but she'd been wrong.

No way was she in love with a logic-loving, wouldn't-know-love-unless-it-was-a-zebra-mussel man. She couldn't love him. No, not couldn't…she could love him with way too much ease.

She *wouldn't* love him.

He had a whole list of reasons why she shouldn't.

She had her own list…although she didn't need to write it down. There was no way they could work it out, so she wouldn't love him.

Even as she thought the words, she knew them for the lie they were, and morosely stuck another large spoonful of ice cream into her mouth.

"You can say you're not in love, but—"

Mary Jo had the uncanniest ability to read her every thought.

"—but it won't alter the truth of it. You love him. It doesn't take a best friend to see that. It's there, written all over your face."

A knock at the door saved Desi from finding a retort.

"That must be Pam," Mary Jo said, squashing any of Desi's hopes that it was Seth.

Desi didn't know why she was hoping it would be Seth. She didn't care if she ever saw that sex maniac again.

Knowing her quiet night was history, Desi opened the door, and Pam breezed right in, a bag in hand. "Hey, Mary Jo, you made it already. I stopped for ice cream, which is why I'm late."

"I brought pralines, what did you bring?" Mary Jo asked.

"Chocolate, chocolate, chocolate." Pam sat on the couch.

Desi walked back into the kitchen and brought out another spoon. "You guys, I'm going to get fat."

"Not a fat bone on your body," Mary Jo said. "And remember, there are no diets allowed on Wednesdays. We might not be at Hazard's, but the rules still apply."

"So what's up?" Pam asked.

"I simply had a small fling with a man, but now it's over," Desi said, digging into the chocolate ice cream.

"She's in love," Mary Jo added. "His name is Seth. That's what she wasn't telling us and it's all I got out of her so far."

"No I'm not," Desi protested.

"Tell us about him," Pam demanded.

"Seth. Tell us about him," Mary Jo reiterated.

They weren't going to let up. And if she was honest, Desi would have to admit she was kind of glad. She needed to talk to someone who'd be sympathetic, and she knew she could count on Pam and Mary Jo.

"He was just dumped at the altar a few weeks ago," she explained. "I should have known better than to get mixed up with someone on the rebound, even if he wasn't in love with his fiancée and was only marrying her because it was logical."

"Logical?" Mary Jo said, mid-bite.

"Yeah, and I told him love wasn't logical—"

"Ah-ha, *love*," Pam gloated. "You said the word."

"No, his loving her, not me loving him, so the fact that I said it doesn't count. Only he didn't love her, which is maybe why I didn't worry about the rebounding, but I should have."

Desi took a hefty bite of ice cream, and Mary Jo and Pam, being the type of friends they were, didn't complain when she talked around it. "And the bride didn't love him either. I've planned a lot of weddings, and I don't think I've ever met a more unenthusiastic bride. Her mom and sister made most of the plans, and she just went along with them, not making waves, right up until the moment she bolted from the church, and took off with Seth's best man."

"Still, even if there was more logic than love, I bet he was devastated," Pam said.

"No, other than that first night when he drank too much—and I think that was more embarrassment than devastation. They were friends and colleagues. That's why he couldn't understand his infatuation—"

"Good word."

Desi ignored Mary Jo's interruption. "—with

me. I mean, we're opposites. And if I'd forgotten that, one look at his list would have reminded me.''

"What list?'' Pam asked.

"The one that I found when I went to use his computer to check my e-mail. A huge list of reasons why we shouldn't be together, and just one lousy little reason why we should.''

"And that was?'' Pam asked.

"I already told Mary Jo, earth-shattering sex. And that's not enough of a reason to be together.''

"It can be,'' Mary Jo assured her. "I mean, that sex in the shower was pretty earth-shattering and—''

Pam asked, "What sex in the shower?'' at the same instant Desi said, "No more talk about your sex life.''

"Oh, we can talk about yours, just not mine,'' Mary Jo said to Desi, and to Pam she said, "Well, let's just say, since Desi's getting all prim and proper, that it was a hot shower…a very hot shower.''

Prim and proper. There was that stupid phrase again.

Realizing Mary Jo was still harping on about showers, she answered her prim and proper retort with, "The difference is, I talk in abstract, not in hard details—''

"Oh, I love the hard details,'' Pam said.

"And since I'm not seeing Seth any more,

there's nothing to even be abstract about," Desi said, ignoring Pam's innuendo.

"Why aren't you seeing him anymore, again? I don't think we're clear on that, are we Pam?"

"Nope," Pam said through a mouthful of chocolate ice cream.

"Because, he was right, we're wrong for each other," Desi said.

What didn't they get? They were both in advance classes in school. Both went to college. They used to be sharp. How could they not get why she'd broken up with Seth?

"That's what you say, but I don't think I believe you. How 'bout you, Pam?"

"Nope, I don't believe you either. You're obviously still hooked on the guy. And hot sex is a good start for a relationship. All men have sex on the brains first...their little brains. The rest of the good stuff comes second."

"So are you going to sit here and wallow in your misery?" Mary Jo asked.

"I'm not miserable. I'm happy." Desi double dipped her spoon and took the large pecan praline, chocolate bite. Yeah, she was going to be happy if it killed her. "Happy I got out before it was too late."

"I think it's already too late," Pam said.

Mary Jo nodded. "But we won't argue the point. So what do you want to do?"

"Let's just watch *West Wing*," Desi said, reaching for the remote and clicking on the television. "I'll ogle Josh and forget all about Seth."

"And I'll ogle Sam," Pam said.

"Who do I get?" Mary Jo whined.

"You're married, you're not supposed to ogle anyone," Desi said.

"Well, you're in love and still ogling." Mary Jo pouted.

"I'm not in love," Desi practically growled.

"Whatever you say," Pam said.

"I'm not."

"Okay. We believe you," Mary Jo said.

"Really," Pam echoed.

"Turn up the volume a little, would you?" Mary Jo asked.

"Will you stop nagging me," Desi said in exasperation. "I'm not in love with Seth, and I'm not calling him."

Pam and Mary Jo didn't seem to register her declaration.

Well, fine. Desi didn't care. She knew she was right, and she and Seth were wrong for each other.

"He has a cat," Desi said, scraping the bottom of the chocolate ice cream carton.

"President Bartlett?" Pam asked.

"No, Seth."

"That's nice," Mary Jo said. "Oh, here comes CJ."

"It's named Schrödinger."

Mary Jo chuckled. "That's funny."

"Yeah, I knew you'd get the joke."

"Well, it's not much of a joke," Pam pointed out.

"It indicates a quiet, refined sense of humor."

"Whatever," Pam said. "If I had a cat I'd name it something pretty like Melody. But since I figure I'm bound to be an old maid, I can't get a cat. It's too cliché."

"What happened to Mr. Right-Now?" Mary Jo asked.

"It seems Right-Now is Long-Gone."

"Sorry," Desi said. "You know the right man is waiting out there for you. Someone with an ear for music, and an eye for the real deal."

"It's taking him long enough to find me," Pam grumped. "I have my life all planned. Marry a wonderful guy, have two boys…I'm going to name them Andrew and Erik, and—"

"He has a boat, too. It's called *The Guppy*—"

"That's nice," Mary Jo said.

Desi said, "Once I got over wanting to barf, I sort of liked it."

Well, she didn't exactly like the boat, but she did like spending the day with Seth. She liked the fact that he'd relaxed with her, laughing and smiling.

"Good," Pam said.

"I didn't like the zebra mussels though."

"Who would?" Mary Jo said. "That's why I like chemistry. No slimy stuff like you get in biology."

"So you think I should call him?" Desi said.

She wondered what he was doing? Did he miss her at all, or did he just miss the sex?

Probably the sex. She missed it. After all, he was right, it was earth-shattering. But she missed him, too. More. She missed seeing him smile. She missed his quiet passion about his work.

"No. Definitely don't call him," Pam said. "After all, you're both all wrong for each other. He loves logic and you love romance."

"He sent flowers," Desi said.

"That's so lame and trite," Mary Jo said.

"Way overdone," Pam said. "Not a bit of imagination there. My dream man will be more original than that."

"No it's not overdone. He called too and left messages."

"Probably just wanted some more earth-shattering sex. That makes him a cad," Pam said. "Men are all cads."

"Well, not my Paul, but you're right, the rest are," Mary Jo defended.

"No he's not a cad. Did I tell you he stood up for me with my family?"

She remembered that moment. He'd made her heart melt. She was pretty sure that's when she started to truly fall for him.

"Really?" Pam said. "Your mom can be kind of scary."

"Yeah, she started in on the old refrain—you know, Desi's wasting her life, blah, blah, blah. Then Seth said they didn't understand. That he respected my choice, that I was following my heart and my aptitude, and they should respect that, too."

"Well, maybe he's not such a loser," Mary Jo said.

"He's not a loser at all," Desi said. "Oh, maybe he sat in the cake, but he rescued it first and found the Barbie dolls."

"I'm not following you," Pam said.

"I don't want to want him," Desi said, then added honestly, "But I do."

"I think we can see that," Mary Jo said softly.

Desi realized that somewhere along the line, someone had clicked off the television.

"We're not right for each other. Only, I worry that if I'm not around he'll forget to laugh, and he won't go out in the rain, or take a swim in the lake. He'll miss so much."

"He needs you," Pam said softly.

"Yes, he does. Why doesn't he see that?"

"He's a man," Mary Jo answered. "They're sometimes slow on the uptake."

"Well, there's that," Desi said.

"So what are you going to do?" Pam asked.

"I'm going after him." She hadn't realized she'd

made a decision until the words fell out of her mouth. Maybe she'd known it from the start and just needed Pam and Mary Jo to show her.

"I'm going after him and making him see that, though we might not be a logical match, we have more going for us than just earth-shattering sex." Desi bounded off the couch.

"You're going now?" Mary Jo asked.

"Yes."

She was going now before she lost her nerve. She was going to tell Seth Rutherford he needed her. He needed her for more than sex. He needed her so that he remembered to enjoy life. And she was going to tell him that she needed him, too, because she loved him.

"Do you mind if I hang out here and watch the rest of *West Wing* with Pam? There are no kids here, and if I wait, Paul will have them all in bed before I get home," Mary Jo asked.

"Stay as long as you like. Just don't wait up for me." Desi smiled at her two friends. "Thanks, guys, you're the best."

The doorbell rang. "Maybe that's him," Desi said, unable to stop the wild careening of her heart.

She opened the door and…

"Mom. Dad. What are you doing here?" She didn't have time for her parents. She was going to ride off and beat some sense into the man she loved.

Loved. The man she loved.

She just didn't whisper the thought, she shouted it in her mind.

"It's nice to see you, too, dear," her mother said, even as she walked past Desi into the living room, her father trailing after her. "Mary Jo and Pam, how nice to see you girls."

"Hello, Mrs. Smith," they said in unison.

"How are the children?" she asked Mary Jo.

"Loud, busy and frequent pains in the butt, but I wouldn't trade them for anything."

"That's how kids are. Mystifying, but even when you don't understand them you just love them anyway."

"And you hope," Desi's father added, "that even if you make a mistake, your kids love you anyway, too."

"And we're thankful your Seth made us see that." Desi's mother beamed.

"He's not quite mine," Desi said. At least, not yet. But he would be. She'd just present her case in a logical way. He'd respect that and he'd have to believe her.

"She was just on her way out to convince him he should be hers," Mary Jo said.

"Because she loves him," Pam added.

"You love him?" her father asked.

"Yes, she does," Pam answered. "She's afraid he only sees her as good sex—"

"Earth-shattering sex," Mary Jo corrected.

"You guys, these are my parents." Desi could feel the heat flood her cheeks.

"And that may have been a little too much information," her father said.

"Oh, come on, Verle, we're both science teachers, and we certainly know about the birds and the bees," her mother said.

"But she's our daughter," he maintained with a frown.

"All the more reason to be happy that she's found someone who's sexually compatible."

"Yeah, earth-shattering sex is important to a marriage," Mary Jo said. "Why just the other day in the shower—"

"Wait a minute, would you all just wait? Mary Jo, no more shower talk. Everyone, no more sex talk. And most importantly, no more marriage talk, Mary Jo. I never said anything about marriage. Seth doesn't even know he loves me yet."

"But he will. How could he not love you?" Pam asked and the other three chimed in their agreement.

"You're all just saying that because you're biased."

"No, it's because we're smart and we know," Pam said.

"Okay, listen, the four of you can just sit here and watch the end of *West Wing* and talk about my sex life. I'm going."

There was another knock.

Desi tried to suppress her groan, but didn't quite manage it. "What is this? Grand Central Station?"

She went to the door, but no one was there.

This time there was a noise louder than a knock. It was a thump.

"I think it's coming from the patio," Mary Jo hollered.

What was going on? Desi had planned to spend a solitary night wallowing in her misery, and instead, she seemed to be hostessing an impromptu party.

She walked over to her sliding glass door and opened the blinds, but didn't see anything. She opened the door and stepped out on the deck.

"Down here, Desi."

11

"DOWN HERE, DESI," Seth called and gave her a little wave.

"You're going to leave a dent on your hood, standing on it like that," she called, by way of greeting.

No, *Seth, I've missed you.* No, *I was a fool not to see that I meant more to you than sex.*

This was going to be harder than he'd thought, and he'd thought it was going to be about the hardest thing he'd ever done.

He couldn't believe he was about to do something so…so…well, something so like his parents would do. How had he ended up here, on his car?

He'd called his parents and they'd accompanied him here with their *plan*…

"This will really wow her," his mother had assured him as he'd climbed up on the hood of his car.

"Really, when Desi said romance, I'm not sure this is what she had in mind."

"Oh, I guarantee she'll love it. Remember that time you stayed out all night bowling, Samuel?"

"How could I forget. Seth, your mother was furious. Thought there was another woman, which of course there could never be."

"Oh, Samuel," his mother crooned.

Standing on the hood of his car watching his parents practically swoon over each other, Seth hadn't felt any more confident. When his father actually pulled his mother into a passionate embrace, Seth actually felt a little sick.

"Um, Mom. Dad. Really, I think I'm going to go."

Immediately the suck-face-fest halted, and as Seth started to climb off his car, his father grabbed his ankle, preventing him. "Oh, no you don't. No son of mine is going to wimp out on wooing the woman of his dreams."

"I'm all for wooing, but not for making a fool of myself."

"Love is all about making a fool of yourself," his mother said. "Why, after that bowling incident, I'd thrown all your father's clothes out onto the lawn, and bolted the door. He hired a guy with a violin—"

"It wasn't a guy, it was a kid from the high school."

"—who couldn't hit a note if it was a broadside of a barn, but your father, just stood out there on the lawn, the terrible violinist squealing as he sang to me. How could I not open the door."

"Seth, I still think you should have gone with some musical accompaniment," his father said.

"No. That's okay." There was no way he was hiring any witnesses to this crazy act.

"Or at least let us help with your poem," his mother added. "No offense, son, but you're not very poetic."

"It's more of a letter than a poem. And I think we should go now. I'll give this some more thought and analysis."

"I don't think so," his father said, even as he lobbed a tennis ball at Desi's sliding glass door.

"Dad!" Seth said. He couldn't do this. It was time to face facts—he was a scientist after all, and used to accepting facts—he was no one's romantic hero.

"Now, Seth, we're just doing this because we love you," his mother said, throwing another ball with even more force than his father had used. It made a satisfying thwack against Desi's door.

"Mom!"

"We'll be here in the car if you need us, son," his mom yelled as she and his father escaped back into their car.

Seth had stood on the hood of his car, his love letter in hand, and knew that he must truly love Desi, because there was no other logical reason he'd be doing something this bizarre.

It had felt like an eternity. He'd known she was

in there. He'd seen her light. She wasn't going to come out. She was going to ignore him.

He had breathed a sigh of relief when Desi finally opened the door, came out to the railing and looked down. Now she was out and he had to say something.

Seth glanced back at his parents who waved their encouragement.

''Desi,'' he called again and gave another little wave.

''Get off the car, Seth,'' Desi called.

''The car doesn't matter, Desi. Only you matter.''

There. That was pretty romantic.

''Yeah, I matter for earth-shattering sex,'' she called down.

He'd been right. She'd read the list. ''I never finished it.''

''What?''

''The list. I never finished it. That's as far as I got with writing it down, but it wasn't everything I figured out. For the first time in my life, I didn't need to record my thoughts to understand them. The clipboard was superfluous. There's so much…''

He pulled a piece of paper from his pocket. ''I sat there, staring at the paper and worked it all out. But I didn't actually write it down, and now you're hurt. So I've gone back and written it down.''

He was going to look silly, but for Desi, Seth

would do it willingly. He took a deep breath and began.

"Desi, before you, I was stagnant, stationary, like the object in Newton's First Law of Motion, which states, 'in the absence of outside force, an object's momentum will remain constant.' I was stationary, and saw no hope of changing that…until you. Like Newton's Second Law, you acted upon my body, forcing me to move and change, but it wasn't just my body, it was my heart. I *thought* I wanted a logical match, someone who was the same as me. I never knew it, but what I've always longed for was you. You were the what I was waiting for. I love you.

"I know I'll never be the kind of man you always thought you wanted. I'll forget to bring you flowers, I doubt I'll buy too much chocolate, because it's not good for you, though I might be persuaded to treat for burgers and shakes on occasion."

He smiled, hoping she'd see the humor in that statement, but she just stood there, watching him, not saying anything.

Not knowing what else to do, he continued, "I know I won't remember birthdays and even anniversaries sometimes, but I also know that no one will ever love you the way I do. No one will ever be able to, because my love for you just keeps expanding exponentially. It just keeps growing and growing, and like an ever-expanding universe, I don't see any signs of it ever stopping.

"I need you. I need you to remind me to go swimming in the lake and to play in the rain. When I was making my list, I started and stopped with earth-shattering sex because that was the easiest part to understand. The rest...well, it's a mystery. You can't measure it, can't list it, can't itemize it, but it's there, it's real and tangible. I don't understand it, but I don't need to. I love you. That's all I need to understand."

He looked up and for the first time realized it wasn't just Desi on her deck, but her mother and father, and two women he'd never met.

None of them were saying a word. Desi wasn't either. She was crying.

It was too late.

He was going to lose Desi, and he knew that he'd never recover from it.

DESI LOOKED AT SETH, standing there on his neon yellow hood, waiting. She felt moisture on her face and realized she was crying. She brushed away the tears.

She wanted to scream her answer, but couldn't seem to force anything past her constricted throat except...*hiccup*.

But suddenly the evening air was filled with

noise. Mary Jo, Pam, her mother and father, all stood behind her in the doorway clapping wildly.

That wasn't all. Two other people got out of the dark car parked behind his and they were clapping, too.

Hiccup.

"Desi," her mother said, giving her a hard elbow. "Say something."

Hiccup.

"I…" she started and then a sequence of hiccups stopped her.

"I love you, too," she said in a hasty blurt before hiccups, friends or family could interrupt her again.

"I'll be right up," Seth called. "I want to hear you say it again."

Her mother pulled her back from the railing.

"Go change," she said. "You can't greet the man you love in flannel pajama pants."

"He won't mind," Desi said.

He wouldn't. He loved her. The pain she'd felt since she read his list was replaced by a warm glow. The man she loved loved her back.

When she was little she'd dreamed of a white knight coming and riding away with her. She'd never, in all her dreams, imagined that her knight would show up in a banana-colored sports car and have a boat called *The Guppy*. She'd never imagined—

"Seth might not mind your pajamas, but I will.

Go put on that dress I bought you a few weeks ago.''

''Mother, I look terrible wearing that.'' Oh it was an utter horror of a dress. Desi didn't have any idea what possessed her mother to buy it.

''Your hiccups are gone,'' her mom said with a smile.

''What?'' Desi asked.

''You forgot you were nervous, and they're gone. Now, go open the door for the boy and give him a big kiss.''

She suddenly realized what her mom had done. ''Thanks, Mom.''

''We like him. He's good for you…and for us. He helped us see what we were missing.''

''Go get him, Desi,'' Mary Jo and Pam cheered.

He father grabbed her and gave her a hug. ''Be happy,'' he whispered.

Desi opened the door.

Seth was bounding up the stairs, taking them two at a time, the two people from the street at his heels. But Desi only had eyes for him.

''I love you, too,'' she said again.

He wrapped her in his embrace. ''Don't ever forget it,'' he said. ''I love you too much to live without you.''

''You can't shake me.''

He relaxed his embrace enough to stare at her. ''Desi, I have a job for you.''

"A job?" she asked.

"Yes. I was wondering if you'd be interested in planning a wedding. I know the holidays are close at hand, in terms of planning a wedding at least. But do you think there's any chance we could marry then? It would be logical. I have a nice long Christmas break and we could maybe honeymoon in Hawaii. I've heard they have some great beaches with interesting aquatic life. What do you say?"

"You and me?" she repeated. Seth was asking her to marry him.

"Is that a yes?" he asked.

This was fast. Too fast. Logic would dictate that they slow down and have a long, lengthy engagement to work everything out. That's what logic might demand, but Desi believed in love, and romance demanded only one answer. "Yes."

"Yes you can plan it, or yes you will marry me?" Seth asked.

"Both."

"Then, I suggest, since we have family—these are my parents, by the way—and a few friends here, we turn this into an engagement party."

"Seth, I'm wearing flannel pajama pants."

"You look *lovely* to me."

"Everyone," Desi said loudly. "I want to announce the impending holiday wedding of Desdemona Smith and Seth Rutherford, Ph.D...

Epilogue

"SEE, I TOLD YOU SIZE MATTERS, size always matters. When you had to pick a cake for yourself, you went all-out. The bigger, the better, eh?"

Desi turned, knowing she'd find Kate's mother, Mrs. O'Malley, behind her, and sure enough she was smiling this time.

"I love the cake," she continued, "but I'm not sure about the cake topper. Aren't those Barbie and Ken dolls?"

Desi laughed. "Yes. Seth insisted we use them."

Arms snaked around her waist and Seth planted a light kiss on her neck. "Well, I told you those dolls weren't ruined. They cleaned right up. I was taken by a little con artist. I priced them afterward, and on top of everything else, she overcharged me for the replacement fee."

"I don't understand," Mrs. O'Malley said.

"Well, when I first started working for Desi, there was this cake and I accidentally sat in it—"

As he talked, Desi tried to collect her thoughts. It had been a perfect day, from the wedding to the reception. She looked over the crowd and spotted her parents dancing together, right next to Seth's parents.

Mary Jo and her husband Paul were out on the floor as well. And Pam was dancing with Seth's buddy, Ralph. Well, well, well. When things settled down, she'd have to see about maybe inviting their two single friends over to dinner. Maybe, just maybe—

"Penny for your thoughts," Seth said.

Desi realized that Mrs. O'Malley had moved on. "Hmm, I think my thoughts might be worth more than a penny. As a matter of fact…" she whispered exactly what she was thinking might be the next logical activity after the reception.

"Why, really Mrs. Rutherford. I'm shocked," Seth said.

"I—"

"Seth, Desi." Mary Kathryn, now Kate, and Tony came over. "We just wanted to say congratulations one more time before we go."

"We've got to get back to the restaurant," he said, his arm draped over Kate's shoulder.

"I'm so glad you both came," Desi said, and surprised herself by meaning it. It wasn't that long ago she'd thought so badly of both of them for hurting Seth, and now she was simply grateful. Not that he was hurt, but that he was hers.

"So are we," Kate said. "I know that everyone was upset when I ran out on the wedding, but I think everything turned out for the best."

Seth loped his arm around Desi. "Me, too."

"Hey," Phil called. Her ex-assistant had taken a

weekend off from the newspaper in order to photograph Desi's wedding called. That was wonderful, but even more wonderful was the fact he'd brought his new fiancée, Debbie, with him. "Everyone look at me."

Both couples turned as the flash momentarily blinded them. They smiled.

Seth said, "You know, this situation is rather like when Mandelbrot theorized that within chaos there is order. I mean, look at us. I thought that the world had turned upside down when Kate left, and indeed it turned itself right instead…"

Desi grinned as she listened to Seth's newest love theory. First Newton, now Mandelbrot.

She couldn't help but smile. She'd always thought she wanted a prince to come carry her away. When all the time what she really wanted was a man who read her Newtonian love letters and took her breath away. A man who named his cat Schrödinger, and who loved her.

The last part, the loving part, that was the most important thing. It was why Desi was sure that she and Seth were destined for their very own happily-ever-after.

"Hey, everyone," Bambi, Desi's new assistant who was running the show today, called. "It's time to cut the wedding cake."

"Did you get stand-ins?" Seth asked.

"Nope, it's just you and me," she replied with a smile. And that was just how it should be.

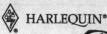

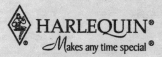

KATE HOFFMANN

brings readers a brand-new,
spin-off to her *Mighty Quinns* miniseries

REUNITED

Keely McLain Quinn had grown up an only child—so it
was a complete shock to learn that she had six older
brothers and a father who'd never known she existed!
But Keely's turmoil is just beginning, as she discovers
the man she's fallen in love with is determined to
destroy her newfound family.

*Look for REUNITED
in October 2002.*

HARLEQUIN®
Makes any time special ®

FALL IN LOVE
THIS WINTER
WITH
HARLEQUIN BOOKS!

In October 2002 look for these special volumes
led by *USA TODAY* bestselling authors,
and receive a MOULIN ROUGE VHS video*!
*Retail value of $14.99 U.S.

See inside books for details.

***This exciting promotion
is available at your
favorite retail outlet.***

Only from

Makes any time special ®

Visit Harlequin at www.eHarlequin.com   PHNCP02

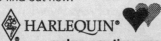
HINTMAG

Princes...Princesses...
London Castles...New York Mansions...
To live the life of a royal!

In 2002, Harlequin Books lets you escape to a
world of royalty with these royally themed titles:

Temptation:
January 2002—*A Prince of a Guy* (#861)
February 2002—*A Noble Pursuit* (#865)

American Romance:
The Carradignes: American Royalty (Editorially linked series)
March 2002—*The Improperly Pregnant Princess* (#913)
April 2002—*The Unlawfully Wedded Princess* (#917)
May 2002—*The Simply Scandalous Princess* (#921)
November 2002—*The Inconveniently Engaged Prince* (#945)

Intrigue:
The Carradignes: A Royal Mystery (Editorially linked series)
June 2002—*The Duke's Covert Mission* (#666)

Chicago Confidential
September 2002—*Prince Under Cover* (#678)

The Crown Affair
October 2002—*Royal Target* (#682)
November 2002—*Royal Ransom* (#686)
December 2002—*Royal Pursuit* (#690)

Harlequin Romance:
June 2002—*His Majesty's Marriage* (#3703)
July 2002—*The Prince's Proposal* (#3709)

Harlequin Presents:
August 2002—*Society Weddings* (#2268)
September 2002—*The Prince's Pleasure* (#2274)

Duets:
September 2002—*Once Upon a Tiara/Henry Ever After* (#83)
October 2002—*Natalia's Story/Andrea's Story* (#85)

**Celebrate a year of royalty with
Harlequin Books!**

Available at your favorite retail outlet.

HARLEQUIN®

Makes any time special ®

Visit us at www.eHarlequin.com

HSROY02